BENJAMIN FORREST AND THE SCHOOL AT THE END OF THE WORLD

ENDINFINIUM #1

CHRIS WARD

AMMFA PUBLISHING

ABOUT THE AUTHOR

A proud and noble Cornishman (and to a lesser extent British), Chris Ward ran off to live and work in Japan back in 2004. There he got married, got a decent job, and got a cat. He remains pure to his Cornish/British roots while enjoying the inspiration of living in a foreign country.

www.amillionmilesfromanywhere.net

ALSO BY CHRIS WARD

For Luna

my moon and my sun
and my world

There is no such thing as magic.
There is only natural order, and unnatural order.
And unnatural order should not be influenced, in any place or time.
For any reason.
By anyone.

Partial text of the Oath of Admission,
Endinfinium High School,
Author Unknown

There are only two concepts of which a pupil need be aware: creation and destruction.
Nothing else matters.

~Anon.

PART I

AT THE END OF EVERYTHING

1

GREETING

A couple of miles from the shore, the sea, a ruffled blanket of blue, grey, and white, appeared to fall over the edge of the world.

Benjamin Forrest sat up and, blinking as though waking from a long sleep, ran a hand through his hair to remove some of the sand. His hair felt longer than he remembered. Unkempt and tangled. His fingers smelled of grease and sea salt.

He was sitting in a bowl of shingle just back from the foreshore. Smooth, grey stones mixed with colourful beads of plastic. Some felt warm to the touch. He didn't remember being dumped here like a piece of driftwood, but that's how it appeared. He still wore his favourite blue T-shirt and the black jeans his mum had bought from Tesco's last February, but they were dirty and ripped and smelled of salt water. A piece of green ticker tape had caught on a thread of denim just below his knee. The laces on his black school shoes had come undone, and even though he felt dry, they were scuffed and stained as though he had spent the morning being tossed around in the shore-break like an old rag doll.

Above him, pale orange clouds floated past, bunching together as they moved toward the horizon. Then, as they crossed an invisible threshold, they elongated suddenly and slid below the line of the sea like streaks of colour from a chalk painting washing away in the rain.

Was this all a dream? Perhaps the sea didn't just fall away into nothing. Perhaps any time now he would wake up in his own bed in his parents' semi-detached estate house in Basingstoke, southwest England, and he would get up to look out the window at the beige council houses on Victoria Road, and not have to worry about whatever was digging its way up out of the shingle by his feet—

'Hey you! Be careful! They're hungry! It's breeding season, don't you know!'

He didn't have time to look for the speaker. The thing climbing up out of the stones was turning toward him, groaning with hunger. It looked like a car crossbred with a turtle, all shiny black chrome and spinning things like wheels with claws. The car's bonnet opened and closed in rapid snaps, metal spikes resembling teeth shining in the afternoon sun.

Something closed over his shoulder. He gave a yelp of surprise, but it was only fingers, someone's fingers, strong and insistent.

'Move! Now! Move—'

The sharp voice didn't have to repeat itself. Benjamin was already moving, heels kicking at the loose shingle, reverse-cycling away from the metallic monstrosity that seemed rather hungrier than any car should be.

'Don't forget your bag!'

The absurdity of the statement registered no more than the reality of his old school bag with the faded picture of Spiderman on its side, lying there on the shingle, its strap perilously close to the chomping maw of the turtle-car. Benjamin stared at it as stones shifted and it tipped toward the monster's mouth, disgorging a fan of dog-eared textbooks. Too late for his math book; it slid into the turtle-car's mouth, becoming a mess of shredded paper in a single snap. His science books were next, but there, on the top, sat his pride and joy: the story notebook he scribbled in while sitting alone at lunchtime.

'No!'

He dived forward, hands closing over the remnants of his

4

schoolwork. He tossed a boring French textbook into the creature's mouth to distract it, then retreated with another backpedalling scrabble of feet as the turtle-car lurched, its hood-maw pointing skyward, emitting an engine misfire that must have passed in this bizarre place as a belch. With a rattle of shifting shingle, it disappeared back into the earth, leaving only a small depression of wet stones to show where it had been.

'Wow! He was hungry! What was that you gave him to eat?'

Benjamin turned, heart still beating like the bubbles rattling out of the pump of his old goldfish tank back in his little Basingstoke bedroom. The girl, hair as red as an evening summer sky, eyes as blue as the dawn, watched him with a wide smile.

'A *Tricolore*,' he said. 'It was the French textbook or me.'

'It was almost you. Don't worry,'—the girl shrugged—'you wouldn't have been the first. Don't think you're special, you know.'

Benjamin stared at the depression in the sand, trying to ignore a niggling that the school would make him pay for the textbooks the creature had eaten. 'I wouldn't dream of it,' he said. Looking up at the girl, he added, 'Who are you?'

'Is that any way to greet someone? I'm Miranda. Is that okay with you?'

'Um, I guess so. We don't get to pick our own names for people, do we?'

'I picked mine, but not all of us, no.'

She turned and started walking off before Benjamin could think of a suitable response. He'd never found it easy to talk to girls, and Miranda already seemed stranger than any of his classmates. He glanced back at the beach, frowning at the piles of washed-up junk along the shoreline. Some of it appeared to be shifting, as though other great beasts hid underneath, and he shivered at the thought. When he looked back at Miranda, she was already some distance ahead, arms straight against her sides, legs stiffly lifting up and down as if she couldn't decide whether she were a marionette or a soldier. Benjamin hurried after her.

'Where are you going?'

'Back to the school.'

'What school?'

'Our school.'

She stopped so abruptly he bumped into her. His foot turned on a loose rock and he sat down heavily on the shingle. Something sharp poked into his back. He pulled out a dirty mantel clock from underneath him and tossed it away. As it bounced on the rocks, it made what sounded like a cry of discomfort.

Miranda folded her arms and glared down at him. 'What are you messing about down there for? I'm late for an appointment.'

He smiled. 'You're like a robot.'

Miranda frowned and, clearly not taking his comment as a joke, aimed a kick at his leg, but he managed to slip backward out of the way. 'What a thing to say to a girl. I am most certainly not. You, Benjamin Forrest, need to learn some manners.'

'How did you—'

A finger rushed across her lips as she made a zipping sound. 'Stop talking. I know your name because I was down on the beach waiting for you. Grand Lord Bastien said you would be arriving some time soon, and that it was best to keep a lookout. I've been coming down here every day for the last month. I've never been so fit.'

'The Grand Lord?'

'Sometimes he knows, sometimes he doesn't. Dreams, he said. I was told you would likely show up on this beach, and it's my job as a first-year prefect to ensure you are delivered to the school safely. It's such a waste of ceremony when a newcomer gets munched by a turtle and ends up turned into a cleaner or a nasty ghoul in the Haunted Forest before they've even met anyone—wouldn't you say so?'

Benjamin lifted a tentative hand as though back in "Dagger" Dangerfield's biology class and afraid those beaming blue eyes would laser-beam off the top of his head.

'Um, excuse me….'

'Yes?'

'One little question, if that's okay…?'

'Hurry up.'

'Where exactly am I?'

Miranda turned with a rapid sweeping gesture of her hands. 'Oh, I'm sorry. I just had things on my mind.' She waved around her. 'This place is called Endinfinium. It's a bit odd, but you'll get used to it. From today onward, you are a pupil of Endinfinium High School. Most of us don't call it that, though.'

'Oh? What do you call it?'

Miranda smiled and, spinning on her heels, held her arms out. Benjamin worried that she might burst into song.

'Isn't it obvious?' she said. 'Most of us know it as the School at the End of the World.'

2

SCATLOCKS

'It wouldn't do to stray too far,' Miranda said, as Benjamin followed her up a steep path rising into the cliffs that backed against the beach. 'At least not until you're familiar with what's dangerous and what isn't.'

Benjamin shot fearful glances into the bushes to either side of them as they walked. All sorts of strange creatures moved about in there—cat-like things; big, lumbering things; small things that jumped from branch to branch and moved with the creak of metal—and every single one seemed to be looking in their direction.

'Is anything else hungry?' he muttered.

'Oh, everything,' Miranda said. 'You'll get used to it. Most things are more of a nuisance than an actual danger, though.'

'That's good to know.'

'Isn't it? Look, I need to drill you on a couple of things. You've appeared on the awkward side of the school. To avoid a very long walk inland that we don't have time for before dinner, you'll have to get past the old gatekeeper before you can be shown to your room and get on with formalities. Gatekeeper has been a bit of a grouch since the new entrance was finished, though; if he smiles, it's probably a bad thing, so just put up with his snarls and complaints and answer his questions.'

'Okay, I'll try.'

'Good. I'll meet you on the other side.' At the top of the path, she turned to head back down.

'Where are you going?'

'I have to meet a friend,' she said. Then, for the first time, uncertainty replaced her brusque exterior. 'Don't tell anyone, will you?'

'Um, no.'

'Promise?'

'I promise.'

'Thanks. See you in a bit.'

With that, she was gone as quickly as she had appeared, jogging back down the path as though the strenuous climb up had been nothing. Benjamin looked around him, feeling nervous. The bushes—oddly coloured, spiny things with strange flowers that reflected the sunlight like shards of glass—seemed to watch him, and without Miranda there for guidance, he felt like a side of sliced beef put out for a buffet.

With a crunch and an electric hiss, something white and square bounced out onto the path behind him, and Benjamin jumped around in alarm. The thing looked like a refrigerator with stumpy, elephantine legs. It turned in his direction, and a fat mouth opened, then snapped shut. Benjamin hurried away from it, and when he glanced back, it had disappeared into the bushes.

A short distance ahead, the path dipped into the lee of a towering buttress of brown rock. Benjamin stepped out of the bushes into a courtyard of cropped couch grass. Overhead, the bluff face reared high enough to leave the courtyard draped in shadows. Set into the foot of the cliff was a large pair of wooden doors too ill-fitting for the space. Away to the left, a battered old tractor lay on its side on the grass, its white bonnet and red chassis shining in the courtyard's only patch of sunlight.

Benjamin looked around for the gatekeeper Miranda had mentioned, but there was no one about. He went over and knocked on the door. The wood reverberated with a hollow tingle, booming as an echo from inside.

No one answered.

Tired from the walk, Benjamin sat down beside the tractor, leaning his back against tires warmed by the sun. With nothing else to do, he opened up his school bag and pulled out his remaining textbooks. His physics book was on top, complete with unfinished homework, while underneath lay his English book, followed by his home economics book. At the bottom was the little notebook with the green cover and the curled corners in which he wrote his stories. He opened it to the first page and read, "Welcome to the School at the End of the World."

'Huh? I didn't write that….'

'Oh, I'm sure you did.'

Benjamin jumped up at the gruff old voice. At the exact same time, the tire beneath him had shifted, and now the tractor was moving, turning over, bending and distorting as if made of flexible plastic.

In a few moments, something rusty and contorted stood in front of him, its hood end bent over to allow a red radiator grill and small circular lights to become a mouth and eyes. The lights blinked at him, and the radiator emitted gusts of warm air like breaths. Small front wheels flapped like ears, while the large rear treads shifted back and forth to keep the creature's balance. Gears and levers poking out of the sides gestured like arms.

'What's so odd? Never seen a David Brown 760 before? Classic model—1967, discontinued in '71. Collectors' favourite. Me, though, I had the personal misfortune to not belong to such an elite. Broke down in a waterlogged field, left there to rust. If you asked me to put a date on it, I'd say '85. May or June? Field got cleared out for a new housing estate, and lucky old me was compactor bound.' The tractor's head shifted sideways. 'In case you were wondering.'

'Oh. It's a sad story.'

'With a happy ending. Of sorts. For a while, at least.'

'Really?'

'Had my second coming as the gatekeeper to the school. Or at least I was, until they built that stupid new entrance. You can call me Gatekeeper, because serial numbers are easy to forget, unless you're really good at math.'

'I'm not.'

'That's settled, then.'

'When did they build the new entrance?'

'Three hundred years ago, by your numbers, I'd guess. I'm no good at math, either. Anytime and all time by mine. Fools. All that plastic and flexi-glass. Like it doesn't reanimate so much quicker than wood? Found that out the hard way, didn't they?'

Benjamin blinked. 'That was silly of them.'

The gatekeeper dipped his head in a sage nod. 'Right you are. Looks like we're on the same page, boy. Who are you?'

'My name's Benjamin Forrest. I woke up on the beach. A turtle that looked like a car ate half my schoolwork, and then tried to eat me.'

The gatekeeper gave a shrug. 'They'll do that, you fool. You have to learn how to talk to them. Don't you know anything?'

'To be quite honest—'

A sudden howl rose up off the cliffs to the east, from the direction of the beach. Benjamin jumped, recalling a school trip to a wind farm outside Swindon and a tour through the generator building. The roar had been so fantastic, so great, Benjamin had heard barely a word the guide had said. The terrible howl reminded him of those whirling, relentless turbines.

'Wow, is that the wind?' he asked the gatekeeper, clapping his hands over his ears.

'Um, no. Small problem,' the gatekeeper said. 'Better make yourself scarce, unless you're not yet tired of being eaten.'

'What is it?'

'Scatlocks. Irritating little things. They like to burrow into your ears and eyes, and just about anywhere else. Best take cover. They'll eat you, but I've heard their mouths are so small that it takes several thousand of them several days to finish you off. Can't imagine that's a great deal of fun, can you?'

The gatekeeper rolled toward the door. A gear lever stuck out, poked into the lock, and the door swung open.

'Come on, get inside, won't you, fool?'

Benjamin hiked his bag over his shoulder and ran for the door. He had almost made it, when the air filled with a blizzard of white-and-grey fluttering things that ripped at his clothes and tore at his bag.

'Hurry! Get inside before they do!'

'I can't see you!' Benjamin screamed, spinning around, trying to cover his face with his hands. The scatlocks felt crisp and dry, like they were made of—

'Here!'

Something metal prodded him in the side, and Benjamin grabbed hold of it with one hand, batting the scatlocks away from his face with the other. The gatekeeper pulled him backward through the door, just as one of the scatlocks ducked down the front of his shirt.

Screaming, Benjamin yanked it out and threw it at the floor like it was a live snake. The door slammed, shutting out the violent noise. A light switched on to reveal a dark, damp cavern with a tunnel leading up a gentle slope to the right. Jagged lumps of rock protruded from the ceiling a few inches above his head.

As Benjamin gathered his breath, the gatekeeper turned around with the white, fluttery thing speared on the end of one of his gear levers.

'Be careful you don't kill them. I'm not sure that's allowed. I'll put it back outside later.'

'It attacked me,' Benjamin gasped.

'It was trying to chase you off its territory,' the gatekeeper said. 'Reanimates don't like humans all that much. You're unnatural, you see.'

'No, I'm not!' Benjamin said. 'This thing's unnatural. Look at it! What is it, anyway?' He poked at what looked like a plastic bag folded into the shape of a butterfly.

'I told you. It's a scatlock. They nest on the cliffs in great colonies, and they get aggressive with anyone who gets too close. One day, they'll inherit Endinfinium, you mark my words.'

'Endinfinium … that's what the girl said. Where are we?'

'We're here, is where we are. There is nowhere else.'

Benjamin took a deep breath. 'Yes, there is. There's England, and there's Basingstoke and there's Victoria Road. That's where my family lives.'

'Well, not anymore. You're here now, and here you'll stay. This is Endinfinium.' The gatekeeper rumbled like a croaky, old engine, which Benjamin sensed was a snort of pride. 'Endinfinium is the end of everything, and it's for infinity, so I'm told. But what would I know? I'm just an old tractor.' The gatekeeper leaned forward, looming over Benjamin's head like a giant, homemade toy. 'Anyone ever told you that you ask a lot of questions?'

'A few teachers, yes. I would have asked the girl, but she went off somewhere.'

'Miranda?'

'She told me to look for you, then ran off back to the beach.'

The gatekeeper's headlight eyes revolved. 'That girl. She'll get in trouble if she's not careful. Always running off, forgetting about the Oath. Well, let me tell you the answers to a couple of questions you'll likely have fairly soon. Right now, you're not anywhere, but the place you want to get to is a couple of miles farther along this way, across a rickety, little bridge.'

'And where's that?'

The gatekeeper sighed as if the answer should have been obvious.

'The only place a boy of your age should be going. Endinfinium High. The School at the End of the World.'

3

THE BRIDGE

The tunnel sloped gently upward, all rough-hewn rock with flickering oil lamps set into natural alcoves. Occasionally a door led off, some with markings and others plain, but the gatekeeper ignored them all as he continued his arduous march. For Benjamin, a soft spot had started to develop for the old tractor who was like a grouchy but beloved uncle, the sort who would ignore a beautiful summer sky to tell you war stories about his misspent youth.

'Are there many other people here?' Benjamin asked after a time, having tired of the gatekeeper's parts' relentless mechanical grinding in the echoing confines of the tunnel. 'Apart from Miranda, everything I've seen was kind of … weird.'

'Of course there are, fool. A right old bag of marbles we are out here. No end to the assortment. Reanimates, wanderers, and humans living in perfectly fractious non-harmony. I'm sure in time you'll find what you're looking for.'

'Miranda said you were a bit grumpy.'

The gatekeeper grunted. 'Huh. I bet she did. Compared to her, the two suns must be grumpy. Always too enthusiastic for her own good.'

'Two?'

'What?'

'Two suns?'

'Yes, the big one and the small one. Don't you look up?'

Benjamin made a note to pay more attention when he next went outside. 'Well,' he said, patting the gatekeeper on the nearest part of his chassis, 'I don't care what she says. I think you're a bastion of sweetness and light. As fresh as summer flowers, with a smile that could out-beam the sun itself.'

'Which one?'

'Both!'

The gatekeeper lurched backward, his radiator grill wheezing. His head struck the roof of the tunnel, and a puff of dust sprinkled down.

'Fool, making me laugh like that. How will you find your way out of here if I keel over and die?'

'Stop calling me fool.'

The gatekeeper leaned down toward him. One headlight flashed in a wink. 'I don't know what it is with you humans. You think you know everything, then you show up and start bumbling around like you've never seen reanimates before.'

'I haven't. Last thing I remember was being in the woods near my house. There was a forest road, and my little brother, David, he was there, and … that's it.'

'And how did you end up here?'

'That's what I'd like to find out, before I get eaten by a burrowing car or suffocated by a flying plastic bag.'

The gatekeeper stopped as the tunnel came to an abrupt end at a large pair of doors not dissimilar to the entrance. 'Well, hopefully you'll find someone who can help you over at the school.' A gear lever poked out. 'Good luck, young Benjamin, and if you find yourself with nothing to do, come and entertain me with a few tales of that other place. Banstock, wasn't it?'

'Basingstoke.'

'Ah, yes.'

Benjamin took hold of his gear lever and shook it. 'I will,' he said. 'Thanks for your help, Gatekeeper.'

'A pleasure. Now be careful out on the catwalk. It can get a little bouncy in the middle if the wind gets up.'

The gatekeeper poked a lever into the lock and the doors swung open to reveal a spiraling stone staircase. Natural light from somewhere above made a circle on the floor. Benjamin stepped forward, and before he could change his mind, the doors swung shut. Through an opening high above, a circle of orange-tinted cloud was visible.

The staircase opened onto a barren outcrop of rock with sharp drop-offs to either side. Behind him, in the direction he had come, was a pretty cove—a semi-circle of sand at the bottom of a steep cliff.

Ahead, the mountainside descended with perilous steepness toward a wide bay. Large, blue-grey rollers battered jagged headlands, while out beyond the line of the breakers, strange creatures moved through the water, some sleek and streamlined, others bulky and angular. From time to time, one would surface in a burst of colour, flop over and disappear back beneath the swell. They were too distant to see clearly, but Benjamin was certain he had never seen anything like them off the pier at Weston-Super-Mare.

And there across the bay, wrapped over the top of a rocky headland, stood a building quite unlike anything Benjamin had ever seen. In some ways a castle, in others a tumbledown ruin, what could only be Endinfinium High was not so much a dazzling display of architecture, but a building clinging for dear life to the crumbling cliff beneath. For every tower reaching optimistically toward the sky, a collapsed wall or an overhanging balcony looked just seconds from a long and painful drop to the rocky shoreline.

Far across on the school's headland, the grey line of a path switched back and forth as it led up to the school. Unfortunately, this lay on the other side of a vertigo-inducing rope bridge that stretched from a thin ledge below Benjamin's feet, to a gate in the castle's outer wall.

Attempting to cross the bridge seemed a quick way to end up as food for the monstrous fish in the water below. With frayed and damaged rope, the bridge swung like a pendulum in the strong wind, at times nearly looping over on itself.

Benjamin scuttled back down the steps and began pounding on the door, screaming for the gatekeeper to let him in, but now that his duty was over and the scatlocks had gone, the old tractor had obviously retreated back to his sunny little spot in the courtyard.

With no other choice, Benjamin sat for a while and stared across at the school, too scared to move. In the end, though, his body made the decision for him: he was hungry, and the school was the only place likely to have food. He remembered eating Coco Pops with David that morning before they had gone to play down in the woods, but since then, the passage of time had scrambled at some point, and now his stomach was so empty, it could have been a balloon at a child's birthday party.

His first step onto the bridge felt solid enough. It was made of wooden slats lashed together with rope and it creaked with every step, but it felt firm enough as he inched out over the bay, one fearful step at a time.

He was a fair way out when the first real gust of wind came. As the bridge swung sharply left, he grabbed hold of the guardrail ropes, wondering if this was a normal, earthly wind, or perhaps a wind caused by having the end of the world just a few miles to the east. Gritting his teeth and hanging on as though the rope might disappear, he waited until the bridge swung back the other way. Then, as it hit the flat, he scampered a few steps forward.

This had to be a dream, and he had to be about to wake up. This realisation helped to quell his fear a little, even as the rope bridge bucked again. Benjamin closed his eyes and wrapped his arms through the guardrail ropes, holding on for dear life, until the bridge swung back again and settled for a few seconds to allow him to race another few steps farther forward.

He was now midway across the bay. The bridge dipped in the middle, at its lowest point close enough to the water below that Benjamin felt spray on his face from the tossing waves. In the brief moments of calm, Benjamin marveled at the creatures that seemed to dance there—great luminous tentacled things; twisted, angular monstrosities that looked like hybrids of beast and machine. Indeed, vessels were down there, too—arrow-shaped ships with billowing sails that bucked and swerved through the surf. Figures that might have been men stood on their multi-coloured decks.

The rope bridge bucked again, then flattened out. Benjamin darted a few more steps forward. The door seemed even closer; he was sure he could make it.

His optimism began to rise, when a howling sound from the headland behind him sent a shiver down his back. He forced himself to look over his shoulder, terrified of what he would see.

The flickering white mass of a flock of scatlocks rose above the clifftop's pinnacle, like a shifting, formless cloud. They bunched into a tight ball, appeared to pause, and then rushed forward across the bridge.

Benjamin turned and dashed for the far side, stumbling and falling more than once as the bridge jerked beneath him. His knees picked up splinters, but he ignored the pain, pushing himself back up in a tumble of arms and legs, forcing himself onward, aware that death by a swarm of angry plastic bags might outweigh death by plunging into monster-infested waters.

He was within a few steps of the far side when a board broke underneath him and, with a howl of terror, he dropped through the slats, wooden teeth scraping at his clothes. Desperate fingers closed over the jagged edge of the broken board, and he hooked his nails into the grooves of the wood while he kicked his legs out, desperately trying to swing himself up.

It was impossible. He had never enjoyed P.E. much and didn't have the upper body strength to pull himself up or the core strength to lift his legs and hook them. If he tried to swing, his hands would likely slip.

He glanced down. Right beneath him, something ominous swirled in the water.

The wind gusted again, swinging him right. Something batted against his hip.

My bag, he thought.

It was still hooked over his left shoulder. Risking losing his grip and plunging into the waves below, Benjamin let go with one hand, using it to unhook the bag. With a wide, arcing swing, it caught on the guardrail and held firm enough take his weight. Steeling himself, he pulled upward with all his might.

He was halfway up through the hole, when the strap on his bag broke. For a moment he felt a great lightness, before the bag sailed away to the water far below. Benjamin watched, wondering why he wasn't tumbling after it. His legs flapped, feeling a thick, jelly-like resistance.

Something was cushioning him. He looked down but nothing was there, though when he looked up again, Miranda was running out toward him. She grabbed his wrists, hauled him up, and both of them fell in a heap on the creaking bridge.

'Don't tell a soul,' she said, her eyes filled with fear. Then, as Benjamin frantically shook his head, even though he wasn't yet sure what she was talking about, Miranda pulled him to his feet.

'Quick,' she hissed. 'The door.'

The cloud of scatlocks hovered right above them. Miranda threw the door open and, in a single motion, pushed Benjamin inside, then slammed the door closed. The howling wind and the buzz of the scatlocks cut off in an instant.

'Come on,' she said. 'Almost there.'

She turned and raced down a tunnel. As she passed, flames appeared in fittings bolted to the wall, as if lit by sensors. Benjamin ran after her, and a few seconds later, she stopped at a door.

'We're here,' she said, flashing him a smile as she twisted the handle. 'After you.'

Benjamin stepped through, then gasped at the sheer size of the room in which he found himself standing.

'Where are we?'

The girl's smile broadened. 'This,' she said, sweeping a hand before her, 'is the Great Hall of Endinfinium. It's where we have assembly.'

Benjamin turned to look around him.

'Wow,' was all he could say.

4

THE GREAT HALL

The hall was at least three times the size of his school's gym, shaped like an old Roman auditorium, with a wide central floor between dozens of ascending rows of seats on either side. Benjamin imagined gladiators racing chariots, or lions and bears eating slaves while a massive crowd roared.

About halfway to a raised stage at the far end, a man quietly swept the floor. Otherwise, the vast room was empty.

'There's no one here at the moment,' Miranda said.

'I noticed.'

With the trials of the rope bridge pushed to the back of his mind, Benjamin descended a set of steps to the floor below, his footfalls echoing around him. The vaulted roof lay in shadow, while seats rose up thirty rows deep to where unlit spotlights the size of dinner tables stood beside black curtains. Alcove lights brightened the hall's dimensions just enough, but he could imagine the place filled with light and theatre.

'What do you do in here?' he asked.

Miranda shrugged. 'Oh, all sorts. You've just missed the school year entrance ceremony. It was last week. You were late.'

'I didn't know I was expected.'

'There's a lot you don't know, isn't there?' she shouted abruptly, loud enough to make the sweeping man stop and turn toward them. He leant on his broom for a moment as though waiting for something to begin, then went back to his work.

Benjamin ignored her. He wandered over to a glass door in between the rows of seats, and as he came level with it, he saw his reflection in a head-to-toe mirror.

He hadn't looked at his own face since he had arrived, but the sight was quite a shock. His hair was a shaggy mop: several weeks' worth of growth longer than he remembered. His clothes were soiled and dirtied, torn in places and even stained on one arm with something that could have been blood. His face was gaunt, eyes bright but bloodshot as if sleep was a distant memory, and his cheeks were scratched as though he'd lost an argument with a bramble.

'What happened to me?' he whispered.

Miranda's hand fell on his shoulder, then sharply pulled away. 'Um, the journey isn't easy,' she said. 'Not everyone makes it. And for those who do, sometimes it can take a while.'

'What's the journey?'

'I think you've asked enough questions. And if I told you the answers, they wouldn't be right, because they'd be my answers. Only you can answer your own questions, right?'

'I don't know.'

'Clearly. I think we've established that all you know is nothing. Lucky you have me to look after you.'

Benjamin sighed. 'Yeah, lucky.'

Miranda scowled. 'No need to be ungrateful. I only left you alone for a few minutes.'

Benjamin wanted to mention that those few minutes had almost gotten him killed multiple times, but he didn't want to risk her running off again. Instead, he said, 'How on earth did you get over here so fast? I had to go through that tunnel, then cross that terrifying bridge, but you just appeared on the other side. How did you do that? And if it was so easy, why couldn't you have taken me with you?'

She crossed her eyes and turned up her nose. 'I told you, I'm the class prefect. I know stuff that other people don't know.' She smirked. 'I'm special.'

'Good for you. What about on the bridge out there?

Something invisible stopped me from falling. You did that, didn't you? What was it, m—'

She clamped a hand over his mouth. Her palm was warm, her skin smelling faintly of salt as though she had washed her hands in the sea.

'Don't say it. Don't say the M-word. You have to remember the Oath, or at least pretend to.' Gone was the brash, confident exterior; her voice trembled with fear. 'I don't want to go into the Locker Room again. Use of it is banned, and even the word will get you a thousand cleans if someone hears you.'

Cleans. The Locker Room. More words Benjamin logged to ask about later. For now, though, best to focus on one thing at a time.

'This thing I'm not supposed to talk about … you used it, right?'

'Don't talk about it. Please.'

'Why?'

'Because I don't want to lose you. You don't know anything. If you fall into the sea, you'll get washed over, and once you're over, there really is no coming back.'

Benjamin put his hands on his hips and took a deep breath. He looked up and down the Great Hall, slowly counting to ten, hoping that Miranda might do the same.

When he felt calm enough to speak without stumbling over his words, he asked, 'Where are we?'

Miranda rolled her eyes. 'I told you. Endinfinium. The School at the End of the World.'

'And where's that?'

'Isn't it obvious?' She shoved at his chest. 'We're at the end of everything.'

Benjamin smiled. 'And I'm supposed to go to school here?'

'That's right. The same as the rest of us.'

'Why?'

'Why not?'

'Where is everyone else?'

She shot him a look that suggested he was the biggest idiot in whatever world this was, and Benjamin wondered if she had any friends. The class prefects he remembered from his old school,

Burnton Secondary, were all snobs who had not so much friends but followers. Perhaps Miranda fit that mould, too.

'They're. In. Class.'

'What class am I missing?'

She looked down at her wrist, at a space where a watch wasn't. 'The same one as me. Trigonometry.'

Benjamin stared at her. 'Trigonometry?' He grinned. 'Oh, what a terrible shame. You must have felt so sad that you had to come and find me.'

Miranda returned his grin, and for the first time, Benjamin felt the hint of a connection, some shared sense of conspiracy that might blossom into friendship. No matter what world you were in, everyone hated trig.

'My instructions were to see that you had the best chance of making it on time. I, you know, did my best. Can't be helped if we're a bit late, can it?'

'If I ever sign up for a camping trip while I'm here, I'll be sure to make sure you're not leading it.'

Her smile vanished. 'What's that supposed to mean?'

'Nothing,' he said with a shrug, then turned away and wandered off down the hall in the direction of the cleaner. After a few seconds, Miranda trotted in pursuit, but Benjamin had already turned his attention to the only other person he had seen who looked human.

'Hello,' he said, offering a hand to the man's back. 'My name's Benjamin. Nice to meet you.'

The man stopped sweeping and straightened the broom in a slow, methodical motion, then turned to Benjamin, lifted his face, and grinned.

Black eyes and a toothless mouth dominated a face long dead, its flesh hardened and leathery. As Benjamin tried to find the breath to scream, a clicking that could have been laughter came up through the dead cleaner's throat.

Miranda's hand closed over Benjamin's wrist, and she dragged him away. He glanced back, but the dead man had already returned to his work.

'Not a good idea to bother the staff,' Miranda said. 'They get easily distracted.'

'He was dead!'

'That's not a very polite way to put it,' she said. 'If he was dead, he wouldn't be very good at his job now, would he? We prefer to say *reanimated*.'

They had reached the end of the hall, where a huge stage rose above them, level with Benjamin's eye-line. In the alcove behind the curtain hung several large flags, strange geometric patterns in a multitude of colours, some faded, all dusty and old. Everything about this place had an air of decay and neglect, not to mention bizarre. Even though he was getting used to it, he still hoped to soon wake up in his own bed back in Basingstoke.

'You have dead people here?' Benjamin whispered, far louder than he had intended, his heart still beating hard.

'Well, they have to go somewhere.'

'But, he's dead!'

Miranda smirked. 'Well, aren't you full of revelations. I'd never have noticed.'

'This must be a dream.' Benjamin shook his head. 'This can't be real. It just can't.'

Miranda shrugged. 'You'll get used to it,' she said.

'Look,' he said, turning back to Miranda. 'Is there anyone here who I would recognise as an actual, normal person? Aside from your wonderful self, of course?'

Miranda rolled her eyes. 'Of course there is.'

'Could you take me to them, please?'

Miranda looked aggrieved. 'Well, you only had to ask. Wasn't that difficult, was it?'

5

ADMISSIONS

Through a door behind the stage was a set of stairs. Miranda switched on a light, and they climbed, emerging through a door into a wider corridor hewn from solid rock. Benjamin sensed they were still inside the cliff itself, yet to enter the buildings he had seen perched on the clifftop. How had these tunnels been created? Very little of this place made sense, so if Miranda told him they had been dug out by giant worms, he would have likely believed her.

Doors and staircases led off at regular intervals. Miranda chose one seemingly at random, and soon they stood inside a tall set of glass doors that opened out to a courtyard on the very top of the cliff. Brightly coloured flowers in ornate pots rested along the edge of a low, stone balustrade overlooking a dramatic coastline. The sky was a familiar ochre blue, and the cliffs looked like regular rock jagging down toward regular beaches. They were on the other side of the headland from the bay, with its strange creatures and rocking vessels, and the sea, fierce and violent, looked like a normal sea … up to a line a couple of miles offshore where everything stopped. Some kind of horizon lay out there, a buttress of rocks perhaps, but after that … nothing. Just a haze of blue-white sky as if he was looking straight up instead of straight ahead.

'It's pretty,' he said. 'I suppose.'

Miranda gave a non-committal shrug. 'We should hurry up,' she said. 'Trig finishes at eleven. Then we have climbing. I like climbing.'

'Climbing? What do we … oh, never mind. I'll wait and see.'

'The school focuses on practical skills,' Miranda said. 'We have no real time for unimportant things.'

'I guess that makes sense. What about trig? Since when has anyone ever needed that, ever?'

'I guess they had space on the timetable. Or they're just sadistic. Come on, we need to get you enrolled and off to class, otherwise we'll be sent to the Locker Room for cleaning duty.' She pouted. 'And I *hate* that.'

Behind them rose a postmodern castle, vast and magnificent. Ancient stonework stood alongside glass walls and steel struts. A wide, mirrored glass front beamed the world behind the balustrade right back at them. Already Miranda was headed for a pair of doors at the top of three marble steps. Benjamin took one last look up at the castle front, at a tower with some kind of glowing light behind it.

Only it wasn't a light. It was a small sun, off-red, just poking out from behind the tower's stonework, hanging low as though too tired to rise far above the horizon. Benjamin turned around. A second sun, a more familiar kind, hung high in the sky.

That explained the orange-tinted clouds, then. He looked down at his feet, where the ghosts of two shadows stretched out, one to either side, one slightly stronger than the other.

'Where on earth—or not—am I?' he whispered, as he followed Miranda to the steps. 'I must be dead. This can't be a dream.'

Miranda was waving him forward with a look of frustration. He hurried over and followed her through the doors.

A woman sat behind a desk. A real, normal woman, fifty-ish years old, greying brown hair bunched up behind her head and spectacles over an aging, lined face. A business suit. Overweight, but not excessively so. Smelling faintly of perfume and scribbling with just too much aggression to be in a good mood.

The urge to shout out loud was so strong, Benjamin slapped a hand over his mouth until he was sure he could control himself. Then, in a quiet voice, he said, 'Mrs. Martin?'

She looked up, and Benjamin stared. It *was* her. Of all the people to find in this odd place, one of Burton Secondary's office secretaries was the absolute last he could have expected.

Even of the three main office staff, she was the least likely. Mr. Bennett was suave and cool, a known jazz musician in his spare time, while Miss Jones with her long legs and strikingly pretty face could have been an actress in another life. No one noticed Mrs. Martin, the engine house, the workhorse, the one in the background, the one who—and it pained him to even think it —couldn't have been anything special at all.

Yet here she was.

'You took your time,' she said, looking up, the hint of a smile on her wrinkled lips. 'I almost threw your paperwork in the bin.'

'I had some trouble.'

'Evidently. I've seen tidier hair caught up in my vacuum cleaner. Welcome, at any case, to Endinfinium. It's not quite as hideous as it initially looks.' She gave Miranda a telling look. 'At least not yet. Not if we can help it.'

'Um, thanks, but how did you—'

A phone on the desk behind Mrs. Martin began to ring—an ancient, black dial phone with ornate brass numbering. It shook as it rang, but tape secured it to the desk.

'Excuse me a moment.' Mrs. Martin spun on a swivel chair and picked up the phone, and as she nodded urgently, Benjamin glanced over at Miranda. When Mrs. Martin looked back, her expression was somewhere between frustration and anger.

'I'm afraid we've got a problem downstairs that I need to attend to with some haste. Can you wait here for an hour or so?'

'We have to get to class!' Miranda protested. 'We're missing climbing!'

Mrs. Martin lifted a sharp eyebrow and observed them for a few seconds. 'Actually, I could do with your help. Do either of you have experience with a vanishing cannon?'

'You mean, one of those things that makes the—'

27

Mrs. Martin lifted a hand as she turned away. 'Yes, yes, those things. I guess you do. Come with me.'

Benjamin, happy to just be going somewhere, asked, 'What's the problem?'

'There's a blockage in one of the rubbish chutes,' Mrs. Martin said without looking back. 'And it's getting violent.'

6

THE RUBBISH CREATURE

Benjamin was quickly lost in the maze of corridors and stairways, but Mrs. Martin strode along with the purpose of someone who had done this a thousand times before. Miranda was always beside him with a guiding hand whenever he came close to straying, caught askew by Mrs. Martin's sharp twists and turns. The postmodern glasswork of the main entrance had quickly reverted into stone corridors, as if the admissions division had been tacked on to some ancient ruin, but from time to time, they passed through sections of quaint, lacquered log corridors that perhaps filled gaps created by giant geological fissures. As they walked, Benjamin's tattered shoes felt alternately warm and then chillingly cold, though he figured best not to dwell too much on the architectural makeup of this wondrous but terrifying place.

'Here,' Mrs. Martin said at last, stopping beside a large, wooden closet that had a set of painted levers protruding at chest level. She tugged and depressed them like someone playing an air-clarinet, then the door swung open.

'We have some unusual locks here,' Miranda said as way of explanation. 'It's not so much to keep people out, but … well, you'll find out.'

Benjamin wasn't sure if he ever would, though he didn't have time to dwell on it as Mrs. Martin thrust a long, vacuum cleaner-like tube into his hands and attached a small box the size of a football to his waist by a strap. It felt warm to the touch.

'How do I turn it on?'

'It's voice-controlled,' Mrs. Martin said. 'My voice. You think I'd let a couple of kids loose with these things? Do I look like a complete idiot?' Before either could respond, she added, 'Just point it and hold it and you'll do fine.'

'Why's it warm?' Benjamin asked, worried it might burn him. The substance didn't feel totally like metal; rather, something molten and viscous but able to dictate its own laws of motion.

'Don't ask,' Mrs. Martin said, and when he glanced at Miranda, she gave him a little smile as if to say, *And you thought I was bossy?*

Mrs. Martin led them to a thick, oak door which seemed to be vibrating, as the heavy, metal crossbeams were blurred and indistinct. Mrs. Martin cursed under her breath, threw the door open, and led them down a steep set of stone steps illuminated by flickering candles stuck into wooden holders that poked out of the wall. Benjamin wondered who had lit them, how they stayed alight, and why none of them seemed to be melting down, but he figured he might as well just add these questions to his ever-growing list.

At the bottom of the steps, they followed a stone passage that led into a massive chamber stinking of smoke and food waste. A circular stone walkway arced to either side of a wide pit, in which flickered the glow of a deep fire.

'The incinerator,' Mrs. Martin breathed, as though it was a personal enemy. 'Some idiot turned it off.'

Benjamin didn't have time to wonder what she meant. A thunderous roar echoed from a tunnel on the other side of the pit, this one broken through into an antechamber one level above, as if something large and unstoppable had really wanted to find a way out.

Mrs. Martin, holding her vanishing cannon across her chest like a fumigator off to war with a rat-infested barn, marched straight around the incinerator pit with Benjamin and Miranda hurrying to keep pace.

'Any idea what's going on?' Benjamin whispered.

Miranda gave him a pained smile. In the incinerator's glow her cheeks shone like red cherries, and her eyes were bright with the thrill of adventure. 'I don't need to answer this one,' she said. 'Look.'

They turned a corner of the collapsed stone tunnel, where something heaving and monstrous lumbered into view. The thing —whatever it was—was an indecipherable conglomerate of rubbish. Crushed boxes flapped like loose skin over crumpled plastic and chunks of metal from old bicycles, refrigerators, gas heaters, garden chairs, musical instruments, clothes horses, and scores of other smaller items all shifting too quickly to be identified.

'Oi, you!' Mrs. Martin hollered. 'I'd like a word, if you please!'

Three lumpy tubes, each the size of a garden shed, swung toward her, rotating around a central lump that had formed into a mouth and eyes. Two massive pillars as wide as a road stumped from side to side as the creature hobbled around in a circle to face them. As it roared, Benjamin gagged at the repulsive wind that stank of kitchen waste. He glanced at Miranda, who was wiping tears out of her eyes.

'What is it?' he gasped.

'It's made of rubbish,' she said, her voice trembling. 'When it gets crushed … if they don't burn it quick enough … it starts to … to reanimate.'

Benjamin stared. Definitely a dream. This had to be. It couldn't have been anything else. He'd never known a dream to smell so putrid, though. As the creature moved toward them, it knocked aside some crumbling sections of the tunnel wall, and only as they fell did Benjamin realise people were down there, moving the rocks away, attempting to clear up the mess as the monster made it.

'Who are they?' he asked. 'Why aren't they helping us?'

'They're cleaners,' Miranda said, and Benjamin remembered the sweeper in the Great Hall. 'They won't harm their own kind.'

Benjamin had no chance to ask what she meant. Mrs. Martin

screamed, 'Fire!' and suddenly the thing in his hands hummed with motion, stinging his hands with its heat as a vague, mirage-like blur fired from its wide nozzle and slammed into the creature. The beast howled and tried to turn away, knocking down another section of tunnel wall in the process, but there wasn't enough room for something of its size to escape. Benjamin stared as pieces of junk and litter peeled off of the creature's body like shed layers of skin.

In barely five minutes, the destructive monster had been reduced to a heap of stinking—but immobile—rubbish. The machine in Benjamin's hands switched itself off, and Mrs. Martin turned to them with a satisfied look on her face.

'Thank you kindly. The cleaners will do what they're supposed to, now that it's no longer wandering about like a lost kitten. I'll see to it that you get notes excusing you from class once we're back up in the office.'

Miranda, at least, looked pleased about this. With her vanishing cannon switched off, she made imaginary grips and handholds with her fingers, as if still hopeful she could make the end of climbing class. As Mrs. Martin led them back upstairs, Benjamin thought it best to hold his questions for a while as he watched Miranda's hair glowing like flame in the candlelight.

They returned the vanishing cannons to the cupboard with the unusual lock, but not before Mrs. Martin pulled from her pocket a canister of something and sprayed them with a liquid that smelt faintly of chamomile.

'That should calm them down,' she said, as if that made any sense.

After the arduous climb back up to the office, Benjamin wanted to rest more than anything, but as Mrs. Martin stamped two pieces of paper and handed them over, Miranda tugged his arm. 'We have to hurry,' she said.

'Can we still make it to climbing class?'

'Oh, no'—Miranda shook her head—'we've missed that.'

'So what are we late for now?'

She grinned. 'Lunch.'

Benjamin nodded. At last, something worth a little urgency.

As he let Miranda take his hand and pull him away, Mrs. Martin's stern demand echoed in his ears:

'Be sure to come back and complete your enrollment forms!'

He gave her a thumbs-up, but couldn't bring himself to reply. He was too hungry, and the mystery of what this strange place might consider food was great enough to push, for now, all other questions out of his mind.

7

CAPTAIN ROCHE

'Eventually you have to start telling me what's going on,' Benjamin said as Miranda pulled him along through corridors that alternated between old and new, cycling through stone, wood, and prefab plastic. 'Isn't that what prefects are for? Orientation and all that? I've been attacked by burrowing cars, chased by flocks of plastic bags, almost thrown off a bridge, and now I've helped to kill some giant monster made out of rubbish.'

She gave him an irritated look. 'So what would you most like to know?'

He grinned. 'What's for lunch?'

Miranda squeezed his hand just too tightly for it to be affectionate. 'Oh, come on,' she said. 'You really think I'd spoil the surprise?'

They passed under a couple of skylights that bathed them in two kinds of natural light, leaving them trailing twin shadows. Benjamin was reminded to ask Miranda about that when he got the chance.

'We should be in time for our sitting,' Miranda said, glancing down at the empty space on her wrist as if remembering the ghost of an old watch. 'The third years are in front of us today, which is unfortunate. Most of them are on the rugby team. If there's anything good, they'll clean it out.'

They turned a corner to a familiar sound coming from up ahead, and the loneliness Benjamin had pushed aside chose that moment to reacquaint itself. He stopped in his tracks, his arm jerking as Miranda halted a couple of steps in front of him.

'What is it?' she asked. 'Aren't you hungry? Quick, we're going in, and we have to hurry up. Sometimes there's broccoli but not always—'

Benjamin squinted to hide the tear in his eye. 'I can hear voices,' he said. 'Kids queuing for lunch. It just takes me back, that's all. Back to Basingstoke.'

'It must be a wonderful place, Basingstoke,' she said. 'I try not to think about where I came from.'

'Actually, it's probably the most boring town on planet Earth,' he said, forgetting himself as another tear made a run for it down his cheek. 'But it is on planet Earth. That's why I miss it.'

'I bet school dinners here beat school dinners there.' Miranda reached up and swiped the tear off of his face with an accuracy that was disturbing, yet comforting. 'Come on, let's go introduce you to some of the other kids. You'll find we're quite a mixed bag.'

She left him standing there, hurrying ahead with an urgency that suggested she was tiring of his company.

When Benjamin caught up with her again, she was pushing her way into the back of a small crowd of about twenty kids—a mixture of boys and girls of roughly the same age. Some looked completely normal, the same types of kids he might have queued with back home, while others possessed distinct traits in the same way Miranda's crimson hair made her stand out. One wore bright green clothing. Another was completely, shiny bald. One girl had arms that didn't look to be real arms.

'Oi, look at the ragamuffin! Hey, bird's nest! Lost your hairbrush?'

A collective cackle rose from the crowd as faces turned toward him. He saw the flaming peak of Miranda's head in there, but she had turned away.

'Someone couldn't find the costume department!'

'I guess they're letting anyone in these days!'

'I bet he washes his hair with scatlocks!'

Like most kids who were underweight, slightly peculiar, or at the wrong end of the popularity scale, Benjamin had been pushed around from time to time. He had quickly learned the bullying survival guide, though: walk away, ignore them, don't react, and on most occasions the bully got bored and moved on to a more entertaining target. And if they didn't, only one option remained. On his first day at Burnton Secondary, Lewis Black, a podgy boy with eyes too small for his face, had snatched a Robert Westall paperback out of Benjamin's bag and waved it around like a trophy. Benjamin had thrown a wild haymaker, then rugby tackled him, but while Benjamin had received a minor black eye for his bravery and suffered the ignominy of a detention on his first day of school, on his second day, Lewis had nodded at him, aloof but respectful, before running off to terrorise some other poor kid and had bothered him no more after.

Sometimes, in order to establish a line of mutual respect, it was best to get a scrap out of the way.

'Hey, dishcloth head!'

From the middle of the pack, a kid with curly, jet-black hair framing frighteningly green eyes that really didn't belong in such a sour, spiteful face pushed his way back toward Benjamin.

'What happened? Mummy forgot to wash up?'

The mention of his mother flicked an anger switch. As the sour-faced boy laughed, Benjamin launched himself forward, hands closing into fists. The crowd parted in disgusted groans, while scrabbling hands shoved his filthy body away, inadvertently directing him right into the path of his abuser.

His fist clumped into the sour-faced boy's jaw. The boy yelped, then pushed Benjamin back into the crowd and came forward, raising fists of his own. Startled by the vehemence of Benjamin's attack and afraid of having whatever authority he enjoyed undermined, he looked ready to settle in for a long battle. Benjamin was wondering if making a run for it wasn't a better idea, when a sudden hush fell over the crowd.

The kids froze. Hands fell against sides and they all turned in a silent salute. Benjamin, scrabbling on the floor among black socks and white sneakers, found himself on his hands and knees in front of a pair of massive combat-coloured hiking boots, easily a size thirteen or fourteen, with soles as long as his forearms.

'What is going on here?' boomed a voice like a grumbling tank engine. 'You queue in an orderly fashion, or you don't eat, either now or at dinnertime, and you get fifty cleans into the bargain. Is that quite clear?' Before a single voice could pipe up, the speaker added, 'Don't you dare answer me.'

Benjamin, heart racing, slowly lifted his eyes. They traced their way up tree-trunk legs to a body nearly as wide as he was tall, over an unnaturally wide chest, up to a head that was so square it could have been a giant Lego brick.

The crew cut on the chiseled head that bent to meet his gaze was so flat it could have been used to play pitch-n-putt.

'Benjamin Forrest, is that you? At long last. Where have you been? We were starting to think you'd rolled right over.'

With the newcomer's defiant assertion still fresh in his mind, Benjamin just stared up at him, trying not to wilt beneath that unforgiving gaze.

'You have permission to speak, boy. No one else does. Only you.'

'I don't know where I've been, sir.'

The man gave a slow nod. His face was so wide, it was impossible to look at both of his undersized black eyes simultaneously, and had he been from some distant planet where gravity was so strong it squeezed people into short, squat lumps, it would have made perfect sense.

'Well, no need to worry about that now,' he said, reaching down with a dinner-plate sized hand and lifting Benjamin up. 'First of all, you need to eat. You can share the Captain's table today. How lucky for you. And you can call me Roche. Captain Roche.'

Benjamin nodded. He wanted to glance back to see if Miranda was watching, but he was too afraid to look away from the captain's over-wide face. Stubble shadow rose and fell on cheeks the size of Benjamin's palms as the captain chewed on something anonymous.

'The rest of you, snap to it. And Godfrey … you irritating punk, you've got the Captain's Eye on you for the next week.'

Captain Roche jerked, one side of his face cocking, and something small and black fell out of his eye. Benjamin turned to follow its trajectory as it landed with a soft thud on the black-haired boy's cheek. Godfrey's eyes widened in terror, as the little black thing sprouted spider-like legs and scuttled up the side of his face, taking up a sentry position in the crutch of Godfrey's ear. Muted gasps of shock and surprise came from the other boys, but not the outright screaming Benjamin would have expected. They had seen this happen before.

'Remember, children, the war is not against each other,' Captain Roche said, squinting on one side of his massive face. 'Where's Miranda Butterworth?'

A reluctant hand rose up from out of the group of terrified faces. 'Here, sir.'

'You were supposed to bring Master Forrest straight here. You were sidetracked. Did you go off to see your boyfriend again?'

Sniggers came, despite the captain's seemingly unbreakable disciplinary rules. Forced resolute faces holding back smiles parted to let Miranda come forward.

'Don't lie to me, Miss Butterworth. Were you or were you not charged with collecting Master Forrest and bringing him straight here to Endinfinium High?'

The girl gave a short nod.

'Then why didn't you?'

'I got … sidetracked.'

The captain let out a sigh that lasted almost fifteen seconds. Benjamin couldn't be a hundred percent sure; he had only started counting after eight, but Captain Roche had to have lungs the size of tents.

'You'll spend a night in the lockers. Five hundred cleans.'

Misery flooded Miranda's face. Her shoulders sagged, and she opened her mouth to protest, but Captain Roche shook his head. 'And you'll go there immediately. If you do not go by your own free will and confess to the sin keeper your reason for incarceration, I will have you escorted.'

The girl burst into a theatrical flood of tears and, glancing once at Benjamin, she stormed off the way they had come.

Captain Roche watched until she was out of sight, then gave a long shake of his huge head and turned to Benjamin, looking rather pleased with himself.

'Now, young Master Forrest, welcome, at long last. I think it's time we used that old teacher privilege of jumping the queue and went to get something to eat.'

8

LUNCH

V egetables.

Some he knew, others he didn't. One bitter-tasting orange thing looked like a ring doughnut but had the consistency of an onion. Another looked exactly like a green banana but with soft, powdery gunk inside that, despite the appearance of icing sugar, tasted like gourd. In amongst such culinary surprises, though, he found simple potatoes and carrots, turnip and cauliflower, pumpkin and radishes.

After the normality of a dinner queue, Benjamin had expected a normal canteen service where he got to pick the items he wanted, but instead, a rotund woman wearing a mask pulled up over her nose and sunglasses covering her eyes dipped a large wooden bowl into a metal bucket of boiled, chopped vegetables, then dropped it without a word onto the tray Captain Roche had given him. A ladle added a scoop of a yellowy sauce which was sweet and resembled custard. For a drink, he had a tall wooden beaker of water.

The Dining Hall was a cozy, low-ceilinged, wooden room with trestle tables surrounding a central open fire flickering out of a granite cauldron. A vent in the ceiling's wooden vaults allowed smoke to escape, and every now and then a fresh log would tumble out of a protruding chute to crash down into the flames, sending up a shower of sparks. A series of arched, wooden pillars with candles flickering in alcoves made it difficult to see anyone else in the gloom, while lending the Dining Hall an altogether romantic air that was awkwardly inappropriate. Benjamin, wondering why the place hadn't burned to the ground years ago, sat opposite Captain Roche, who took up two seats—one hip perched on each chair—at a table in one corner with a RESERVED FOR STAFF sticker on the deeply varnished hardwood surface.

At the opposite end sat a couple of other teachers talking quietly over their food. Over the captain's jutting headland of a shoulder, Benjamin had a view of both the entrance door from the serving room and the nearest table of pupils, on which two girls and four boys sat. One of them—Godfrey—glared at Benjamin between mouthfuls of food as though his personal space had suffered an invasion.

In some ways it felt good to have made an enemy; it gave the school more normality. In others, it made him a little nervous to have established an opposition before he had built up a circle of friends, particularly considering the only person who had seemed friendship-inclined now languished God-knew-where in some punishment cell.

'We're very glad to have you here with us,' Captain Roche said around mouthfuls of food large enough to have suffocated a smaller man. 'We've been expecting you for some time. You look like you need a chance to settle in, though, so I'll make sure of it that you are excused from afternoon classes and are shown to your room. That fool girl Butterworth was supposed to have done that.'

Benjamin sensed the only way to get answers was to start small, and gradually build up to the more pressing questions.

'What's the Locker Room?' he asked. 'I'm worried that I got Miranda in trouble.'

'That fool girl doesn't need any help. Rest assured, she'll be fine. The Locker Room will give her time to think. It's her own fault; she shouldn't have dithered about getting you over to the school. It can be perilous out there for newcomers. We're hardly bursting at the seams here, are we?'

Captain Roche's shirt looked as though it was, quite literally, bursting at the seams, but Benjamin felt it best not to mention it.

'Miranda told me she had to … go to a class.'

'Don't be fooled by the colour of her hair. She's a sneaky one, that girl. How's the food?'

Benjamin shrugged. 'It's—'

'Missing a couple of bangers? A decent slice of bacon?' Captain Roche gave the kind of guffaw Benjamin associated with men in panama hats from old black-and-white movies. 'Call it as you see it, lad. Don't feel the need to hold back. Not like we can change anything about it, so you might as well say what you see.'

'Is it the same every day?'

'The same.'

'No meat?'

'No.'

'Ever?'

'Ever.'

'Why not?'

Captain Roche speared a lump of carrot as if it were a deserter running for enemy lines. The fork clunked, embedding itself into the wooden bowl.

'Because we don't trust it. Meat doesn't like to stay dead here in Endinfinium. Nothing much does. Hence the woodwork.'

'The wood doesn't come alive?'

'Boy, where have you been? It's already alive. It's just not all that interested in causing trouble.' When Benjamin frowned, Captain Roche pointed at the tabletop. 'Go on, have a feel. It's warm.'

Benjamin put down his fork and placed the flat of his palm onto the table. Captain Roche was right; it did feel slightly warm, but he assumed that was due to the proximity of the fire. Then, before he lifted his hand to resume eating, he felt a barely perceptible motion—like a tiny pulse.

'Did it just move?'

The captain shook his head. 'Not, it's just breathing. It doesn't move anywhere. Unlike a lot of things, it's content to just sit there.'

The captain lapsed into silence, munching on his bowl of vegetables like a cow chewing in its stall. Benjamin tried to eat his own without looking up every few seconds to see if Godfrey watched him. The other boy was, of course, but with feigned innocence, staring without as much as a wrinkled nose to suggest aggression. If a manifestation of Captain Roche's eye really sat on Godfrey's shoulder, in amongst the tendrils of greasy black hair that hung like seaweed over the boy's ears, it kept him sedated. At some point, though, Benjamin would find himself stuck in a rematch, and with the territorial advance stacked so heavily against him, he was unsure he'd come off victorious a second time.

'Well, I guess you could say that filled me up.'

Benjamin looked down. Captain Roche's oversized bowl was empty; just a little puddle of the cream sauce pooled in the grooves at the bottom. Afraid of being left at the table on his own, Benjamin punched the fork into his last stray piece of potato and thrust it into his mouth.

'I'll take you back to admissions,' the captain said, standing up. 'Once you've filled out your forms, Mrs. Martin will show you to your room. You're probably looking forward to meeting your roommate.'

'Roommate?'

A comb-sized eyebrow rose over the captain's non-squinting eye. 'Oh, didn't you know? Scatty Miss Butterworth was supposed to tell you. There was only one spot left in the first years' dorms, I'm afraid, so we didn't have much choice. I imagine in time you'll get used to rooming with him.' Then, with a muttered aside that probably wasn't supposed to be overheard, the captain added, 'The little brat.'

9

WILHELM

Mrs. Martin seemed no more excited to see Benjamin than she had before.

'I'm afraid the headmaster is away on business at the moment,' she said as she emerged from the office with a big metal key in her hand and a bag over her shoulder. 'Have I already mentioned that? He should be back in a day or two, so at that time you'll be taken to his office for a short orientation meeting.'

Her voice held a hint of frustration, as though the headmaster should have already returned. 'Will I find out why I'm here?' Benjamin asked.

Mrs. Martin arched her eyebrows. 'In a sense, as best as any of us know,' she said, as if the answer should be obvious. 'And I'm sure a few far more important things.'

'Why are *you* here?' Benjamin blurted before he could stop himself. 'Yesterday—at least, I think it was yesterday—you were sitting at a desk in the office of my school in Basingstoke, and now you're sitting at a desk here, in this school at the supposed end of the world. There are two suns in the sky, everything dead seems to be coming to life, and some of the people aren't really human. Why aren't you still in Basingstoke, too?'

'You've had a long journey,' she said, turning her eyes down. 'The adrenaline has set your mouth to motoring. A good night's sleep will sort that out.' She shrugged. 'If Wilhelm lets you sleep,' she muttered, voice trembling. 'Heavens, couldn't they have picked someone else?'

'I'm sorry,' he muttered, looking at his feet.

Mrs. Martin sighed. 'We all have our stories. Soon you'll have yours, and you'll have to deal with it the way we all do, in any way you can.'

'I'm just … it's all so confusing.'

Mrs. Martin smiled. 'Look, give me a question. If I can answer it, I will. Only one, though. Most of them you'll need to figure out for yourself. The answers aren't all the same for each of us.'

Benjamin thought for a while. Which single question would give him the most insight into this place? Already, he was back to thinking this was all a bizarre dream, even though his mouth still tasted of cauliflower dunked in custard. But just in case it wasn't, he needed some way to get inside his guide's brain to pick out the best clue that this place was, indeed, real.

In the end, the question picked itself. 'Why … is Captain Roche so wide?'

Mrs. Martin laughed, a hollow clucking sound like a chicken getting strangled. 'Isn't it obvious? I assume you didn't play truant from every science class back in Basingstoke?'

'Not all of them.'

'Diversity. Do you look exactly like me? It wouldn't be much fun if we were all … um … the same. You'll just find that Endinfinium has a wider range to choose from than you're probably used to. Anyway,'—she gave a little shake of her head —'enough of that.'

'But—'

'I said one question.' She wagged a finger at him. 'You can grill the headmaster when you see him. First of all, I have to talk you through negotiating the walkway to the dormitories without alarm.'

Benjamin gulped. 'There's not another rope bridge, is there?'

'Oh no, nothing like that horrible old thing. One of these days they'll get around to replacing it.'

'But…'

His voice trailed off. They had reached the end of a corridor, where a wide pair of glass doors opened out onto a jagged cliff. To their left, the cliff rose in spines and tight gullies; to their right, it dropped almost vertically toward a grey beach far below. A thin path barely as wide as a person led straight out, following the cliff's arc until it reached a craggy, windswept headland.

A four-storey wooden building stood atop the headland, so close to the edge, its foundations were literally undermined and loose boards flapped back and forth in the breeze.

'You've got to be joking….'

'The dormitories. It's the best place for them. If something happens to the school, then the pupils will be safe.'

'You call crossing that precipice to get to class "safe"?'

'Oh, you'll get used to it. It's not that far, is it?'

Benjamin looked down at the grey curve of beach, and gulped. He'd vomited on a school trip to Blackpool Tower, while the lift was still sitting on the ground. If he ever made it across to the dormitories, there was little chance he would be coming back.

'You'll get hungry,' Mrs. Martin said, as if reading his thoughts. 'A lot of pupils get scared, but they all get over it. You'll be dancing across blindfolded before you know it. In fact, that used to be the rugby team's initiation, until Captain Roche caught wind of it, and that was only because of poor … anyway. Let's get moving.'

She had barely touched the door when a huge, fluttering cloud rushed up the cliffside, engulfing the path for a few seconds before banking toward them and disappearing over the top of the school. One solitary plastic bag—*scatlock*, he reminded himself—flapped against the glass doors like a giant moth, did a pirouette, then fluttered away.

'That's something else you should know,' Mrs. Martin said. She tapped a hand against a wooden cupboard door beside the entrance. A click sounded, and it swung open. 'Don't forget your scatlock cape.'

Inside hung several brown cloaks. Mrs. Martin picked one out and dropped it over Benjamin's head. He let out a startled cry, blinded until he realised the cape had a thin mesh on one side of the head portion for him to see out.

'Step into the foot holes,' Mrs. Martin said, tugging on the cloth until his battered shoes were inside. 'Then you zip it at the back. Here.' She pulled across a zip, and he was completely enclosed in the cloth bag.

'What's this for?'

'It keeps the little blighters out. They're mindless, but they have a certain intuition. They like to block things. Eyes, ears, nose, you name it. If they can, they'll wrap around your face and suffocate you. This is a happy hunting ground for them because of the wind that rushes up the cliff face. All the kids who've fallen off have had some sort of trouble with scatlocks.'

'Fallen off … why not just build a tunnel or something?'

'The rock strata on this part of the cliff won't handle excavation. And even if it could, don't get me started on trying to organise such a thing.'

'I guess I won't.'

'Right. Off you go.'

She pulled open the door and pushed him outside. As he started to turn, Mrs. Martin slammed the door shut, putting a solid wall of glass between them.

'Sorry, got to keep out the draft,' she said, voice muffled. 'Room thirty-five. Third floor, near the back. The housemaster will show you. And tell Wilhelm to make sure he shows up for braiding class. Professor Eaves said if he doesn't show up by the end of the week, he'll braid him a new … well, just tell him.'

'Sure.'

'Hurry up, now. You hear that buzzing noise? Scatlocks.'

Benjamin tugged on the door handle, but Mrs. Martin held it shut from the inside, leaning back to put her considerable weight into play. The buzzing came closer; the scatlocks would be on him in seconds if he didn't move. In the stupid cape he felt rigid and inflexible, aware that one strong gust could send him toppling down to the beach, but Mrs. Martin still held the door shut, face stern and unsympathetic.

Benjamin took a deep breath and stepped forward. The drop fell away in front of him, interspersed with jagged, rocky outcrops that would beat him up a bit on his way down. Far below, the beach appeared to shimmer, as though high tide had come in a sudden rush. Then he realised. Not water. Scatlocks. Millions of the accursed things, preparing to catch the next up-gust and rip him off the cliffside.

He started moving, left hand out near the rock face but not touching, in case he accidentally pushed himself off. The other he held out in front of him like a guide. The buzzing from below loudened as a rushing grey cloud swarmed up the cliff. Back by the door, Mrs. Martin gestured in ever more frantic hand motions toward the far side.

'Hurry! They'll knock you off!'

Benjamin turned to look for the voice. The door to the dormitory had opened, and a cherubic face now peered out.

'Do I sound like I'm joking?'

The boy was about twelve, but small for his age. Dark brown hair in tight curls created a sheepskin-like mop around his head. He wore green pajamas and a light blue dressing gown secured by a bright yellow belt.

'I'll fall!'

'Not if you get moving, but you will if the scatlocks catch you. Quick!'

Miranda had saved him on the rope bridge, but no one could save him now except for himself. Benjamin stared down at the rising tide of suffocating death, gritted his teeth, and raced across the rest of the path. He barreled through the entrance, past the boy, who laughed and slammed the door shut moments before a grey cloud pattered against it.

'Nice one!'

As Benjamin fell, the scatlock cape twisted, the back of its hood covering his face. He scrabbled at it, trying not to panic.

'Relax, you're safe. I've got it.'

A cool gust of air tickled his back as the boy unzipped the cape and helped him climb out. The boy then dusted down the cape and hung it up in a cupboard by the door.

'Wilhelm,' he said, sticking out a hand. 'You're Benjamin, right? My new roommate?'

Benjamin shook a wiry but strong hand. 'That's right.'

Wilhelm nodded. 'Let me guess, the old bag gave you a message for me?'

'Show up at braiding class.'

Wilhelm rolled his eyes. 'Old Dusty Eaves won't mind if I don't. He hates me anyway.'

'What's braiding class?'

'Where you learn to make those stupid rope bridges.'

'What for?'

'In case one of them falls down.'

'I had to cross one to get here. Are there others?'

'That's the big one,' Wilhelm said, nodding. 'But yeah, there are a few about. Not so many near the school, though.'

'Why can't they build proper bridges?'

Wilhelm laughed. 'Why can't they do most things you would do in a normal place? A bunch of reasons. Come on, I'll make you a cup of tea. Since we're going to be roommates, we might as well get to know each other.'

'You have tea?'

'Of course. It's the best. Not everything sucks in this horrible place.'

THE DORMITORIES

The little common room was on the bottom floor nearest to the cliff edge. 'Just don't sit by the windows,' Wilhelm said. 'If it collapses, you'll drop straight over. Stay near the middle of the room and you'll have a chance to run. They say it's safe, but I'm not so sure.'

'Thanks for the advice.'

A fire burned in a grate near the back wall. Wilhelm filled a metal kettle from a tap and placed it into the flames. They sat on wooden stools around it, warming their hands until the kettle began to whistle, when Wilhelm filled two wooden mugs with water then spooned in some powder out of a bowl.

'It's chamomile,' he said. 'The stuff grows wild just back from the headland, but I've heard there are farms of it farther inland. They put it in all the food because it's pretty much the only flavouring they've got.'

'Mrs. Martin sprayed the vanishing cannons with something that smelt like it. She said it would relax them.'

'Yeah, it's pretty good for doing that.'

'Whatever that means.'

Wilhelm shrugged. 'You'll figure it out. As much as anyone knows, at any rate.'

The tea tasted pretty good, and Benjamin was reminded of evenings at his grandmother's house. How he would kill for one of her homemade chocolate biscuits now, the ones with the oversized lumps of Dairy Milk in them because she said regular cooking chocolate was too bland…. He pushed the thought from his mind and turned to Wilhelm.

'Do you have any idea what's going on? I've found it impossible to get a straight answer out of anyone. Every time I ask anything, I get brushed off. Where on earth are we?'

'Or aren't, is the better question. I know some, I guess. But not much. I've only been here for a couple of months, and I've spent most of that time causing trouble.'

'Am I dreaming?'

Wilhelm shrugged again. 'I don't think so. If you are, it's a really long dream.'

'Why do I keep seeing all these weird things like tractors that can talk and hordes of flapping plastic bags—'

'Scatlocks.'

'Why are they called scatlocks? That's such a ridiculous name.'

Wilhelm laughed. 'No one seems to know why. At least, they won't say if they do. I've asked a bunch of people.'

'They're flying supermarket bags. And why are they flying? Nothing … makes … sense.'

'There's a fundamental rule to this place,' Wilhelm said. 'Better if I demonstrate.'

He slid open a window, balanced his cup outside on the ledge, then pulled the window closed again. For a couple of minutes he sat in silence, watching it, then pulled open the window and brought the cup back in.

'Dip your finger in the tea.'

'It's cold!'

'Of course it is. Now feel the cup.'

Benjamin took it from Wilhelm, nearly dropping it in surprise. 'It's warm!'

'Yup. That's because the wood itself is alive. Feel anything made out of wood. It's the same.'

'How? I mean, I've seen all these things, but … I don't get it.'

'Endinfinium is this place where stuff people made comes back to life. Don't ask me why, or how. If the professors know, they're not telling. It happens to everything. It starts to get warm, then it starts to move about. Some things just shake a lot, others eventually grow personalities. They're called "reanimates." How reanimated they can get depends on how complicated they were to start with, and whether or not they get fused with anything else. Some, like the old gatekeeper, have memories and intelligence, and they choose whether or not to be nice to you. Others, like the scatlocks, are mindless, instinct-based.'

'But that's crazy. It can't happen to everything! What about the buildings?'

'If they get too reanimated, they start to shake and break up. Wood is pretty sedate, that's why you see a lot of it. Rock is inanimate, of course, but all the metal and plastic … anything humans have played around with at some point, it gets a bit jumpy after a while. They have periodic re-spraying parties. There was one just after I arrived. No one knows what happens if it goes untreated for too long. I don't think they want to find out.'

'Why not?'

'Because they don't want to know.'

Benjamin sat brooding over this for a few moments. From what he'd seen it made sense, but the why of everything would have to wait until he met the headmaster.

'How many kids are there?'

Wilhelm shrugged. 'About eighty. Fifteen or so in each year. The older kids are pretty gung-ho about everything, as though they've forgotten all about where they came from. Don't expect any allies, if they talk to you at all. My guess is that the dissenters get weeded out. I've been here for two months, and after the first week, I refused to attend any classes. I'm hoping dissenters get sent back, but if they don't, I'll take the alternative.'

'Which is?'

Wilhelm whistled and made a falling motion with his hand. 'If I had to guess, it would be over the edge, with the rubbish.'

Benjamin stared out the window. Clouds had rolled in, but from their viewpoint, he could clearly see where the roiling ocean just stopped and gave way to sky. It wasn't that far; swimmable on a fine day.

'What if that is the way back?' he said, pointing. 'What if that's the only way?'

'It's crossed my mind. I'll wait them out a bit longer before I try it, though. Come on,'—Wilhelm stood up—'I'll show you our room. You made any friends yet? Other than me, of course.'

Benjamin shrugged. 'A girl called Miranda met me on the beach.'

Wilhelm nodded. 'Red hair? Blue eyes? About this tall? Aggressive? Yeah, I know her. She's the prefect of the first year because the previous kid disappeared one day and no one else wanted to do it. Or so I heard. She's you're friend, is she?'

'I'm not sure, to be honest,' Benjamin said. 'Captain Roche sent her to the Locker Room for disobedience.'

'He likes to do that. I have a couple of thousand cleans outstanding on my account. I'm pretty sure he'd drag me down there himself, but he's too wide to get across the path.'

Benjamin sniggered. He could imagine the captain leaning half out over the edge, one eye squinting down as a flock of scatlocks raced up toward him.

'And I've made an enemy,' he said. 'Godfrey.'

'Ah, don't worry about him, he's a chump. He's a year ahead of us. Has a massive chip on his shoulder.'

'And now he has one of Captain Roche's eyes.'

Wilhelm laughed. 'Ouch. I've heard about that. Apparently if the captain closes his other eye, he can see out of the one he sticks to people, like a camera. It tends to keep the bad kids in line, and gives him plenty of excuses to send them to the Locker Room.'

'Isn't it kind of unusual to be able to do that?'

Wilhelm smiled. 'You seen anything you would describe as usual yet?'

Benjamin shrugged again. 'You?'

'Ha! I'll take that as a compliment. Well, this is it. Our mansion.'

A tatty wooden bunk bed stood against the wall nearest the door. A table with two chairs sat beneath the window, with a couple of units of drawers and a wardrobe taking up the other wall, a strange cross between a prison and a mountaineering hut.

A few items of dirty washing lay scattered around, and beside the door, some crumpled pieces of paper sat at the bottom of a litter bin.

'Yours is the top bunk. You didn't have any stuff except for your bag, which I hung up to dry in the laundry room at the end of the corridor.'

Benjamin started. 'What bag? I dropped my school bag in the sea.'

'Someone fished it out and brought it up here. I don't know who, but it was in your post tray in the lobby. I brought it up to your room because it was dripping on mine below it. Benjamin Forrest. Wilhelm Jacobs.'

'Thanks.'

'Don't get excited. It was sopping wet. Your books will be ruined, but you might be able to use the bag again. You're lucky it didn't get eaten. They're hungry, those things in the water, and they will quite literally eat anything.'

Wilhelm excused himself to go to the bathroom, leaving Benjamin alone in their room, which was a far cry from his cozy little room in Basingstoke, with its Disney posters, Transformers bedspread, and shelves of his favourite books. But it could have been worse.

Then the floor creaked, and the whole room seemed to shift.

'Don't worry about that,' Wilhelm shouted from down the hall. 'It does that from time to time. The beams will straighten themselves out in a couple of hours or so.'

Feeling a little uneasy in their room that tilted toward the sea, Benjamin left to explore the rest of the building, which had four floors with around twenty bedrooms on each. Next to each door was a name plate, and it appeared they were roomed in alphabetical order. Many of the names were unusual, some foreign-sounding, others a mixture of numbers and letters like lines of computer code. The last few rooms on each floor, the names reset back to A, so he assumed these were assigned to the girls.

All of the doors were wide open, as if ready for inspection, but only some rooms had been made up just in case. Most were typical kids' rooms—all discarded clothing, dog-eared textbooks, and dusty furniture.

Two toilets sat on each floor—one for boys, one for girls. The first floor housed two shower rooms, with a timetable for morning showers taped up beside the door. First year boys at 5.45 a.m. Benjamin balked at the early time, but then wondered if the days here were the same length as they were back in Basingstoke, what with having two suns and everything.

A noise came from a room at the far end of the corridor, nearest to the inland side of the building. Benjamin pushed through a door marked LAUNDRY to find himself facing a large, wooden cauldron filled with a spinning whirlpool of steaming water. Items of clothing circled like fish, repeatedly pushed under by a jet of water from a wooden pipe poking out of the wall. Underneath, used water trickled into a plug hole and gurgled down a drain.

'Put your dirties in there first thing in the morning, then ladle them out when you get back,' Wilhelm said from behind him, making Benjamin jump. 'They don't use washing powder, so you have to soak them. For a new kid like you, best to get back early, or Godfrey and his crew might leave you shirtless. They've done it to a couple of others.'

'I'll try to remember that.'

'Oh, and I left your bag over there. It got kind of smashed, I'm afraid, but your guidebook should still be in there.'

'My what?'

Wilhelm pointed to the far side of the room, where several items of clothing on a series of racks and hangers dried in front of an open fire behind a grill. His bag hung from a hook nearest to the fire. Wilhelm had taken out his books and neatly arranged them in a semi-circle, but even from a distance the water damage was obvious, their covers crinkled and pictures blurred. Benjamin shrugged. He probably wouldn't need them anyway.

Lying on top of everything, though, was a thin book he didn't recognise. It was nearest to the heat, but so damp, opening it would tear the pages.

'Do you have one like this?' he asked.

'They're from the Grand Lord,' Wilhelm said. 'He gives one

to all of us. It's nothing much, just a bunch of details on the classes. No one knows how he does it, but he seems to know when we're coming. I've never actually seen him close up, but there's definitely something odd about him.' Wilhelm grinned. 'Even for here.'

Benjamin picked up the thin book and turned it over in his hands. It was definitely made of paper, but of a kind older than any he had ever seen.

'Mine's a lot thinner than yours,' Wilhelm said. 'Perhaps you're special, I don't know. All mine talks about is what happens in each lesson. Braiding, climbing, woodwork, engineering … all sorts of boring stuff. I liked the idea of the orienteering lesson, but I don't want to break my standard and show up for just one thing.'

Benjamin tentatively lifted the front cover of the book. Underneath, a damp circle in the centre threatened to rip out the hearts of the subsequent pages if he tried to open it any further. It could take days for it to dry out completely, but Benjamin sensed this book might offer his own way out. He would lift one page at a time, drying them out one by one, until the whole book was dry. It was the only way. On the first page, handwritten in black ink, it said:

Welcome, young Master Forrest, to the School at the End of the World! Herein you will learn everything you need to successfully graduate from the most unique school of all time, the school that stands at the edge of everything, a school that is threatened daily with its own end, an end that only the love of our wonderful teaching staff and pupils can help to prevent! Turn the page to find out how you can help!

Yours, and welcome,
Grand Lord Sebastien Aren
Headmaster

Benjamin was just wondering whether to risk turning the page, when a loud thump came from downstairs.

Wilhelm grabbed his arm. 'Quick,' he said. 'Back to the

room. Pretend to be unpacking or something. If we get caught messing around in here, we might get sent to the Locker Room.'

'Who is it?'

Wilhelm gave the widest smile Benjamin had yet seen.

'Gubbledon Longface.'

'Who?'

'The housemaster.'

11

THE HOUSEMASTER

Something that couldn't walk properly stumped up the stairs. Benjamin listened to the heavy footfalls as he sat on the top bunk and pretended to make his bed. They sounded too awkward to belong to a man. Wilhelm had scurried off to the dormitory kitchens, where he said he had been on permanent cleaning duty since his refusal to join any classes.

The footsteps paused at the top of the stairs, and Benjamin, heart thudding, risked a glance down. Something long and brown appeared in the doorway. Huge nostrils flared, and through eroded fur and flesh appeared white slivers of bone. Two large eyes flickered at him. One remaining ear bent and then straightened.

Benjamin gulped as a hoof poked out from a purple silk shirt and rapped on the open door.

'Mr. Forrest,' whinnied the reanimated corpse of a horse that wore human clothes and stood upright like a man, 'I was given word that you had arrived.'

Benjamin climbed down. As he stared at the housemaster, he didn't know whether to be terrified or amused.

'Nice to meet you, sir.'

'My name is Gubbledon. I am the housemaster of these dorms.' The horse stuck out a hoof, and when Benjamin hesitated, the housemaster said, 'Shake it, please. I expect common courtesies from my charges.'

Benjamin took hold of the hoof—which was bone cold—and gave it a quick shake. 'I'm sorry, sir.'

'No need for that. Did you bump into your worthless roommate? He should be here somewhere. Doing his chores, I hope. I can't force him to go to class, of course, but I can force him to work his useless butt off while he stays here. His only alternative is to sit outside and play with the scatlocks.'

'Yes, I met him.'

'You have been excused from all duties for the rest of the afternoon. Have you been drilled on procedures?'

'No, not really.'

The horse rolled his dead eyes, and one took a little longer to bounce back into place than the other. 'No surprise. The transfer of workable information is one way this school lets itself down.'

Benjamin nodded. 'I have, um, noticed.'

'Breakfast is served in shifts in the common room downstairs. You'll be assigned to a breakfast rotor for duties, although you'll start off with simple tasks, such as serving and clearing away the utensils. Be aware that causing trouble or shirking your duties is not tolerated and will result in a harsher punishment.'

'I understand.'

'Lunch and dinner are served in the Dining Hall in the main block. You are expected to be out of the dormitories by eight a.m. except in ex … ext … ex … extenuating circumstances.'

Hearing the horse stutter over the word 'extenuating' tipped Benjamin over the edge, and he let out a snort of laughter he had been bottling up inside, then clamped his hand over his mouth, making a pitiful attempt to convert it into a cough.

When he looked up, the housemaster was glaring at him. Gubbledon gave a light whinny, the visible bones in part of his face vibrating like piano keys.

'Is something funny?'

Benjamin shook his head. 'No, nothing at all.'

'I run a tight ship here, Master Forrest. Dissent of any form will not be tolerated.'

'I'm sorry.'

The reanimated horse stared at him for a long few seconds. 'I think it would be best if you joined Master Jacobs in the dormitory kitchen for the rest of the afternoon. There are always pots to scrub and floors to clean.'

Benjamin apologised again, then followed the housemaster down the stairs to the kitchen, where Wilhelm was up to his elbows in frothy water that filled a massive sink.

'It appears that your union is one made in the two heavens,' the housemaster said. 'I shall return in an hour to survey your progress.'

Gubbledon stumped off into a room beside the entrance, closing the door behind him with a soft click. Wilhelm turned to Benjamin, unable to keep the grin off of his face.

'You laughed, didn't you?'

'I couldn't help it. What was I supposed to do? He's a dead horse and he was talking to me about chores.'

Wilhelm gave a vehement shake of his head. 'No, no. He's a dead *race*-horse. Believe me, you'll hear that one. He won some famous race in a previous, um, life. Or so he says. And don't ever call him Longface to his, um, face. That's a kids-only term. Don't even allude to it, as in "Why the long face?" I did it once and he made me clean all the dormitory windows.'

'That doesn't sound so bad.'

'From the outside.'

Benjamin thought about the flocks of scatlocks and the treacherous drop to the sea far below. 'Ouch,' he said. 'Why is everyone here so weird?'

'Believe me, after a while, you'll begin to appreciate whatever normality you can find. Even clowns like Godfrey don't seem so bad after a couple of weeks.'

Benjamin shook his head as he plunged his hands into the water and felt around for a bowl that needed washing. 'Where on earth are we?' he said.

'I have no idea,' Wilhelm answered. 'But I've made it my mission to find out.'

12

DINNER

The larger of the two suns had just set, disappeared into the haze beyond the edge of the sea, leaving the sky awash with orange, when other pupils' voices began to sound downstairs. During their afternoon of washing pots and pans, Wilhelm had told Benjamin a little about the classes' structure, that there were 'core' classes that everyone—himself, by personal choice, excluded—had to attend, while others were elective, some of which ran into the evenings or even happened late at night. As a result, the dormitory was never really quiet; someone was always coming or going. For the most part, though, pupils returned around five o'clock, got changed for dinner back in the Dining Hall at six-thirty, then returned to their rooms to study or engage in light free time activities until the official lights-out at ten p.m.

Just after five, the housemaster called all of the kids together in the breakfast common room and made Benjamin stand up on a stool at one end. Most of them looked tired, reluctant to have their free time interrupted, rolling their eyes and talking amongst themselves as Gubbledon called for order. The reanimated horse appeared to have forgiven Benjamin for his earlier transgressions; he waxed lyrical about how the others should look after Benjamin, and help him get to grips with life in Endinfinium. Then he asked Benjamin to say a few words.

Neither Miranda nor Godfrey were in the crowd. At the back, Wilhelm also stood on a stool so he could see, smirking while Gubbledon glared at him from the front.

'Um, thank you,' Benjamin stuttered. 'It's been an interesting day so far. This morning, I woke up on a beach and had a car almost eat me, and now I'm standing in front of all of you. It's nice to meet you all, I guess, and I hope to enjoy my time here in Endinfinium … wherever here is, of course.'

Some kids at the front sniggered. Benjamin cleared his throat and continued. 'I'm from a place called Basingstoke in the UK. My father is a train driver for Great Western Railways and my mother works in Lloyds TSB. They drive a Honda Civic and a Ford Explorer and like to go for a pub lunch on Sundays. My dad always complains about the texture of the roast potatoes, no matter what pub we go to, and my mum always insists on taking a scenic route home, which usually involves us getting lost. I have a six-year-old brother called David. He has learning difficulties and has to go to a special school. He cries if mum cooks turnip and it touches any of his other food, but he can complete math equations quicker than my dad. My birthday is January the thirty-first. I, um, don't like moths or boiled cabbage.' He grinned. 'Or boiled moths.'

The sniggers from the front were more mocking than amused, and Benjamin immediately regretted his attempt at a joke. The housemaster sighed and waved him down off of the stool.

'Well, I hope you'll all make Benjamin feel at home. Now, go and get ready for dinner. I apologise that we're now running a little late, so if Captain Roche throws a tantrum, you can blame it on me.'

The crowd dispersed, and Benjamin was relieved. He'd seen more than a few disapproving glares, and thought he had recognised a couple of kids from Godfrey's crew. Of the others, at first glance, most seemed normal.

Wilhelm met him up in their room. 'This chest of drawers is yours,' he said. 'There are two types of clothes: school uniforms and bed wear. You have to wear a uniform whenever you're outside the dorms, but there's a casual one for dinner. It's the one with the zip-up jacket instead of the buttoned one. The loose ones with the elastic pants are for gym-type classes, which includes stuff like climbing, both rock and tree, and orienteering.' He grinned. 'I've never worn mine. I really want to go to orienteering, but you know, I can't break my protest for just one thing. It's kind of like going on hunger strike but only eating steak.'

Benjamin smiled. He hadn't really paid much attention to what the other kids had been wearing, but when he thought about the crowd downstairs, he realised that the kids had been divided into six shades of blue, from a light grey-blue to a dark blue that bordered on purple. The older kids had been wearing the darker colours, and his suspicions were confirmed when he pulled open his drawer to reveal several light blue jackets and slacks, as well as white underpants and shirts. Everything was made of cotton, except for the undershirts, which were silk.

'Natural fibres,' Wilhelm told him when he asked. 'Polyester or acrylic gets a little jumpy. The natural stuff just keeps you warm.'

There were two pairs of shoes: a smart pair he assumed was for indoor classes, and a tough, durable outdoor pair. Both were leather-made with cork soles and no discernible brand markings. Other various items sat in the drawers, too: a toothbrush and a jar of paste, a hairbrush, nail file, several pencils.

Benjamin realised he'd done no personal grooming at all since waking up on the beach, so he rushed off down to the shower rooms to brush his hair and teeth. Stray bits of vegetation were stuck in his hair, as well as half a twitching scatlock, which he pitched out through a little window in the bathroom. Then he grabbed himself a quick shower under a surprisingly hot and powerful jet of water.

Afterward, while he brushed his wet mop of hair, Benjamin stared at his face in the mirror and realised how quickly everything was reverting to normal. At his best estimate, he'd been in Endinfinium for less than eight hours, yet here he was, preparing for dinner with a group of strangers—some he wasn't sure were even human—as if about to settle down for lunch with his family.

Don't forget them, whispered a voice in the back of his mind, and he suddenly felt the urge to cry, something he had not done since he had fallen off of a swing on his eighth birthday and split open the front of his right knee so badly it had needed five stitches. So far, he had directed all his questions forward: Where was he? What was going on? Why was he here? He'd barely had time to think about what might be happening in his absence.

Were his parents looking for him? Were they even aware yet that he had disappeared? What about David? He had a love-hate relationship with his little brother, but if David had vanished, he would certainly miss the little tyke.

'None of it's your fault,' a voice behind him said. He spun to find Wilhelm standing there, curls bouncing after brushing. 'I know what you're thinking. I spent the first week thinking the same. Why am I here? Who brought me? What do they want? How can I get home?' Wilhelm came forward and patted Benjamin on the shoulder. 'I mean, is this place even real? How can it be? But just remember: you didn't do anything. It's not your fault that you're here.'

Benjamin forced a smile, but inside, he was wracked with doubts. 'How do I know that?'

'How could it be? If every kid who imagined himself waking up in some *Alice-in-Wonderland* mystery place actually did so, there wouldn't be any kids left.'

'I guess so.'

'Just hang in there, and you'll figure everything out.' Wilhelm shrugged. 'That's what I keep telling myself, anyway. Come on, let's go eat. I go stir crazy cooped up in here, and dinner is the only reason I'll set foot in that accursed place.'

Crossing the precipice to the main building was just as terrifying as the first time, but stuck in the middle of a line of other kids. Benjamin had no choice but to brave it. There were whoops and cheers as each kid made it to the far door, more of a thrill kind than of absolute fear. Just as he squeezed inside and let out a deep breath, someone screamed, 'Scatlocks!', and the line of kids behind him all crouched down in regimented fashion, their arms over their heads as a flock of the fluttering creatures filled the air.

'Shut the door!' someone growled beside him, pushing the door out of his hands to slam it shut, and Benjamin realised he had been staring. The older boy glared at him for a few seconds longer, then rolled his eyes and set about taking off his scatlock cape. Benjamin watched through the window until the air had cleared and the rest of the kids resumed their crossing.

'You have to guard me,' Wilhelm said as they followed the other kids to the Dining Hall. 'A couple of teachers have it in for me. Dusty Eaves is one; Captain Roche, the other. I've done five spells in the Locker Room, one for a day and a half, but they can't break me. Whenever they let me out, I go straight back to the dorms and refuse to go to class. I'd stay over there, but breakfast leftovers won't keep me going all day, will they?'

Having not yet had breakfast, Benjamin wasn't sure how to answer, so instead he said, 'Wouldn't it be easier to just go to class?'

Wilhelm shook his head. 'Nope. It's the principle. I didn't ask to be here, so they've got another thing coming if they think I'll comply. I'm not some dog that will do tricks at a click of their fingers. If I get some straight answers, I'll think about it, but you know what the truth is?'

'What?'

Wilhelm leaned close. 'No one knows what's going on. None of them. Not even the mighty Grand Lord Bastien himself. I got to meet him, you know. Kind of. He stayed behind a screen so all I could hear was his voice, but he didn't tell me anything straight up. Just gave me a load of vague answers. They're only pretending to know what's going on because knowledge is power and all that, right? If they told us straight out that they have no idea why any of us are here, they'd have no control over us.'

Benjamin was going to point out that they already had no control over Wilhelm, but they had reached the front of the queue, where one of the masked, sunglasses-wearing dinner ladies was scooping brown gunge into a bowl and putting it onto a tray in front of him.

'Great. Curry night,' Wilhelm said. 'A shame it's not spicy and there's no meat in it.'

'Why do they wear sunglasses?' Benjamin asked as they made their way to a far-corner table.

'Can't you guess? They're reanimated. Do you really want to look at a corpse while it serves your food?'

'I suppose not.' Benjamin dipped a piece of lumpy bread into the brown gunge, gave it a sniff, then a tentative bite. It was actually pretty good, even though Wilhelm scowled as though he'd found a cowpat on his plate.

'You said you'd been in the Locker Room,' Benjamin said. 'What is it?'

'It's on one of the basement levels, western side of the school. There aren't any actual lockers, just cubicles for you to sit in. You have to do menial work for a few hours. Kind of like detention. I'd refuse to go, but they've cornered me a few times, and those cleaners, they're stronger than they look. Once you're in there, you're stuck.'

'Can you take me down there? I want to see Miranda.'

Wilhelm rolled his eyes. 'Can't you wait until tomorrow? How many cleans did she get? If it was less than five hundred, she'll be out by the morning.'

'I want to say sorry for getting her put in there.'

Wilhelm sighed. 'Okay, but only if you do something for me.'

'What?'

Wilhelm's answer came in a rush: 'Tell Captain Roche you don't know where I am.'

'Jacobs!' boomed a loud voice from behind Benjamin just as Wilhelm ducked down under the table. Captain Roche threaded his way awkwardly through the tables, a task nigh on impossible for a man of his considerable width.

'Stand up, Master Forrest,' the captain instructed. 'Don't you dare let the little mite escape.'

Benjamin did as he was told. He peered under the table as Captain Roche reached him, but Wilhelm had vanished.

'Where did he go?'

'Who?'

'Your little friend. Tell me the truth, or you'll be spending your first night in the Locker Room.'

Benjamin peered up at the squat, squinting face. 'Sir, I

honestly have no idea. Did you want him for something?' Then, unable to resist, he added a little icing to the lie. 'He talked so highly of you and your classes. I'm sure he'll be sorry he missed you. Perhaps he went to the bathroom or something? It is curry night, after all.'

Captain Roche glared with his one remaining eye. 'You just be careful about spending too much time with that little runt,' he said. 'I'll have him scraping the bark off my climbing shoes before the term is out, you mark my words.'

'I'll be sure to let him know.'

As the captain scowled and stomped off, Benjamin felt something tug on his ankle. Under the table, Wilhelm appeared to be sticking up out of the floor. Benjamin stared, then realised his roommate had removed a wooden floorboard and slipped down into the space beneath.

'How did you know that was there?'

'I made it. It's the only way I can eat in peace sometimes. The good captain is supposed to eat on third sitting, with the fifth and sixth years, but sometimes he tries to catch me out. Pass down my bowl, will you? Even this dirt starts tasting good when you're starving.'

'Here.'

'Listen, he's watching for me now. Meet me near the stairs to level four in about fifteen minutes. I'll show you where the Locker Room is since you helped me hide and all. Go out of the Dining Hall, first left, then first right.' Wilhelm winked. 'Enjoy dinner.'

Benjamin couldn't help smiling. As the floorboard clunked back down, he figured, if he was going to spend the next however long in this bizarre place, it was good at least to have a friend.

13

THE SIN KEEPER

Benjamin had just left the Dining Hall when a bell rang and a voice came over a public address system from a speaker above his head:

'Captain Roche, Professor Eaves, Mistress Ito, Professor Loane, Doctor Coach, and Mistress Xemian … please assemble at Room one-oh-three on level four at once. Thank you. Repeating message.'

The voice sounded a little like Mrs. Martin's, but with the amplification, Benjamin couldn't be sure. He wondered what was going on, but when he reached the rendezvous point Wilhelm had explained, the curly-haired boy jumped out from the shadows of a cleaning closet alcove with a big grin.

'Did you hear that?' he said. 'That's a roll call of practically every authority in this place, with one notable exception who is supposed to be back by now. Something must be up. But who cares? It means we'll be able to get down to the Locker Room without worrying about ending up doing any cleans. Let's go.'

'How did you get out of the Dining Hall?' Benjamin asked as Wilhelm led him down a stairwell into the bowels of the school. 'I thought you got stuck under the floor.'

'This isn't just one building,' Wilhelm said. 'There're dozens of them, all built on top of each other, going back hundreds of years. Build one: over time it breaks; build it up again. There are whole suites of rooms just lost and abandoned down there. Some of it's really rather creepy, and some of the guys who live down there … well. On the plus side, it makes it easy to escape from the teachers.'

'You know,' Benjamin said, 'in the hours I've been here, every now and again I'll have this kind of epiphany that this is all a dream, and I'll wake up in my own bed any minute. Then something else happens, and it just seems all the more real, and as time passes, I get the epiphanies less and less.'

'Something in the water,' Wilhelm said. 'That's what I reckon. Just don't forget your family and you'll see them again, I'm sure.'

'Do you think about yours a lot?'

Wilhelm turned and looked back. 'Me? No. Not at all. I don't have a family. I grew up in an orphanage.'

'But I thought—'

Wilhelm gave a bitter laugh as he pulled open a heavy, wooden door, holding it aside for Benjamin to slip through. 'My parents died, or gave me up, I'm not sure. I only have a vague memory of what they even looked like, and I can't remember much of my early childhood. Even so, that doesn't mean I want to stay here. The orphanage wasn't so bad. None of the horrible stuff you read about from time to time. The wardens were all pretty friendly, and the food was way better than it is here.'

'That's sad.'

'About the food? Too right it is.'

'No, about your family.'

Wilhelm shrugged. 'Don't beat yourself up. I got over it ages ago. Made me a little more argumentative, perhaps. At least that's what my teachers at school always said.' He winked. 'I'll tell you what, if they wanted cooperative pupils here in end-of-the-wherever-we-are, then they made a mistake picking me. That's why I don't think you should worry. We're here at random. I went to sleep in my bunk in the orphanage, and woke up in this really creepy forest inland from the school. I was all tangled up in the roots of a tree, and for some reason, I felt like I'd been there for years and years.'

'And someone rescued you?'

'Captain Roche found me. Some people just show up. Others —like yourself—are expected. Don't ask me how. I was a random. They send out regular search parties looking for new arrivals, as too long wandering about out there with no clue what's going on will get you in trouble.' Wilhelm grinned. 'When Captain Roche showed up, I was terrified. First thing I did when I opened my eyes was call him a monster. He's hated me ever since.'

'That's too bad.'

'My life here started off bad from the outset. At least you got picked up by Miranda. She's kind of pretty, if a little sharp around the edges. Ah, here we are.'

The candles replacing the electric lights had thinned out as they descended deeper into basements carved out of solid rock, so the tunnels now became creepy and dark. Through a door up ahead came the sound of machinery.

'That's the gatehouse,' Wilhelm said. 'If you want to see Miranda, you'll have to confess to the sin keeper to get into the Locker Room. There's no other way in or out. Trust me, if there's one person—or thing—you don't want to mess with in this place, it's the sin keeper.'

'What kind of confession?'

'A personal one. The teachers usually give you a card or call the sin keeper so he anticipates your arrival. If you're a rat like me, you'll get something brutal like a thousand cleans. But if it's personal, you can get away with ten or fifteen. It won't take long, and you'll have a chance to talk to Miranda.'

Benjamin spread his hands. 'You've lost me.'

'Oh, too late. He here comes. Tell him you didn't try hard enough on your homework or something.'

The patter of running feet behind him signified Wilhelm's disappearance as the door up ahead flew open, the light behind framing a metal-clad man in a fedora-style hat.

'You have come to confess a sin?' rattled a metallic voice that sounded like a gust of wind ripping through a metal tube at an incredible velocity.

Benjamin's first instinct was to follow Wilhelm's retreat, but as the man came closer, his feet refused to move. The man's legs and feet, arms and hands were covered by a metal armour plating. His body was a crimson red waistcoat of chainmail with strips of black metal that made a shirt around the sin keeper's waist which rustled as he walked. The hat, Benjamin now realised, was not a fedora but a helmet, one with a central crown and sloping sides to protect the wearer's ears and neck. By far, the most fearsome part of the sin keeper's costume, though, was the face mask. Benjamin remembered a kid from school who had collected model soldiers from around the world, and one he had brought into class had resembled this. A Japanese Samurai, with a mask designed to terrify the wearer's opponents. Now, the snarling mouth and pointed teeth of a red-skinned demon approached him, hollows where eyes should have been—

'What is your confession, boy?'

The mouth didn't move and there were no eyes inside the red-and-gold-rimmed sockets. Benjamin gaped. There was no one inside the armour at all. The sin keeper was the reanimated armour itself, and his voice was the whistle of air through his hollow body cavity.

The curved Samurai katana that he drew from his belt in a sudden swift motion was certainly real, though.

'Confess, or be struck down where you stand!'

'My math homework!' Benjamin screamed. 'I only got a B plus! I wanted an A! I need to work harder! I'm a lazy, lazy boy!'

The sword hung in the air for a moment longer, then the sin keeper replaced it into the scabbard on his belt.

'Your punishment?'

In his panic, Benjamin tried to remember what Wilhelm had told him. Something about cleans, whatever they were. A low number.

'Ten isn't enough!' he shouted, thumping a hand against his stomach for dramatic effect. 'I should do fifteen!'

The sin keeper crossed his hands over his metal chest plate. Several other weapons hung at his waist, deterring any thoughts of escape. Benjamin counted three knives, a crossbow, and something with a spiked head that looked very unpleasant indeed.

'Locker Number Four,' the sin keeper said.

14

PUNISHMENT

Beyond the door guarded by the sin keeper, who stood just inside on a little pedestal, looking for all the world like a harmless suit of Samurai armour, ran a row of covered cubicles, each with a small door that rose only to the average person's chest, and each with a number on the side. On the other side was an arm's-length-wide conveyor belt that appeared out of the wall, then disappeared into the wall again just in front of the entrance. Sliding past came a random assortment of items, from cups and bowls to shoes, little toys, and even books.

The sounds of activity came from several of the cubicles. Benjamin was just wondering where he would find Miranda, when the door of Locker Seven opened. The girl's head appeared as she turned to place something on the floor outside the cubicle—a bucket filled with random objects—but before Benjamin could wave to her, a door at the far end of the Locker Room opened and one of the strange, dead cleaners entered. The man lurched to the bucket, picked it up, and carried it back through the door.

'Don't stare.'

Benjamin jumped. The door was still open and Miranda stood watching him, her sunset-coloured hair tied back into a pony-tail.

'What are you doing here?'

Benjamin glanced back toward the sin keeper.

'Don't worry, he won't move unless you try to escape before you complete your cleans. Did you get punished for something?'

Benjamin shook his head. 'I came to see you.'

Miranda frowned. 'What for? What's the point of us both being down here?'

'I wanted to say I'm sorry.'

Miranda's eyes narrowed as if she were preparing to attack, then she relaxed. 'It's okay,' she said. 'It's not the first time I got sidetracked.'

'I'm not quite sure what you're doing down here, but I'm sorry for whatever it is.'

Miranda smiled. 'How did you get in?'

'Wilhelm helped me. He told me I had to confess.'

'That little punk. He's your roommate, right?'

'Yes.'

'Don't get too close to him. He breaks all the rules so they add on ten cleans to everything we get punished for as a kind of warning. Professor Eaves has threatened him with ten thousand for when he next catches him. The sin keeper knows it. That's a week sleepover. They bring your meals down from the Dining Hall, but I heard it's just slops scraped off all the unfinished plates.'

'Oh, yuck. That sounds awful.'

Miranda nodded. 'Godfrey and his mates always lick their plates just in case.'

A few cubicles farther along, the door opened and a tall boy Benjamin hadn't seen before leaned out. 'Hey, shut up over there! Some of us are trying to concentrate so we can get back upstairs before breakfast!'

'Buzz off, Derek, you clown,' Miranda snapped. 'If you're lucky, Godfrey's underpants will come past in a minute. You wouldn't want to miss out. You want them clean for next time you kiss his butt, don't you?'

The tall boy scowled, but before he could reply, Miranda pulled Benjamin into her cubicle. She closed the door behind her, and Benjamin found himself in a tiny room with a single flickering candle on a table just in front of the conveyor belt moving past the open far end. Attached to the wall on the left was a rack of sprays and brushes. There was only one chair, so Benjamin sat down on the floor next to a pile of stacked buckets.

Miranda pointed at a ticker counter on the wall above Benjamin's head. And as he watched, the tickers flapped over, the number changing from 306 to 291.

'Getting there,' she said, giving him a tired grin.

'What are you doing?'

She plucked a plastic ruler off of the conveyor.

'Feel it.'

The plastic was warm, and as Benjamin looked at it, the ruler twitched. With a gasp, he dropped it on the floor.

'Quick, pick it up!'

Benjamin scooped it up as though it were a frog or a beetle, and plopped it onto the table in front of Miranda. He rubbed his tingling fingers on his trousers.

'It's alive!'

Miranda grabbed a spray can and doused the ruler with a fine mist that smelled of chamomile. Then she gave it a quick polish with a cloth, and when she held it back out, the warmth was fading away. This time it didn't move.

'Put it in the bucket, please.'

'Is it dead?'

Miranda laughed. 'Don't be a fool. It's a ruler. It was starting to reanimate, so I cleaned it with this deanimation spray. Another two-hundred and ninety and I can go.'

'You're killing objects?'

She slapped him on the shoulder hard enough to make him yelp. 'You can't kill something that wasn't ever alive! It doesn't have a brain; it's just got a few nerves and stuff.'

'How do you know it doesn't have a brain?'

'I don't! But if it does, it'll grow back if you wait long enough. That's the whole point. The cleaners collect stuff that's started to get a bit jumpy and dump it on the conveyor for us poor kids to deanimate. Then they take it away again. This place is just for small stuff. All of the big stuff, like the rooms themselves, get deanimated during monthly cleaning parties, and the stuff that's reanimated too many times gets sent to the incinerator. The Locker Room is just for the fiddly bits and bobs that we use over and over again.'

'Oh. Don't you find it a bit weird, technically killing stuff?'

Miranda glared. 'No, I don't. See how you feel after you sit here all afternoon cleaning hundreds of these stupid things. You'll quickly stop caring. Spray on, brush and polish. Toothbrush in the tight places. In the bucket. Next.'

Her nostrils flared in the flicker of the candlelight.

'Perhaps I should leave you to it, then,' Benjamin said.

Miranda glared a moment longer, then sighed. 'Thanks for coming to see me,' she said. 'I appreciate it. It's my fault; I wasn't supposed to let you go across the bridge on your own. I just had to … meet someone.'

'It's okay.'

She smiled. 'I thought you'd make it okay. I didn't expect the wind to get up. I thought I'd get away with it, though, and I didn't. I'm sorry.'

'I'm sorry, too. Friends?' Benjamin stuck out a hand.

'You didn't shake Wilhelm's hand with that, did you? He's always getting dirty. He likes climbing up walls to spy on teachers through their windows. Scatlocks poo on those walls.'

'I washed it after.'

'Good.'

She shook his hand. 'Look, I'd better get on with this. If I hurry, I can be back in the dorms by eleven. If you have a chance, can you grab me some dinner? For anything less than a thousand cleans, they don't bring you food.'

'I'll try.'

'Thanks. I'm on the second floor, room twenty-three. Just leave it with my roommate. I owe you. Go on, you'd better hurry. How many cleans did you ask for?'

'Fifteen.'

Miranda rolled her eyes. 'Easy life. Still, it always takes ages on your first time. Once you're up to speed, you can do two or three a minute if you don't get all the fiddly stuff. Thanks again for thinking of me. I'll see you tomorrow, I hope.'

Benjamin headed for Locker Four. The sin keeper still stood immobile next to the Locker Room entrance, and Benjamin gave him a smile anyway as if to say 'sorry for wasting time,' but the suit of armour didn't move.

Inside his cubicle, the ticker on the wall said 15. A little cat statue sat waiting for his attention, as if someone had put it there to get him started. He picked it up, turned it over, feeling a warmth seep through the hard clay. When he put it down onto the table and reached for the spray, though, one porcelain paw slashed at his hand in a slow, lazy arc, easily avoidable had he been paying attention.

'Ow!'

He pulled his hand back as the paw slashed at him again. Luckily, the rest of the cat couldn't move, but it was too late; a line of blood cut from the back of his thumb across to his little finger. He licked away the blood, then hugged his throbbing hand.

The cat's paw started moving again. This time, Benjamin grabbed the spray from the rack and doused it. The paw stopped moving. He gave the cat a tentative touch, but the statue was already cooling down.

Trying to ignore the ache in his hand, Benjamin rubbed over the cat statue with a cloth until it felt cold all over. Then, worried that it might remember him during a future reanimation, he placed it carefully into the bucket.

As he watched the conveyor, he wondered why nothing coming past seemed easy. Everything consisted of oddly shaped items, things with sharp edges or difficult-to-reach insides. Then he remembered that, because the conveyor moved from left to right, kids in the higher-numbered cubicles had the first pick of the easy stuff. *It would really suck to be in Locker One when a lot of kids were being punished,* he thought. He grabbed a metal colander with a revolving centrepiece to spin salads, and as he put it down, the insides spun threateningly.

Quite a hazardous job, he thought, rubbing the back of his scratched hand, which continued to throb. Then, almost as an afterthought, he gave the scratch a quick squirt from the spray can.

Can't do any harm. Can it?

THREATS

Miranda wasn't joking. Even with only fifteen on his ticker, it was an hour before Benjamin had finished. He had nearly gotten into trouble at one point because he had naively gotten up and headed for the door after he put what he had counted as his fifteenth item into his second full bucket and saw a cleaner carry it away. As he reached the sin keeper, the reanimated suit of armour pointed his crossbow at Benjamin's chest.

'You're not finished. Return to your locker.'

Thinking there was some mistake, Benjamin went back to Locker Four to check, only to find his ticker still showed the number 3, and with a sigh, discovered he hadn't cleaned some of the items well enough to deanimate them. This time, when he put out the bucket, he stayed in the cubicle until the ticker started to move: 3 … 2 … 1 …

The word GO appeared in red lettering, and Benjamin breathed a big sigh of relief. This time, the sin keeper stayed on his pedestal as Benjamin opened the main door and went out, casting one last regretful glance back at Miranda's cubicle as he closed the door behind him.

With no sign of Wilhelm down in the corridors outside, with the hum of the conveyor receding into the distance, an uneasy quiet fell over the bowels of the school. Far fewer candles flickered than before, and Benjamin remembered what Wilhelm had said about whole suites of rooms being forgotten and unused. What if he stumbled into some long-lost section of the school? He might never find his way out.

He passed staircases leading both up and down, some wide and grand, others tight and twisting. Some had dusty marble steps, the lack of footprints betraying their disuse, while others were just wooden ladders ascending tight shafts leading into subterranean attic space. Benjamin figured up was best and chose whatever well-lit, rising staircases he could find. Heading toward sound also seemed like a good idea, so when a loud rustling came from behind a door at the end of a corridor, he ran to it and threw it open, only to teeter on the edge of a rocky ledge with the sea tossing below and thousands of roosting scatlocks for company. The sound, he realised, had been coming from the creatures, which now began to stir like windswept leaves on some giant, grey-white tree. Benjamin slammed the door shut and quickly retraced his steps before any could rouse themselves for a pursuit.

He was beginning to despair he might be lost forever, when he heard metal clanking on metal, and at the top of the next staircase, found himself around the back of the kitchens, where a handful of cleaners were washing up. The Dining Hall itself was empty, the central fire's embers lending a dim flicker of light. He cut through it to the front entrance, where he managed to get one cleaner's attention.

Unmasked and without their sunglasses now that the pupils were gone, they were terrifying to behold as they stomped back and forth behind the empty food displays, carrying pans, stacks of trays, and boxes of cutlery, occasionally frowning and throwing something into a large crate on a central preparation table.

The cleaner, responding with jerky nods and grunts, did as Benjamin asked and found a bowl of leftover food for him to take up to the dorms for Miranda. As he headed out of the kitchens and into the dark corridors, the sounds of activity were soon lost. The school was silent, and as Benjamin passed staircases and intersecting corridors, he began to wonder where the teachers lived. There were no signposts or maps anywhere.

After several wrong turns, he finally emerged onto the concourse at the main entrance. Mrs. Martin's office was unlit, but inside, a light flashed on a console at the back that was otherwise dark. Benjamin paused.

Though he was desperate to return to the dorms with the food for Miranda and then finally get some sleep, what if something inside that console could give him a clue as to how he had gotten here and how he could get home? If he was careful and didn't move anything, would it cause any trouble to take a quick look inside?

Benjamin moved for the door before he could stop himself. It wasn't locked, although the handle was uncomfortably warm. Inside, Mrs. Martin's office looked like any other office—all computers and fax machines and photocopiers. In fact, it was so normal, he felt a certain kind of retro shock at the mundane nature of everything—a paperweight shaped like a duck holding down a stack of papers, a mug still a third full of a liquid that smelt of chamomile—

Then he spotted it: the telephone.

While everyone on their street was obsessed with the newest smartphones, his parents had kept an old-fashioned landline in the hallway by the door. Benjamin glanced up at a clock just visible in the dim light. It was nearly ten p.m., later than he'd realised, but not so late as to wake anyone up. Assuming, of course, that time here worked the same as it worked there.

The warm receiver had a dial tone when he pressed it to his ear. His family's phone number was engrained on his memory, forced into his head by rote memorisation almost as early as he could speak. And even now, the numbers came easily to his tongue: 01732-243-9213.

Before he could stop himself, his fingers moved across the buttons, and he wondered dumbly whether he ought to use the international code. However, in this world of two suns, he figured his number would either work or it wouldn't.

He held his breath, waiting. Surely it wouldn't work. He felt like he was calling home out of a dream.

A ringing tone. His heart beat almost too loudly to hear the *brrr* from the other end of the line. Would someone answer? What would he say if they did—

'Hello?'

Benjamin froze, phone shaking in his hands. He pushed it against the side of his head as the voice came again, and this time he managed to answer in a croak: 'Lo?'

'Hello? This is the Forrest household. May I take your name?'

For a moment, Benjamin had no idea who he was speaking to. He had never heard the words spoken in this way before, and after a moment of hesitation he realised why: he had always been in the room, not on the other end of the line.

'Mum? Is that you?'

'Who's this?'

'It's me, Benjamin.'

A short pause, followed by: 'You should be ashamed of yourself, calling like this. How dare you—'

'Mum, it's me—'

'This isn't funny. I'll be checking this number and calling the police in the morning. I'm not putting up with this any longer. This is harassment.'

'Mum! Wait!'

The line went dead. In his frustration, Benjamin slammed the receiver against the desktop. It let out a little squeal, and when he lifted it again it snapped at his fingers like the head of a snake, the plastic having folded over to form crude jaws. He dropped it, backing away in terror, but it had gone still again.

Obviously she had not recognised him. If he could just speak to her again, he could make her understand. He reached for the receiver, then paused.

Someone was walking through the lobby area, coming toward the office.

A thin figure, dressed in black, face hidden beneath a hood.

Benjamin held his breath, overcome by a sudden dread. It sounded ridiculous, but he'd become almost accustomed to seeing the zombie-like cleaners wandering about. They moved with a lethargic stagger, and since none had shown any interest in eating him, he felt no real fear.

This, however, was something quite different.

It walked with an arched back like an old man, though with greater haste. Thin, almost skeletal fingers shifted like crab's claws drifting in an underwater current, their deathly pale colour gleaming, reflecting the dim night-lights in the lobby ceiling.

The creature appeared to be looking for something: as it crept from one wall to another, its fingers brushing over the curves and contours of every surface as if searching for the lock to some hidden door. Benjamin peered out from behind a filing cabinet as it walked in front of the partition window, its fingers scraping as they brushed across the glass. Benjamin, heart pounding, inched back into the shadows, terrified of being seen.

A desk bumped into his lower back. He reached behind him, feeling for it, and knocked a tray of pens to the floor.

The clatter was impossibly loud, and Benjamin yelped, sinking to his knees, cowering back from the window as the creature spun toward him, hood lifting. Metallic robot eyes glowed orange, peering out of a bleached human skull, jaw opening to emit a sharp gasp that could have been either surprise or a warning. Then it was gone, bolting down the corridors, cloak billowing in a sweeping wave that blended into the dark.

Benjamin didn't move for a long time. Whatever it was, it had looked right at him. All he wanted to do was hide, but he wasn't safe here. What if it came back with others?

Shaking hands pushed him back to his feet. He could barely grip the door handle to turn it, and only when he had gotten outside in the lobby he realised he had forgotten to replace the spilled pens. No matter. He would happily confess his trespassing in exchange for a thousand cleans in the Locker Room, if he got back to his dorm room unharmed.

Once again, silence had descended upon the school. The main entrance was before him, twin staircases rising up to a wide concourse at the rear. In the shadows beneath them stood half a dozen doors and intersecting corridors. Other than the one to the extreme left leading to the Dining Hall, Benjamin had no clue where they went.

Unsure of what he was doing, Benjamin pushed through the main doors and out onto the wide courtyard on the clifftop in front of the school. Despite the gloom and shadow of the building's interior, outside it wasn't totally dark, with the orange sun still visible on the far horizon, lighting up the clouds beyond the edge of the world in a rainbow of brilliant colours.

Benjamin walked to the wall surrounding the courtyard and looked left back toward the bay where the rope bridge hung now in shadow, its location pinpointed by a handful of solar lamps hanging from its underside. Back and up to his right, the cliff rose to near vertical behind the school, with the headland on which the dormitory stood cast in its shadow. The building itself was just visible, a couple of lights glowing in the downstairs common room windows, but by now, most of the pupils had probably gone to bed.

Despite near-freezing air, Benjamin didn't want to go back in. That creeping thing, and whatever other horrors he was yet to meet, waited through those doors. Perhaps it would be better to just let the elements claim him. After all, his mother hadn't recognised his voice, and if his family no longer wanted him, he was as good as lost anyway.

He walked to the edge and looked down at the shadow of the ocean, a blend of greys and dark blues until it suddenly no longer was. Without a horizon he felt robbed in a way; symbolic of a future that no longer existed. Nothing over there, nothing to wish for, nothing on which to pin his hopes—

A black shadow rose up over the cliff's edge and huge, billowing wings wrapped around him, pulling him forward and knocking his knees against the balustrade, almost toppling him over. Benjamin screamed and beat at them, slapping away the massive flapping creature. It rose up, then turned and swooped at him again, falling out of the night sky like a great black tarpaulin.

He ran, making it to the main entrance just ahead of the creature, and ducked down as it slammed into the glass. Then he pulled the door open and slipped through as the creature retreated to make another pass.

Back inside, he pulled in deep, desperate breaths as the shadow creature battered against the glass a few times then rose and disappeared into the sky.

'Too close,' he muttered under his breath.

Now, the idea of returning to the dorms really appealed. He wasn't quite sure how to get there, but up the stairs to the concourse, then left in the direction of the headland, seemed the right way to go. Benjamin moved at a gentle jog, looking over his shoulder every few seconds in case the sinister creature followed.

Voices from up ahead came like a sudden downpour after a long drought. Unable to help himself, he started into a run, calling out to them.

He didn't see what tripped him, but he felt the hard stone floor as it cracked against his forehead, then felt strong hands wrap around his mouth and pull him back into the shadows.

16

SETUP

'Hello again, mophead. I bet you thought you'd seen the last of me, didn't you?'

Benjamin struggled in Godfrey's arms. 'Let go of me!'

'Not so fast. I just wanted to let you know that I'm watching you.'

'And Captain Roche is watching you. You'll end up in the Locker Room if you don't let me go!'

'Captain Roche is a fool. Didn't you hear the alarm? All it took was a little deanimation spray to put his eye to sleep for a while.' Godfrey held up a little drawstring bag similar to the one Benjamin kept marbles in at home. 'Easy.'

'He'll find out.'

'Not while they're having one of their little councils of wizards. They sit in there all night.'

'Wizards?'

'Or whatever those freaks are. Who cares?' Godfrey pushed Benjamin back against the wall. 'Look, all you need to know is that I'm the boss around here. You do what I say, or I'll make life difficult for you.'

Godfrey was a head taller, but Benjamin was tired of being pushed around. As Godfrey tried to put the little bag back into his pocket while holding Benjamin still with his other hand, Benjamin swung a knee up into his stomach.

Godfrey grunted and bent double, letting go of both Benjamin and the bag containing Captain Roche's eye. Darting forward, Benjamin kicked the bag away down the corridor.

'No!'

Godfrey's scream reminded Benjamin of when one of his classmates, a prudish type called Melissa, had found a frog in her lunchbox. Despite all of his bluster, Godfrey was clearly terrified of Captain Roche. He dashed after the little bag as it rolled over the top of a flight of stairs, and while Godfrey's cronies watched dumbly, Benjamin sprinted toward the other voices.

At the end of the corridor, lights were on by the doors leading to the dormitory path. Several dozen pupils stood around, talking animatedly in voices thick with frustration. Benjamin spotted Wilhelm standing near the edge of the group, and he ran over, tapping his friend on the back.

'Hey! Where did you go? You'll never guess what I saw—'

Wilhelm turned to him with a borderline look of anger. 'Benjamin. Please tell me it wasn't you who left the bathroom window open.'

Benjamin opened his mouth to reply as several other pupils turned to follow the conversation. He remembered brushing his teeth and combing his hair, then opening the window to toss out a piece of scatlock from his hair. He'd definitely shut it again … hadn't he?

Doubts rushed in like a thick, black tide. He must have. But what did it matter anyway?

'Scatlocks,' Wilhelm said in a tone that made the flying plastic bags sound like disease-ridden vermin. 'Someone left the bathroom window open and they got in. Dozens of them. We're lucky Gubbledon found the window and shut it before an entire colony got inside.'

'It wasn't me….' Benjamin muttered, though he wasn't so sure now.

'Some cleaners are in there shooing them out,' Wilhelm said, 'but it could take a while. They get everywhere. It says on the

85

first page of your handbook: "Never, ever, ever leave doors or windows open."'

'My handbook got wet,' Benjamin protested.

Wilhelm looked down at his feet and sighed. For the first time, he looked like a little kid rather than a twelve-year-old troublemaker. Benjamin lifted a hand to put it around Wilhelm's shoulders in a gesture of comfort, when a clacking of hooves behind him was followed by the whinnying voice of Gubbledon Longface: 'There you are!'

Benjamin turned as the reanimated horse reached him. The housemaster wore a red satin nightshirt and a grey woolly cap perched between the remains of his ears.

'You were the last person seen using the bathroom,' Gubbledon said, shaking his big, zombified head back and forth. 'You must have left the window open. Perhaps it was an honest mistake, but that's one of the worst things you can do with all of those pesky scatlocks about. I'm afraid it carries a set punishment of a thousand cleans down in the Locker Room. Have you been acquainted with that place?'

'Who saw me?' Benjamin shouted, anger boiling up. He wasn't stupid. He would never have left the window open. Someone must have set him up. He looked around the assembled sets of eyes as if daring someone to own up to it.

'You were seen by Simon,' Gubbledon said, pointing to a large, dopey-looking boy with an upturned nose. 'And, of course, by Godfrey.'

Benjamin turned. Godfrey was walking up the corridor toward them with a wide grin on his face. He gave his pocket a surreptitious little pat, then cocked his head and said to Benjamin, 'We felt really bad saying anything, but we don't want you to repeat your mistake. It's the only way we can all get along here.'

Benjamin scowled, and while the urge to cuff the smirk off of Godfrey's face was overwhelming, there was nothing he could do. This time, they had gotten one over on him. Someone must have sneaked into the bathroom after he'd left and opened the window. It was the only possible answer.

'So sorry to hear your handbook got wet,' Godfrey added.

'You can borrow mine if you like, when you get back from the Locker Room. Assuming you don't clean yourself to death.'

Benjamin lifted a hand to strike him, but Wilhelm stepped between them. 'Just forget it,' he whispered, leaning close. 'Don't make him worse.'

'Are you familiar with the way down to the Locker Rooms, Benjamin?' Gubbledon said. 'There's no point sitting around. You might as well get started. Perhaps Godfrey here would be kind enough to instruct you on the quickest way.'

Benjamin scowled again. 'I can find it myself.'

He turned to leave, when what he had seen earlier returned to his thoughts. 'Wilhelm,' he hissed as he passed the smaller boy, 'I saw something wandering about downstairs. Something with metal eyes that glowed orange, and a skull for a face.'

Wilhelm turned pale. 'You're joking right?'

'No. I wish I was. What is it?'

Wilhelm opened his mouth as if about to divulge some great secret, then snapped it shut again.

'What?'

Again, Wilhelm opened his mouth to answer, but whatever he was about to say was drowned out by a collective cheer from the kids standing by the doors.

'Okay,' Gubbledon announced in a loud voice. 'We're all clear. Capes on, everyone.'

'Don't say anything to anyone else,' Wilhelm said. 'We need to find a teacher.'

'Can't we just tell Gubbledon?'

Wilhelm glanced over his shoulder at the housemaster, who was struggling to get his hooves into his own oversized scatlock cape. Godfrey and Simon were trying to hold it open for him while suppressing a series of sniggers.

'Do I even need to answer that?'

Benjamin nodded. 'Let's go find a teacher. Where will they be?'

Wilhelm gave an involuntary shiver. 'Teachers' block.'

'Which direction is that?'

Wilhelm grimaced, and he lifted a finger to point up at the ceiling. 'The tower,' he said.

17

TRAP

'It can't be that difficult to get to,' Benjamin said. 'There's a staircase, right?'

'There's another gatekeeper. The teachers' tower is strictly off-limits to the pupils at all times. Even I've never been up there.' He shrugged. 'Not officially, anyway.'

'Then how do you know where to go?'

Wilhelm grinned. 'I didn't say I didn't know the way, did I? At least, I know a special way.'

They edged to the side of the group, and as soon as no one was paying attention, they made their escape back through the corridors, where Gubbledon's frustrated commands to form an orderly queue gradually faded out.

'It probably won't attack if there're two of us,' Wilhelm said. 'But best to stick to the lit areas if we can, just in case.'

'What was it? What did I see?'

'A ghoul.'

'A what? Aren't ghouls a kind of ghost?'

'Not this kind. That's just what they're called. You know how you see all those dead people wandering around the school?'

'Yeah, the cleaners, right?'

'That's them. And you know how machines and stuff come to life if they're not sprayed by chamomile?'

'The reanimates.'

'Well, sometimes they get mixed.' Wilhelm wiped sweat off his brow. 'Ghouls are part corpse, part machine. Most of them come out of the Haunted Forest—hence the name—but they sometimes show up in or around the school. If someone knows why, they're not telling.'

'How exactly do you know this?'

Wilhelm grinned, even though his eyes held no humour. 'I was bored up in the dorms while everyone else was in class and I found some storybooks in the common room. One or two of them featured ghouls.'

Benjamin scoffed. 'All you know about these things comes from storybooks?'

'The pictures were exactly as you describe. And the book said they were based on true legends.'

'That's a load of rubbish.'

Wilhelm smirked. 'I haven't let you down yet, have I?'

'Well, if you'd waited for me, I might not have bumped into one.'

'And then no one else might know what danger we're in.'

'If we're in any danger at all. Perhaps it, you know, lives here? Not like this place isn't full of other strange things, is it?'

'Let's put it this way: was it scary? Was it the scariest thing you've seen so far, out of a lot of scary things?'

Benjamin shuddered as he remembered the skull and the glowing orange eyes. 'It was terrifying.'

Wilhelm gave a satisfied nod. 'There you go, then.'

They had reached the balcony that overlooked the lobby. Both of them peered into the dark around the closed admissions office, but there was no sign of the creature.

'Which way did it go?'

'I didn't see for sure, but I thought it went right.'

Wilhelm gave a frustrated grunt. 'That's the same way to the teachers' tower, unless we circle around through the basements. That would take longer, and we might run into it anyway. Or we could go outside. There's a path.'

'No way am I going out there again. I got attacked by this black thing, like a giant scatlock.'

'A haulock.' Wilhelm nodded. 'They're reanimated refuse

sacks. You're not having much luck, are you? You've certainly made things interesting since you showed up.'

'It wasn't intentional.'

'Don't worry, once you've been here for a few days, you'll get the hang of how to avoid things like that. Haulocks are quite rare around the school, and they're nocturnal. You were lucky, though, because they're big enough to drag you off the top of the cliff.'

'I don't think—'

'Shh! Do you hear that?'

Wilhelm pulled Benjamin down into a crouch as footsteps echoed up from the lobby below.

'It's come back!' Wilhelm hissed. 'Let's catch it. Then no one will be able to call us liars.'

'You're crazy! How?'

Wilhelm held up a scrunched up scatlock cape. 'You go to the bottom of the stairs and hide behind that rail there. When it appears under the balcony, I'll drop the cape. You grab it while I run down to help. Zip it up if you can. These capes are pretty solid.'

'Why can't I drop the cape?'

'Because it's my plan so I get to choose who does what. Go on.'

Benjamin grimaced, but tried to take comfort in Wilhelm's confidence. He skipped down the steps and ducked behind the railings where the stairs opened out on to the lobby floor. From here he couldn't see who was approaching, but the footsteps grew louder as someone emerged from one of the central downstairs corridors.

From the balcony, Wilhelm grinned and gave him a thumbs-up. 'Get ready,' he said.

Off to Benjamin's left, the school office windows reflected a couple of dim night-lights back in the corridors beneath the concourse. Something bobbed as it moved toward him, little more than a wavering shadow. He tried to stick his head out and peer round as it came level with the bottom of the stairs, but Wilhelm screamed 'Attack!' and the scatlock cape came billowing down.

As the cape fell over the creature's head, Benjamin jumped out of his hiding place and wrestled the shape to the ground, quickly zipping up the opening at the back. He was just wrapping his arms around it to hold it tight, when a hard, lumpy object struck him between the eyes, making his head spin. Someone roared in anger. Then he was tumbling over and over as if blown by a strong wind. He struck the edge of the lowest wooden step, and he sat up, dazed, rubbing his forehead.

Miranda stood in front of him, face like a thundercloud, the scatlock cape in pieces around her feet.

'You!' she shouted. 'What were you thinking of? You brainless twit!'

'I was trying to catch a ghoul,' Benjamin protested as Miranda came forward, hands bunched into fists. Benjamin put up his own hand to protect himself as a warm wind struck his face. He winced as an ache flared where the cat statue had scratched him.

'What ghoul? What are you talking about?'

Wilhelm came running down the stairs. He stopped a couple of steps from the bottom, but Miranda still towered over him, her flaming hair like a fire at the top of a tall building. One strand stuck straight up like the nearly invisible wire of a puppeteer's controls.

Miranda glanced from one boy to the other. 'Benjamin? You two were in on this together? What did I tell you about hanging around with *him*?'

Benjamin wanted to tell her that she had no right to pick his friends for him and that he agreed with her, but her expression forbade him to open his mouth.

'What's going on?'

'I saw a ghoul. We were on the way to see the teachers when we heard a noise——'

'Storybook rubbish.'

Wilhelm bent down and picked up a piece of the destroyed scatlock cape. He held it out to Miranda, eyes wide, while a wisp of smoke rose from a charred corner of the blanket.

'So is magic,' he said in a small, frightened voice.

18

THE TEACHERS' APARTMENTS

'I have no intention of forgiving you,' Miranda said, glaring at Wilhelm, who was at least a head shorter and looked significantly younger. 'And you'—she turned to Benjamin —'you've disappointed me. I thought you would choose better company.'

'Hang on a minute! You can't talk, running off and leaving me!'

'I had a good reason.'

'What?'

Miranda turned on Wilhelm. 'You be quiet. And don't let me hear you say the "M" word again. If someone hears you, we'll both get tossed over the edge of the world.'

'So you did use it, didn't you?'

Miranda gave a vehement shake of her head. 'I don't know what it is, only that it happens … sometimes. When I'm angry, usually.'

'Well, make sure you use it if we run into another ghoul.'

'What ghoul? What are you talking about?'

Benjamin explained what had happened to him after he had left the Locker Room. He decided not to mention the phone call, and instead, told them he had seen the ghoul while looking at the sky through the window.

When he was finished, Miranda gave a frustrated sigh. 'So what if you did see a ghoul? What are you going to do now?'

'We're going to tell a teacher.'

'They won't believe you. And they won't appreciate being woken up at this time of night. It's nearly midnight.'

Benjamin stifled a yawn. 'I know.'

'Didn't you hear that alarm call?' Wilhelm said. 'They're all in a special meeting right now. They might be talking *about* the ghoul. We have to tell them we saw it.'

'*Benjamin* saw it.'

Wilhelm shrugged. 'Guilty by association. Look, we might get a reward or something. If you want in on it, you can come with us. You can protect us with your magic.'

'Don't say that word! Remember the Oath!'

'The Oath is a load of rubbish. I had my fingers crossed the whole time.'

Miranda looked from one to the other. Wilhelm winked at her, provoking a scowl. Benjamin just shrugged.

'Just for the record,' she said, 'I hate you, and I've begun to go off you, too.' She glared first at Wilhelm, and then at Benjamin. 'But it's better if we stick together. Just in case. We'll go and tell the teachers what Benjamin saw, then go back to the dorms together. Deal?'

'Sounds good,' Benjamin said. 'Except that I'm supposed to go to the Locker Room to do a thousand cleans for leaving the bathroom window open. Even though I'm sure I didn't.'

'Don't worry,' Miranda said. 'The teachers will probably let you off after this.' Wilhelm grinned and held up a hand, looking for a high-five. Miranda ignored him. 'No more stupid surprise attacks, though.'

Before either Benjamin or Wilhelm could reply, she strode off toward the middle corridor, head held high.

Wilhelm hurried after her, with Benjamin coming last, holding one hand with the other. The back of it was red and sore, maybe infected, and the scratch had begun to sting again after Miranda had used her … whatever it was.

Miranda didn't seem concerned at all by the prospect of being attacked by a strange beast as she led them through parts of the school Benjamin had never seen. On the way they passed classroom-lined corridors, and he wondered if he would even survive long enough to take a class.

At the top of a long flight of stairs that left all three of them puffing, Miranda stopped. She pointed at a door at the far end.

'That's the way into the teachers' apartments. I've heard there's a gatekeeper, but I've never seen him. Any ideas?'

Wilhelm lifted a hand as if addressing a teacher. 'I've heard there's one, too. There's a way on the outside, a kind of fire escape. Perhaps we could try that.'

'And go outside with all those scatlocks and heaven knows what else? Are you crazy?'

Benjamin looked from one to the other. 'Why don't we just knock?' he said.

'But—'

'You can't disturb the teachers!'

'Why not?'

Miranda waved her hands, then slapped them against her sides. 'Okay, fine. But I'm staying here.'

'Me, too.'

Benjamin shrugged. 'I'll do it on my own, then.'

He marched toward the door. Great shuttered windows leaned in over him, candles flickering in alcoves between. The wooden floor creaked beneath his feet as the walls projected their cold onto his arms and legs; only the scratch on his hand felt warm. He was sure this must be a causeway between one part of the headland and another, and the enormity of some great chasm that began just below his feet was enough to make his knees tremble. All of a sudden, nothing mattered—where he was and why, what had happened to bring him here. All that mattered was that the people around him were in some kind of danger and he had to do what he could to help.

Footsteps echoed behind him. Miranda's fingers closed over one arm, Wilhelm's over the other.

'It's creepy back there,' Miranda said. 'I think we should stick together.' She indicated Wilhelm with a nod. 'I told him to keep watch, but he's a coward.'

'You keep watch,' Wilhelm said. 'I'm not staying back there on my own.'

Benjamin smiled. 'Well, thanks.'

The door rose in front of them. Up close, it was at least ten feet tall. Benjamin lifted a hand to knock … then stopped.

His feet had begun to tingle.

'I can't move,' he said as his feet began to sink into the floor, the wood having taken on the consistency of mud. It felt like the riverbank near his house after a particularly heavy rainfall, squelching around his ankles, but when he tried to pull his feet out, the wood hardened, trapping him.

'What's happening?' Wilhelm cried, scrabbling at Benjamin's shoulder. 'I can't get out!'

'We're in trouble now,' Miranda said with a resigned sigh, tugging on one knee and then giving up. 'The floor is reanimating. I'd guess this is the gatekeeper you were talking about. We'll be stuck here until they find us, and then we'll be sent straight to the Locker Room. Anyone want to wager on how many thousands of cleans we'll have to do for this? We could be gone for weeks.'

Benjamin patted her arm. 'Calm down. There must be some way out.' He tested the consistency of the surrounding boards with his finger. 'It's hard over there, around the edge. There must be a safe path that the teachers use. If one of us can just get free—'

'Too late.' Wilhelm's voice was hollow, hopeless. 'The ghoul. It's found us.'

Benjamin twisted to look over his shoulder, hips aching as his stuck legs resisted. At the far end of the corridor, standing at the top of the steps, was the thing he had seen in the lobby. The ghoul. It lowered its head to the floor as if searching for a scent, then swung it toward them. Twin orange lights flickered under its hood, and it started into a run.

19

MEMORIES

'Blast it!' Wilhelm screamed at Miranda. 'Like you did before!'

'I'm trying! I can't just switch it on and off! That's the whole problem!'

Benjamin, in between his friends, didn't and couldn't move. The creature ran straight toward him, its glowing eyes and the bleached white of its clacking jaw flickering in the corridor's gloom. He stared it down, knowing he could do absolutely nothing other than wait for it to rip his body away from his trapped ankles and leave his severed feet stuck in the floor, twitching and lonely.

'Help!' all three screamed together. The ghoul had covered half the distance. Arms with bird's talons instead of hands emerged from under the folds of its cloak, vicious clacking claws ready to start tearing into human flesh.

'*Help!*'

The door flew open with a loud crash, slamming against the wall hard enough to snap one of the hinges clean through. The room inside looked like a small, cozy library where shelves of books filled every wall space, and comfortable chairs upholstered in faded, red leather sat in quiet alcoves. In the centre, a cast iron staircase spiraled into the ceiling.

And standing right in the doorway, dominating everything, was the most terrifying woman Benjamin had ever seen.

Her hair was a chessboard of black-and-grey—the black strands straight, the grey curled—so it appeared as though some poor animal had been thrown onto her head in sacrifice. Her face was pinched, her nose so thin to be near invisible from straight on, her eyes black with piercing blue pupils like a mutated snake. The motley patchwork of black-and-white quilting that hung to her ankles couldn't hide the plaster cast on one leg that appeared longer than the other. She leaned on a gnarled metal staff that glowed as her eyes flared like an extension of her own anger.

'Out!' she roared at the ghoul, which skidded to a stop and started to turn back. 'Leave!'

The woman jabbed the end of her staff into the floor. Around Benjamin's feet, the wood liquefied again and he pulled them free, scrambling to the safe section of floor, then reached back to help Miranda and Wilhelm. As the three of them cowered against the wall, the woman lifted her staff and jerked it in the direction of the ghoul. A waft of warm air brushed past Benjamin's face.

The ghoul wailed, its feet yanked out from under it, and it spun around in midair as if caught on some invisible wheel. The woman scowled, stomping a few steps forward, her plaster cast landing heavily on floorboards jellified just moments ago. The still-spinning ghoul tried to reach her, but she jabbed her staff into its midriff, and there was a sudden burst of blinding light. Benjamin flinched, and when he opened his eyes, the ghoul was just a few steaming pieces of cloth and bone that quickly began to dissolve into the floor.

'Who is she?' Benjamin hissed into Miranda's ear.

The girl's smile was full of adoration. 'That's Ms. Ito,' she said. 'The art teacher.'

Wilhelm was also staring at Ms. Ito, whose stern, almost disdainful gaze had turned on them. 'Magic,' he said.

'Idiot boy,' Ms. Ito snarled. 'That's a thousand cleans right there for breaking the Oath. There's no such thing as magic. People once thought fire was magic. Then electricity. Phones.

97

The Internet. Space travel. No! No magic! There's only science, fool.'

Then she stumped away, back to the stairs as three other teachers appeared, Captain Roche among them. An older, slightly hunchbacked man on his left, with huge, tufting grey hair pressing out from beneath a brown Christmas hat, snarled at the sight of Wilhelm. The third, a younger man with neat brown hair in a centre parting who looked almost normal compared to the others, waved them to come inside.

'You're letting out all the heat,' he said in exasperation, as if that explained everything.

Miranda grabbed Benjamin's hand, and he in turn took hold of Wilhelm's, before the smaller boy could entertain any serious thoughts of fleeing.

Captain Roche dragged the heavy door closed, frowning at the broken hinge and muttering something unsavoury about Ms. Ito. The woman, for her part, had already headed back up the stairs, the clanking of her plaster cast on the metal steps echoing down from above their heads.

'Well, what do we have here?' the thin, brown-haired man said, waving the three of them toward a leather sofa. 'Three little Indians, looking for smoke signals, no doubt. Miranda Butterworth, she of sky and fire. Wilhelm Jacobs, king of reluctance. And who might you be?'

Benjamin covered his scratched hand with the other. 'Benjamin Forrest, sir.'

'Came in this morning,' Captain Roche said. 'Miss Butterworth failed spectacularly to bring him here safely, after which the knock-on effect got him into all sorts of scrapes. Isn't that right? Not yet here a day, and already with a thousand cleans hanging over your head. Quite the start, isn't it?'

'We become those with whom we keep company,' the older man said, glaring at Wilhelm. 'I've already set the sin keeper the task of setting up a bunk down in the Locker Room for you, my errant lad.'

'Well, I'm glad you're still alive.' The brown-haired man pointed long, piano fingers at his own chest. 'My name is Robert

Loane; Professor Loane to you. You've met Captain Roche, and this is Professor James Eaves.'

Professor Eaves just grunted, eyes briefly flickering across to Benjamin before returning to Wilhelm, who was positively squirming.

Captain Roche finished his assessment of the door, then went over to a corner table and picked up the receiver of another ancient phone. He dialed a number, spoke into it for a few minutes, then hung up.

'The rest of them are accounted for,' he said to Professor Loane. 'I've commanded those in the Locker Room to have today's punishments waived and be escorted back to the dormitory. All night classes are canceled. We'll do a flushing of the school tomorrow.'

Professor Loane didn't look convinced. 'Where there's one, there will be more,' he said. 'The situation is worse than we thought.'

Miranda raised a hand.

'What is it, Butterworth?'

'What was that thing, sir?'

'A ghoul, as your friend said. A rather base creature. They hail from the forest to the west. They are scavengers, hunting for reanimated mutations, upon which they feed. They smell them like we might smell fresh bread in the morning. They're nearly mindless, which is what makes them deadly.'

'Reanimated mutations?'

Professor Loane looked from face to face, his gaze eventually settling on Benjamin. 'Young Master Forrest. Let me see your hand, if I may.'

Benjamin held up his good hand, but Professor Loane smiled and shook his head. He held up the other, and the three teachers gasped.

'How did this happen?'

'I got scratched by a reanimated cat statue.'

'How?'

'I was in the Locker Room. I wasn't sure what to do. I picked it up, and it swiped me.'

'What were you doing in the Locker Room? You had no

99

punishment. No one is ever given cleans before receiving thorough instruction on how to clean safely and successfully.'

'I wanted to see Miranda. To apologise for getting her into trouble.'

Professor Eaves snorted. 'Miss Butterworth finds her own trouble, don't you? Forrest, didn't you read your information manual? All of this is explained.'

'It fell into the sea.'

The two professors exchanged a glance. 'Quite the catalogue of disasters, you've had, boy,' Professor Eaves said. 'I guess we'll have to figure out a plan for you, won't we?'

Benjamin wondered if it involved any time in the Locker Room. He looked from one teacher to another, but didn't say anything.

Professor Loane looked about to say something else, when a clanking rang out again from overhead and the crunch and thud of a plaster cast on metal steps announced the reappearance of Ms. Ito. The other teachers appeared to shrink back from her presence, even Captain Roche.

Ms. Ito leaned on her staff and glared at Benjamin.

'Come here.'

He did as he was told. He was tall for his age, but the wizened old woman with the wild hair and the plaster cast seemed like a giant.

'Kneel, boy.' As he squatted down, she turned to the other teachers and said, 'Should we make him take the Oath in the Grand Lord's absence? I know Sebastien always does it, but—'

'A bit late for that,' Professor Loane said.

Professor Eaves replied with a groan, while Captain Roche looked at his feet.

'Well, let me just see what I can. See if I can figure out what's going on, why that thing was after him.'

'They always—'

'Quiet, James. This is not an ordinary situation.'

Professor Eaves opened his mouth, then closed it again. As Ms. Ito glared at him, he tugged at his collar, then shrugged and wandered off, idly picking out a book from a shelf and turning it over in his hands.

Benjamin glanced at Miranda and Wilhelm. Neither returned his gaze. They were staring at Ms. Ito as though she had sucked all the light out of the room.

A cold palm fell on the top of his head. Too afraid to look up, he stared at her plaster cast, the surfaced lined and scored, the colour dulled with age. Whatever ailment she suffered from, she wasn't likely to recover soon.

His eyelids grew heavy. He had never wanted to sleep like he did now, and he found his eyes closing, while everything he thought he understood about the world disappeared—

It's very cold. You lie there on the ground, feeling the hard press of the concrete beneath your calves and heels. You no longer remember where you are, or how you ended up here. White markings among the tufts of grass suggest an old tennis court. You try to lift your head, but nothing happens, so instead you turn it to the side and there you see the creature, crouched at the edge of the forest, watching you. Twin orange lights glow beneath its hood. You can't see anything of its face other than a white jawbone.

If it has come to kill you, you don't want to know. You turn your head to the other side, looking away, and you see a bicycle lying in the weeds. It's new, the blue paint of the frame not yet flecked with dust. On some of the spokes, luminous clips that you got out of a cornflakes packet just this morning slide up and down as the front wheel continues on a seemingly endless spin, and you remember your dad oiling up the mechanisms as you prepared to take it out for its first ride.

That's it, it's your birthday. You're twelve years old.

Behind the bike, the other half of the old tennis court has been torn up. In its place are a series of earth mounds and kickers, tangled with brush, but with clear bicycle trails on each. Of course. The old bike park. You came down here to test out your bike while all the biggest kids are at school. Your parents have let you pull a sickie because it's your birthday. You feel a momentary surge of regret that you didn't just go to school, and it takes a moment to remember why you didn't.

That's it. The other kids would have pulled some nasty stunt on you. Some special birthday treat. You still remember the pain from last year when a couple of big kids tried to stick a melted candle to the top of your head. The little scar took weeks to fade.

No, all alone down at the old bike park in the forest is your idea of a great birthday.

Except for the fall.

You can hear a hissing sound. You're sure the creature is still there, but you don't want to look. The top of your head hurts, and you know you landed on it. You might even have drawn blood. You wonder if the creature might be attracted to it, like one of those forest cats that can smell a wounded animal, but on another level you sense that it has been watching you for some time. Not just today, but for years and years. Perhaps even all time.

It's been waiting for you, waiting for its moment to reveal itself.

In the end, you have to know. You turn your head, squinting just in case, and there it is, looming over you, its face a skull with metal robot eyes that glow orange, the teeth still stuck in its jaw, jagged and sharp. It snaps at you, a growl coming from its throat as it reaches down toward you, bony fingers closing over the crest of your head, then at the last moment, you hear David, your brother, your kid brother who goes to the special school that you feel at times both envious and embarrassed about, you hear him shout—

'Stop!'

Benjamin opened his eyes. Ms. Ito had pulled her hand away, staring him as though he had just tried to bite her. With his body soaked with sweat and his heart racing faster than a boulder bouncing downhill, he looked around him. The room was dim, lights turned down low. Captain Roche was nowhere to be seen, though Professor Loane and Professor Eaves sat on wooden chairs in a small semi-circle around where he crouched in front of Ms. Ito. Over in the corner, Miranda and Wilhelm slept soundly, curled up on two sofas and covered with blankets.

Ms. Ito looked up. 'They were hunting him,' she whispered. 'Ghouls. Somehow they got across … and they were hunting him. He escaped, but how?'

'Someone must have helped him. Someone who could—'

'Don't be ridiculous, Robert. You're starting to sound like that fool, Caspian.'

'Perhaps they're still looking for him? What else could explain why that ghoul was inside the school?'

'There's more,' Ms. Ito said. 'I lost my hold on him before he revealed how he got here, but he's extremely important. I can feel it.'

'What could they want this little boy for?'

'We'll have to see what Sebastien has to say,' Ms. Ito said.

'Only that old fool will have any answers, but they'll be as vague as ever. Whatever happens, we mustn't forget our duty. The school, and the pupils in it, are too important.'

'This boy is a pupil like any other,' Professor Eaves said. 'He deserves the same treatment as the rest.'

'Yes, but—'

'What do we do?' asked Professor Loane. 'Now that the Grand Lord—'

'That's no help to us now. First things first,' Ms. Ito said. 'He's infected, so we have to get him cured before that gets any worse or he'll end up like one of them.' She frowned. 'I felt … there's something about him I can't understand. Something special. We have to protect him.'

'How?'

'By teaching him how to survive.'

'But what about the Oath? We can't talk about m—'

'Professor! We have to set an example, even when alone.'

'Fools,' Ms. Ito said. 'They'll find out in the end, won't they? Why not just get it over with?'

'We took the Oath, the same as you.'

'Well, I think—'

Their arguing continued, but Benjamin had zoned it out. Over the last couple of minutes, an incredible itch had developed in his lower back and, unable to move, he had suffered for as long as he could. Now he had no choice but to scratch it.

'Do you think it could have something to do with why the Grand Lord—'

Benjamin jerked, trying to rub his back against his school uniform, and the three teachers flinched. Apparently they hadn't realised he was awake.

'What's going on?' he asked.

Ms. Ito put a hand on his shoulder and he felt an immediate sense of calm. Her palm was unnaturally hot, but this heat seemed to spread out through him.

She glared at Professor Eaves and Professor Loane in turn, as though defying them to speak, then turned back to Benjamin. 'You've had a long first day in Endinfinium,' she said. 'And the most important thing for you right now is to get some sleep.'

PART II

THE ROAD INTO DARK
PLACES

20

EDGAR

The old wizard lived in a cave under the headland, halfway across a wide bay an hours' walk south of the school. It wasn't just any cave, carved out so cleanly as to be perfectly smooth and decked out with an assortment of furniture and personal items that their owner had reclaimed from the arms of the sea and lovingly restored. He had fitted in a snug door that kept out the draft, and was in the process of carving out a window so he could see the edge of the world and watch the red and yellow suns in their sunset dance, though he was still waiting for something that resembled glass to wash up onto the beach before he knocked through the last little bit of rock.

He called himself Edgar Caspian. It wasn't his real name. He didn't know what that was, but from the day he had woken up in Endinfinium without a name, he had decided to choose one for himself. He had played around with the sounds of names from the spines of storybooks in the school library until he found one that sounded right.

And then he kept it.

Almost every day—unless she had a special evening class—Miranda made her way down a crumbling cliff path to the beach to knock on Edgar's homemade door. After letting her inside, he would offer her something he had caught or baked that day—

Edgar lived entirely from what he caught in the sea and plants growing on the stepped cliff ledges—and then she would sit down and continue to learn how to control the strange pulses of energy she called magic.

'He isn't really a wizard,' she said, stopping to wait on a ledge farther down as Benjamin picked his way carefully over an especially treacherous outcrop. 'He just doesn't know what else he should call himself. Hurry up, won't you? We have to get back before the yellow sun sets, or we'll be in trouble.'

This far south were fewer scatlocks; it seemed the creatures stayed near inhabited places, like irritating next-door neighbours who would call in for the sole purpose of making a complaint. As Miranda constantly reminded Benjamin, though—and he had experienced plenty on his first night for himself—other creatures were far more dangerous.

'Why does he live down here?'

'We're not allowed to admit to the existence of magic. They'll send you out to the Haunted Forest and the ghouls if they so much as catch you talking about it. I've seen other kids disappear. Edgar used to be a professor, but he didn't agree with how the other teachers viewed magic.'

'But magic is everywhere. All that reanimation, deanimation stuff. It's all magic. I can't explain it. Can you?'

Miranda shook her head. 'It's not "real" magic, you idiot. It's "science" magic. At least that's what they expect us to believe.'

'What's the difference?'

'That's simple,' came a gruff voice from above them. 'One is easier to control.'

They both looked up, and Benjamin gaped at an elderly man floating in the air, arms folded. He was neater than the storybook kind of wizard that Benjamin knew well, with a short, manicured beard not even all grey, tidy hair, and clothes that looked more akin to a Medieval pub than a mountaintop.

'So, you're Miranda's friend. Nice to meet you, I'm—oh, sorry, got to go!'

He began to drop straight down, like a lift, and Benjamin leaned out over the cliff edge to watch. The old man gave him a smile and a wave before he dropped out of sight.

'I forgot to mention he's a little crazy,' Miranda said. 'I think it's the solitude.'

By the time they had reached the beach, Edgar had disappeared back into his little house. The door stood ajar, which Miranda said was a sign they should enter. Inside, the old wizard stood at a bar counter, cutting into strips something that smelled fishy.

'All they let you eat up there are vegetables out of their school gardens and from the fields behind the school,' Edgar said. 'I bet you're desperate for a bit of variation, aren't you?'

Benjamin and Miranda both nodded, and Edgar handed them each a strip of dried meat. It tasted like tuna jerky, but the flavour was so strong, Benjamin finished his in a single bite. A hundred times better than anything he'd been served for school meals.

'What is this?'

'Why, it's fish. The same kind of fish you might have eaten back home.'

'Captain Roche said they don't trust meat.'

'It's true. Didn't your mother ever tell you never to eat anything you found in the garden that looked like a mushroom? Just in case it was poisonous?'

'Yeah, but—'

'Same thing. Reanimates are incredible things. Many of them can breed just like anything else that's alive, but you have to be careful what you eat, because something evolved from a plastic box or a tin can isn't exactly fit for human consumption. Too many mercury-laced steaks on the menu, and the whole school will end up with mad hatter's disease.'

Benjamin took another offered piece of the dried fish. 'But this is—'

'Fish. Just like I said. That's an ocean out there, and oceans have fish in them. You just have to be really, really sure that it's what you think it is.' He grinned. 'Allowing myself the freedom to do what those clowns up in the school refuse means I'm far better than they are at figuring out where something came from.'

'Well, it's good,' Benjamin said.

Edgar smiled. 'Miranda here says you might need my help.'

'I think I'm in danger.'

Edgar laughed. 'Really? Isn't that the very definition of this place? We live within a couple of miles of the edge of the world. We could slide off it at any time.'

'The teachers … Ms. Ito … she said something that I wasn't supposed to overhear. They thought I was unconscious.'

Edgar leaned forward. Old fingers stroked his chin. 'Tell me.'

Benjamin relayed, word for word, what the teachers had said. 'And when I asked them to explain what they meant, they just brushed it off. Told me I was hearing things. That they were just speculating.'

Edgar frowned, leaning forward on his hands and staring into Benjamin's eyes until Benjamin became unnerved and looked away. His head had started to ache.

'Are you reading my mind?'

Edgar laughed. 'Goodness, boy. No one can do that. No one I know of, at any rate. I'm just picking up on your feelings.' He turned to Miranda. 'Do you ever think about going home?'

Miranda gave a powerful shake of her head. 'No! I don't want to go back. The only people I remember … I don't want to see them again.'

The wizard nodded. 'I've been here for a long time, and perhaps soon I'll take my own personal trip over the edge of the world. But what memories I do have—as vague as they are—were the same. This place … Endinfinium … it was a second chance for me. A place to be—' He paused, cocking his head and frowning. 'Hmm. A place to be … repaired.'

'I don't want to stay. I want to leave. That thing was looking for me, I'm sure of it.'

'The ghoul?'

'Or whatever it was.'

Edgar nodded. 'I can sense your inner turmoil. You're like a glowing ball of anger and frustration. The truth, as you've probably figured out by now, is that if anyone knows why they woke up here, they're not telling. Endinfinium is a country that makes its own rules. And you, my dear Mr. Benjamin, appear to have broken them.'

'How?'

'If I knew that, we could swiftly end this discussion.' He turned to Miranda, who sat on a rug at his feet, the swirling colours of an old mosaic that had been almost entirely bleached out by the sea. 'Miranda here is what, in my day, we called a miscreant. Someone who refuses to honour the Oath and deny the existence of what passes for magic here in Endinfinium. Such people were considered dangerous. Back when I first arrived, miscreants were given the choice of leaving by their own accord, or being forced out. Don't ask me to explain in what ways such things were executed. Believe me, Ms. Ito, Loane, and the others might appear harmless, but they've continued with the same old witch-burning tradition as their predecessors. If they think the school is threatened by someone who won't toe the line … over you go.'

'I don't get it,' Benjamin said. 'What magic? I have none. I can't move things. I can't look into people's minds, or see the future.'

Edgar smiled. 'You'd be surprised what each of us can do that we don't yet understand,' he said. 'We each have what we consider normal, but just look around you. Have you seen anything you consider normal?'

'Not really.'

'Yet in Endinfinium, where the very buildings are coming alive, it is you, a simple human, who is the deviant from the norm. Everything is connected, but here, in Endinfinium, it is connected in a different way. Things that one wouldn't expect to have sentience are not just walking and talking like us, but in many cases, they are setting the rules.'

'Is that what Endinfinium is? An entire world that came alive?'

Edgar laughed. 'Your guess is as good as mine, but it's possible, I suppose. I'm an old man now, but when I was young like you, I hunted for answers, too. They're out there. Never give up on them.'

Miranda nodded at Benjamin. 'Show him your hand.'

Benjamin pulled off the thick plaster the school nurse had given him. A little ointment still congealed around the scratch, but even now, three days after the event, there was no sign of healing. The skin was red and sore, the scratch itself so dark as to be almost purple.

'Hmm. That's not good. Not good at all.'

Miranda sniffed. 'It's my fault. I came here to see you, and left him to cross the bridge alone. His book fell into the sea; otherwise, he would have read the warnings about the Locker Room.'

Edgar shook his head. 'Not at all, my dear. By coming here to see me, that makes it my fault.'

'I didn't mean—'

'And by coming to see you in the Locker Room, that makes it a fault of Benjamin's very sense of kindness. You see where I'm going with this?'

Miranda gave a confused shake of her head, red hair rustling like leaves in the wind.

'He means you shouldn't blame yourself,' Benjamin said. 'It's not your fault.'

'Oh.'

Benjamin looked back at Edgar. 'The nurse keeps telling me it'll heal. I'm supposed to see Professor Loane tonight. I'm worried they'll throw me off the edge of the world, or worse, give me to the ghouls.'

'I don't think you have to worry about that. I think they're more interested in seeing what happens. Have you met the headmaster, Grand Lord Bastien, yet?'

Benjamin shook his head. 'They keep telling me he's gone away on business, and that I have to wait until he comes back.'

Edgar frowned. 'They do, do they? And where exactly is he supposed to have gone?'

'I don't know.'

'I do!' Miranda blurted. 'Wilhelm told me something—'

'Wilhelm? The curly-haired boy who refuses to go to classes? I thought you didn't get on with him.'

Miranda blushed. 'I-I-I decided to give him another chance.'

Benjamin felt a strange knot in his stomach, and Edgar glanced at him, flashing a smile. The old wizard felt his feelings, too: jealousy.

'What did he say, Miranda?'

'He was spying again. He said that Grand Lord Bastien went west, on a diplomatic meeting.'

'When?'

'Five days ago.'

'I'd be happy to talk to young Wilhelm. Could you not have brought him, too?'

Miranda shook her head. 'He got caught. He's in the Locker Room now.'

Benjamin smiled. 'He volunteered to do a thousand cleans.'

'Volunteered? Is that so? I heard he was quite the rebel.'

'He was, until he met Ms. Ito. Now he sits at the front of every art class. I think he's got a crush.'

Edgar gave a wistful smile. 'Indeed. Quite a woman, she is. Back in the day, I was rather taken with her myself. That monstrosity of a woman has broken every rule of attraction ever written. There's just something about the way she drags that oversized plaster cast….'

The old wizard appeared to have drifted off into some ancient memory, and Benjamin exchanged glances with Miranda, who quietly got up and sneaked a couple more pieces of the dried fish off the plate. They had both finished eating before Edgar sat up with a jerk.

'Well, where was I?'

'We were talking about Grand Lord Bastien.'

'Yes, yes. Indeed. Well, I think we need to investigate where exactly the old chap has gone, and why he's not back yet.'

'What's to the east?' Benjamin asked.

Edgar let out a long sigh. 'Things you don't want to know about, believe me.'

21

MESSAGE

'On the count of three … climb!'

Benjamin was slow out of the marks. Godfrey, two ranks to his right, was nearly at the foot of the cliff before Benjamin had even taken two steps. By the time Benjamin had his fingers on the first handholds, the taller boy was already ten feet up, and moving fast.

Fifty feet above, holding on to her harness, Miranda leaned out, one hand cupping her mouth. 'Come on, Benjamin! Hurry *up!*'

Behind her, Wilhelm had wrapped his arms around their bracing pole, feet digging into the dirt. Benjamin pulled himself up as quickly as he could, but he had no chance; Godfrey's team was simply too strong. As Benjamin scrambled, wheezing and gasping, over the edge—managing to beat just two of the nine other teams—Godfrey and his crew had begun to howl with laughter.

'You're useless!' Godfrey shouted. 'You couldn't even climb stairs!'

Benjamin was getting tired of Godfrey's constant goading over the last few days. They didn't share every class together, but when they did, the bigger boy made it clear who he considered was at the bottom of the class. While some of the teachers—Ms. Ito and Captain Roche, in particular—were quick to crack down on any obvious bullying, others turned a blind eye, pulled in by Godfrey's otherwise flawless class performance.

Miranda put a hand on Benjamin's arm. 'Leave him,' she said. 'Just let it go.'

Benjamin shook his head. His body ached from the climb, and the scratch on the back of his hand throbbed.

'I'm tired of this.'

Captain Roche was still down on the beach, supervising the next climbers. Benjamin glared at Godfrey, wondering if the crab-shaped teacher could scuttle quick enough to catch someone if they were pushed off the edge.

'Okay, time to unharness and get back up to the school,' the captain bellowed. Benjamin breathed a sigh of relief. Their next class was advanced math taught by Professor Loane. Godfrey was in the lower group, so for a couple of hours, at least, Benjamin would have some peace.

He was walking back up the steep path toward the school when someone tapped him on the back. He turned to find Simon, one of Godfrey's regular wingmen, and whom, on account of his nose, Benjamin had learned everyone called Snout, standing at his shoulder. Benjamin had quickly discovered that, while harmless and relatively amiable when alone, Snout wasn't the sharpest knife in the rack; therefore, he was perfect cannon fodder for Godfrey's errands.

The dopey-looking boy grinned a smile so wide it stretched his nose, flattening it out a little like a ski jump.

'Hey, Forrest.'

'What do you want?'

'Godfrey says he has something important to tell you. He wants you to meet him in the disused gym on level four.'

'But I have math.'

'Skip it.'

'No. Go take a hike.'

'He says someone called David has a message for you.'

Benjamin stumbled, his heart feeling like it had skipped a beat or two, while a sudden flush of heat filled his cheeks.

'What are you … what are you talking about?'

Snout shrugged. 'That's all he said.'

'I'll be there.'

Snout grinned. 'Good.'

As the other boy slowed and slipped back behind him, Miranda came up alongside Benjamin, her crimson eyebrows folded together in a frown like two crayons trying to reach each other.

'What are you playing at?' she snapped. 'He's just going to beat up on you or something. I'll come with you. And Wilhelm.'

'I'm not going!' Wilhelm protested. 'I don't want to get my butt kicked. I suggest we all just go to math as planned, then straight back to the dorms.'

'He said David has a message for me. David is my little brother. Back … home.'

'He's lying.'

'How could he know my brother's name?'

'A lucky guess?' Wilhelm said. 'You were shouting stuff out in your sleep the other night. Maybe he heard you.'

'What did I say?'

Wilhelm shook his head. 'I don't know. I stuffed bits of tissue in my ears and went back to sleep.'

'Benjamin, promise you won't go,' Miranda said. 'At least not alone.'

'All right, all right.'

'Promise?'

Benjamin sighed. 'Okay, sure.'

They had a twenty-minute break before the next class. Math wasn't his favourite, but it was better than quantum physics or philosophy or particle mechanics, none of which he could even spell, let alone understand. Art was okay, even if Ms. Ito was a loose cannon ready to explode the moment anyone said a word out of place, and he enjoyed biology and ecology well enough, even if they ignored the glaringly obvious: that certain things that shouldn't be were alive.

He enjoyed the physical lessons most, though—sculpting, tree and rock climbing, rope making, survival techniques. They were easy to lose oneself in, something he found himself doing more and more as the days passed. Alone in his bunk at night, with Wilhelm snoring beneath him, it was all too easy to roll over and tug back a corner of the curtain to reveal a sky never truly dark and an ocean that ended halfway to a natural horizon. Wilhelm and Miranda both claimed that, in time, he would forget his past —or at least learn not to pine for it—but with every minute and hour that drifted by, his mother's voice on the other end of the phone line became louder and louder until his ears seemed to ache.

Miranda and Wilhelm were both in the advanced math group, one above his own. The three of them walked to the classrooms together, but then Benjamin excused himself to go to the toilet. He ducked through the toilet door, then listened for their classroom door closing. As soon as he was sure they had gone inside, he slipped back out and bolted down the corridor in the direction of the stairs to level four.

Benjamin, on his trips around the school, had so far located nine gyms in various stages of disorder. Three were still actively used, replacing three now filled with old furniture and smelling of the chamomile sprayed from the ceiling's sprinkler system to keep all of those disgruntled tables and chairs quiet. Of the oldest triumvirate, two were in the bowels of the school, carved out of the rock, and had partially collapsed. Warning signs stood outside of their locked doors.

The final one was on level four and looked pretty much like a regular gym except, apart from a natural skylight, it was almost devoid of light. When Benjamin arrived, Godfrey was standing just back from the small, orange circle cast by the skylight, his back to the entrance, arms folded as if he had been waiting for hours.

Benjamin slipped in through the door that hung ajar to wait in the shadows, watching Godfrey and peering around for anyone else who might be ready to jump him. The gym, though, was silent, apart from Godfrey's shallow breathing, and, aside from the dust motes dancing in the single beam of light, empty.

Taking a deep breath, Benjamin stepped forward.

'I'm here.'

Godfrey shuddered as if awakened from a daydream and turned in a slow circle. Benjamin stared at the sight of Godfrey's glazed eyes and dazed smile.

'Where's this message?' Benjamin lifted his fists. He had cracked Godfrey once and he would do it again if he had to. Alone with no one to break them up, he didn't stand much of a chance against a boy who was older, taller, and stronger, but he would give it his best shot. 'If you're joking with me about my brother, I'll—'

'Bennie? Bennie, where are you?'

He froze. The voice coming from Godfrey's mouth was his brother's. Godfrey continued to stare as if looking through a portal into the future.

'I'm coming, Bennie. I'm so sorry, Bennie. I just wanted to look after you. I didn't know what else to do. Do you forgive me, Bennie?'

'David—I mean, Godfrey—I mean, David—what are you talking about?'

'Those things in the woods … I don't know … they wanted you and knew I could stop them … the truck … it was so big … it hurt so much … I'm sorry, Bennie, but I'm coming … I'm coming to find you and bring you home. Mum and Dad … they're so worried, and I'm so sorry … I just didn't want it to—'

'David? Is that really you? What are you talking about?'

Godfrey didn't answer. Eyes still glazed, he cocked his head slightly, gave another vacant smile.

'It's so dark, Bennie. I'm so scared. There are orange lights in the trees. I see them every day. I see them all around. They're watching me.'

Orange lights?

'No!' Benjamin grabbed Godfrey and began to shake him. 'No! Leave him alone! Leave my brother alone!'

He let go, and the older boy slumped to the ground. The floor gave a sharp lurch, the force knocking him to his knees, while from above came the crash of breaking glass followed by a flurry of gigantic beating wings, black and shiny, that filled every available space. Benjamin curled up into a ball, covering his face with his hands, screaming at the top of his lungs. Only once did he open his eyes, and through the pulsing, beating mass of living darkness, he saw the mocking glow of twin orange lights.

22

TIME SLIPS

The zombified horse's head flinched back at the same time Benjamin did. 'Oh, you're awake,' Gubbledon Longface said. His huge head swung around, and his hooves clacked together to attract attention.

Miranda ran in through a door that led out into a dark corridor, while Benjamin pushed himself up onto his elbows and took stock of his surroundings. He wasn't in the dorms, but in a small hospital ward with five foldout beds, of which his was the only one occupied. Curtains hung, ready to seal him off from the world. Across the room were desks and a variety of medical equipment, all old-fashioned and a little musty.

'Well, if you're awake, I'll trot along and help with the clean-up,' Gubbledon said, standing up. 'Good to have you back in the land of the living.'

'Is it?' Benjamin said as the reanimated horse went out, ducking through the door, then closing it behind him.

'What are you wittering about?' Miranda asked, taking the seat Gubbledon had just vacated. 'You fool. I told you to stay away, and you promised me. You could have been killed. There was an earth tremor and the east wing of the school woke up. That old gym was a roost for haulocks. A couple of kids who were late for their braiding class heard you screaming, otherwise those things would have ripped you apart.'

'Godfrey spoke to me in David's voice. I think my little brother is in danger from the ghouls.'

'What are you talking about? Godfrey didn't go down there, he went to his math class. He got Snout to tell you to go there as a trick. He wanted to make you late for math so you'd get sent to the Locker Room again. He's really sorry.'

Benjamin tried to sit up, but his body ached as if he'd just run a marathon. 'What? He was there. He knew my brother's name, and I saw him, right there, in the centre. In the shaft of light.'

'What shaft of light? That gym is in complete darkness. You could have died, Benjamin. I know you think this place isn't real, but you can still die.' She looked down at her hands. 'And if you ever come back, who knows what you'll become.'

As if to illustrate the point, a cleaner ambled past the door, pushing a mop along the corridor floor. The man's head swung slowly from side to side, eyes glazed.

'I have no idea what's going on,' he whispered.

Miranda looked set to answer, when the door swung open and in strode Professor Loane, immaculately dressed as always in a black blazer, pinstripe slacks, and a tweed jacket. His hair was neatly brushed over to the side, gelled so tight as to be immovable.

'Well, there he is, our little adventurer. Feeling better?'

'Not really.'

Professor Loane looked perturbed at Benjamin's stilted response. He gave a wide grimace, then asked Miranda for some time alone with Benjamin. The girl's expression said she wanted to refuse, but a teacher was a teacher. Standing up, she gave a curt nod.

When the door had closed, Professor Loane sat next to Benjamin's bed.

'We've been talking about you,' he said.

'Who's "we"?'

'Those of us in the teachers' inner circle. Myself, Professor Eaves, Captain Roche, and Ms. Ito. We're worried about you. Things are happening to you that have never happened before. Not in anyone's memory, at any rate. For the time being, we'd like you to move into a special suite within the teachers' apartments so that we can keep a better eye on you.'

'Why?'

'Other ghouls have been spotted in the school grounds. If one can get in, others can. We need to protect you until we figure out what they want and what we can do about it.'

'What about the other pupils? What about my friends?'

'We're quite sure the ghoul was hunting you. Ms. Ito said it showed no interest in your friends. If you're with them, they're in danger, but if you're apart—'

'Do I have a choice?'

Loane shook his head. 'No. Your things have already been moved.'

'But that's not fair! I didn't ask for the ghoul to chase me. I want to go home!'

The professor looked pained. 'Unfortunately, for the time being at least, that's where you already are.'

Benjamin refused to humour Professor Loane's attempts at small talk, so after a few more fruitless minutes, the professor said his goodbyes and left. No sooner had the door closed, when Miranda reappeared.

'Were you listening?'

The girl nodded. 'As best I could, although the walls are pretty thick. It sucks, but don't worry. I'm sure Wilhelm can find a way in so we can visit you.'

Benjamin had been in Endinfinium for less than a week, and if there was anything he didn't totally resent, it was the evenings in the dormitories after classes and dinner were over, when his friends would get together to play trumps, tell ghost stories, or battle over one of the many board games that filled a couple of the common room's cupboards. He couldn't imagine Dusty Eaves and Ms. Ito haggling over poker hands, although he had Captain Roche, with his large sleeve size, down as a surefire cheater.

'Thanks.' Benjamin sighed. 'Even though Wilhelm is probably the messiest person I've ever known, and he snores like something undead, he already feels like my second brother. I'll miss him. I know that we've only known each other for a few days, but you and Wilhelm … you've become a second family to me.'

'I'm honoured.'

'Do you ever think about going back?'

'Never.' Miranda shook her head. 'It wasn't for me like it was for you. It's difficult to explain. I didn't enjoy being a child. I just dreamed of the day I could grow up and go off-world, find a better place to live without all the smoke and the junk everywhere—'

'Huh?' Benjamin frowned. 'What do you mean by "off-world"? Overseas, right?'

'No, to the colonies. The orbiters and the moon base.'

'What colonies? What moon base?'

'Benjamin, surely you know—'

'I have no idea what you're talking about. When I woke up here, it was April fourteenth, twenty-fifteen.'

Miranda laughed. 'Ah, I forgot about that. We don't tend to talk about our past lives all that often. Not much point, really.'

'You're not from twenty-fifteen?'

Miranda shook her head again. 'I was born on August the sixth, twenty-eight eighty-seven.'

Benjamin stared. 'That's crazy. I'm more than six hundred years older than you.'

Miranda smirked. 'You look it, too.'

'I'm serious.'

He wasn't sure whether Miranda believed him. The girl shrugged. 'What does it matter? We can't go back, can we? It doesn't matter if we're from a million years in the future, we're all stuck in the same place.'

Benjamin's mind whirred almost too fast to keep up with these new revelations. Endinfinium was like something out of a storybook. What if it wasn't a real place, like Basingstoke was, but a place between places, a world that existed alongside the real world and that could pluck people out of any date in history?

He tried to explain this theory to Miranda, but he was so excited, he stumbled over his words.

'So what?' she said. 'It just means we have a different view on the world. It doesn't make anyone better than anyone else. It might matter if one of us came to the other's time, but here, we're all the same. And as far as I can gather, everyone comes here as a kid, so it's not like any of us are super-scientists or anything, is it?'

'No, you don't understand,' he said. 'If people can exist from multiple points in history, then surely machines can, too? I've not seen anything more dangerous than a few animated cars, but what if there's real danger out there? The kind of danger that can destroy us all and smash the school to pieces?'

Miranda watched him, her eyes guarding a thousand possibilities that Benjamin didn't even want to guess at. 'If there was, what could we do about it?'

He gave a slow shake of his head. 'I have no idea.'

23

RISING ARMY

Professor Loane's use of the word "suite" was a gross exaggeration. The box room at the end of the corridor was barely big enough for the single bed and a small washbasin. The room itself sat next to a dusty cleaning closet and had surely once belonged to a janitor, one whom, from the floor's grimy look, had never once removed his shoes before entering.

The biggest difference, however, between Benjamin's new room and the old one which he shared with Wilhelm was that it was situated in a tower room rather than on the clifftop, and now faced inland. If he got up early enough, he could watch the yellow sun rise over the hills behind the school and the red sun slide across the horizon in a slow, lazy arc that never took it higher than a mid-morning forty-five degree angle. In those early mornings, before the haze of day took over, the faint outline of distant mountains became visible beyond a vast expanse of forest. The forest itself was separated from the undulating hills by the dark line of a wide river flowing languidly from north to south. Surrounding the school, the hills were a series of outcrops, gullies, and patches of farmland where lethargic figures worked from dawn until dusk, and perhaps even long into the chilly, red-tinged night. Occasionally, Benjamin spotted vehicles: low, wide things with oversized wheels, ferrying produce and tools back and forth.

Within a couple of days it became apparent that he was under guard. During regular class hours inside the school he could relax, but whenever the lesson took the pupils outside the main building—for climbing, maintenance, or brush walking— he sensed a presence tailing him, staying just out of sight. Often, he would pretend to tie a shoelace in order to steal a glance at the path behind, but whoever or whatever was back there was practiced at the art of stealth and stayed well-hidden.

If indeed, it was a real person. He began to suspect he might be under the surveillance of one of Captain Roche's mysterious eyes, and before changing for bed thoroughly checked his clothing every night for something beady and spidery. Yet, he found nothing. His mysterious tail remained just that—a mystery.

Without even realising it, he grew distant from his friends, and his mood wasn't helped by the endless nightmares, or that every morning he had to sit at the teachers' table for breakfast, eating in reluctant silence while a few seats away, Wilhelm and Miranda made small talk about their day's lessons, and Godfrey and his friends made jokes and jibes about his misfortune.

He wouldn't have minded so much if the teachers got better food, but it was the same bowls of vegetables with the sweet, custardy sauce, day after day after day.

'Look, this is getting ridiculous.'

Miranda had one foot propped onto Benjamin's belly as he lay flat on the course grass beside the path. The roundhouse chop had come out of nowhere—one moment, they were hunting through the gorse and heather for a variety of wild mushroom they had eaten once or twice for lunch; the next, Benjamin was sighing just a little too loud and his feet were swept out from beneath him.

Benjamin picked a broken sprig of bush out of his armpit.

Luckily he had bounced off a bank of heather, rather than a far spinier one of gorse.

'What did I do?'

'It's what you didn't do. You're moping so much, you've driven Wilhelm to start sucking up to Dusty Eaves. Look at him over there, being all leech-like. He's asking questions and showing interest. I feel utterly disgusted.'

Farther along the path, Wilhelm was squatting in the dirt beside Professor Eaves, nodding attentively as the professor scrabbled for some hidden gem just below the rocky surface.

'I think it's nice that he's started to go to classes. He couldn't stay holed up in the dorms forever. I admit he's sucking up a bit too much, but—'

'You have to snap out of it, Benjamin.'

He sighed. 'I'm trying. But you don't understand. I hate being stuck in there.'

'Look on the bright side. You're safe. You've got the teachers to protect you if anything bad happens. All we've got is old Gubbledon. You know, he almost fell in the washing tank yesterday morning because he got a hoof caught in his shoelaces. I mean, it's not like he even needs them, being a zombie horse and all that. A bit of dirt isn't going to hurt him, is it?'

Benjamin shrugged. 'But it's the same old deal up there. No one will answer my questions. All they'll tell me is that they think I'm here by mistake, even though no one seems to know the rules as to why anyone is here at all. And if that's true, why can't I go back? And I keep dreaming of David. Last night I dreamt that he was wandering about in a dark forest, being chased by ghouls, and that it's somehow all my fault.'

Miranda looked thoughtful. 'Perhaps they're waiting to see what happens,' she suggested. 'If they say something too soon and it's wrong, they'll look like idiots.'

Benjamin shrugged again and sat down on the ground beside Miranda, who suddenly gave a long frown. She reached out for the nearest patch of heather and, after tensing her fingers, a popping sound came from inside the bush, followed by a large, bulbous mushroom that appeared in her hand.

'Wow! I didn't know it was there, until … just before,' she

said, holding it up. 'Look, it's huge. It's the biggest one we've found so far.'

'Edgar seems to be helping you,' Benjamin said. 'It's a shame I'm being followed, or we could get away to see him. Say, can you do something about that? If you concentrate, can you feel if someone's tailing me?'

'I don't know. I've never tried before.' She dropped the mushroom into their basket. 'But I have to be careful. If Professor Eaves knows I'm using … *special influence* to find mushrooms, I'll end up in the Locker Room again.'

'How do you do it? What does it feel like?'

Miranda shrugged. 'I don't know, really. I think about it, then imagine it a little bigger. And there it is.'

At the front of the group, Professor Eaves had stood up. 'Gather,' he cried, holding his arms wide, like a preacher calling to his flock. 'Gather, quickly. The weather's taken a turn.'

Over the last few minutes, clouds had come rolling in and the red sun was completely obscured now behind a cloudbank more dark purple than pink. Five minutes ago the skies had been clear. Now, a shadow was racing across the land, bringing with it fat drops of freezing rain.

'Back,' Professor Eaves shouted. 'Back to the school. With haste.'

Wilhelm came running up, holding something under his jacket. 'Look at these big ones old Dusty let me have,' he said, pulling back his jacket to reveal a cluster of fat mushrooms. 'He said I could get Longface to add them to tomorrow's breakfast. He's not so bad, really. You know, for a teacher.'

The other kids were already hurrying for the door in the school's outer wall, a five-minute walk back up the path. Miranda took one each of Wilhelm's and Benjamin's arms and dragged them like two slacking children up the path to the castle, stamping her feet as if threatening punishment for any dissent.

'You're the best of friends now, aren't you, Dusty and you?' Miranda said.

Wilhelm shrugged. 'You get used to the old blower.'

'Perhaps you can form a mushroom club together. Won't that be nice—'

A lightning flash lit up the grey sky, leaving the rest of Miranda's sentence unheard. Farther up the path, Professor Eaves waved the pupils toward the door. It was the only way into the castle for a long way in each direction. The other pupils were running now, leaving Benjamin, Miranda, and Wilhelm behind.

Rain had begun sheeting down, and the air had gone quite dark. Another lightning flash lit up the sky, and in that split second between light and darkness, Benjamin caught Professor Eaves' gaze. The smile had dropped, and the professor's mouth closed, jaw set hard. With a look that was part regret, part relief, he followed the last of the other pupils inside the door and slammed it shut.

'Wait!' Miranda shouted. Turning to the others, she added, 'He didn't see us in the rain.'

'Oh, he did,' Benjamin said, kicking at a clump of couch grass. 'He left us. That old git left us outside.'

'Look over there.' Wilhelm pointed at the clifftop to their right. 'What are those orange lights?'

Amidst the dark green grass, hundreds of what might have been flowers on a less sinister day blinked on, shifting back and forth and rising up through the rain, slowly bringing with them lumps of brown earth and grey rock encasing the metallic spines of ancient buried machines.

'Ghouls,' Miranda whispered. 'Oh, wow. There's so many.'

'Yeah, we, um, need to run,' Wilhelm said.

Benjamin stared as the creatures rose out of the ground, shaking off the dirt to stretch out stiff, rusty limbs.

'They're all so different,' he said, remembering the creature that had attacked them. 'It's like they can't decide what form they want to take.'

'Doesn't matter what they look like,' Miranda said, voice trembling. 'They'll rip us apart if they catch us.'

The otherworldly horde rising up out of the ground was a sea of human remains fused with broken machines, mechanics and bone and rotting flesh, wire-cloaked and veiled, with only the uniformity of their orange glowing eyes out of bleached human skulls to give them a shared identity. Some walked like men, others bounded on all fours, still others slithered on the ground.

'Benjamin!'

He gasped and staggered back as something hard struck him across the face. He looked away from the lights to see Miranda lifting her hand to slap him again.

'Don't stare at them! Edgar said they can hypnotise you, and then you're dead!'

She jerked his arm, turning him back toward the school. Wilhelm had already reached the door but no matter how hard he jerked on it, it wouldn't budge.

To either side, the school's stone outer wall rose like a castle's keep; there was no way up the vertical climb to the lowest circling promenade without scaling equipment. To the right, around the wide arc of the outer wall lay the cliff's edge with paths leading down to the beaches, though they were treacherous in bad weather. Left was inland, around the base of the school's outer wall to where it straddled a deep gully, the tower of the teachers' apartments rising over it like an ice cream cone above a pit of coal. There was a way down, with an entrance into the basements beneath the school, but it was always kept locked.

'Stick close to the wall,' Miranda said. 'We have a head start. We make for the gully, and then, when I say, we turn toward them, outpace them to where the gully's shallow enough to cross. Then we head around the north side of the school to the main doors.'

She glared first at Wilhelm, then at Benjamin, searching for agreement. Though Wilhelm's face was streaky with rain, sobs betrayed the tears that hid there. Benjamin said nothing. At his nod, they turned as one and raced for the gully, boots sloshing in the waterlogged grass.

They had gone no more than a few steps, when a bounding creature much like a tiger but with metal poles for legs barreled into Benjamin from behind, knocking him to the ground. Spiked front arms swung toward him, but then it was rolling away, knocked aside, and Miranda stood nearby, shaky hands raised and eyes filled with terror.

Another creature that rolled like a bulbous, out-of-control

cable wheel knocked Wilhelm over, then spun, its metal outer wheels leaving a muddy trail behind them. It shuddered as it found purchase, then raced at Benjamin, who avoided it with a sideways dive. He had barely gathered his breath before Miranda was pulling him up again, dragging him along behind her.

They made it to the edge of the gully, though too slowly to cut back to where it was shallow enough to cross. Instead, they found themselves at the top of the steeply meandering path that led down into its dark depths and to the door that would almost certainly be locked.

'The door's our only chance,' Wilhelm gasped, bounding down the path without waiting for Miranda and Benjamin to follow. Something looming and dark that looked like an old, upended carpet had risen up to block their path, twin orange eyes glowing out of worn and frayed threads, before it blew apart in a flash of silver, showering them in lumps of damp, musty fabric.

'Nice one!' Wilhelm shouted.

'That wasn't me,' Miranda said. 'Someone's helping us. Come on. This is our chance.'

The lightning regularly splitting the darkness had been joined by other flashes of light from the battlements above—arrows of silver that blew apart the ghouls on impact, turning them back into lucid smears of light and substance that the drumming rain dissolved back into the earth. Their anonymous helper was doing what he or she could, but for every ghoul that exploded into a quickly dissipating cloud of metal and flesh, two more appeared to take its place.

'I've almost got it!' Wilhelm screamed from the door farther down the path, hands jerking at a stick he had poked into the heavy lock. 'Come on!'

Benjamin found himself on a set of crude steps cut into the gully's side. Wilhelm and the door were right ahead. Miranda was behind him, but then she cried out as something with hooks caught hold of her school blazer and dragged her back toward the edge of the precipice. Wilhelm screamed. Benjamin tried to reach her, but something else knocked into him from behind, and then Miranda and the creature were tumbling into the gully, locked in a tangle of limbs and metal.

'*No!*' Benjamin roared, and a blooming pain filled his head, seeming to rend him apart from within. A blinding, glorious light split the sky, the clouds parted, and then there was silence.

24

SANCTIONS

'You say you have no idea what you did?'

Benjamin shook his head, jaw set, resolute. 'No.'

Professor Loane uncrossed his legs, then crossed them again. Beside him, Ms. Ito sat on another chair. Captain Roche paced up and down, while Professor Eaves stood behind Professor Loane, arms folded. Benjamin couldn't look at him. Professor Eaves had claimed not to see them out on the cliff, believing them already inside, but Benjamin could see the lie sitting in his eyes.

'Benjamin, this is very serious. The kind of power you displayed should never be used. Don't you understand the Oath? That the existence of the beyond powers can never be acknowledged or used, for the safety of everyone? Such power can jeopardise this school. It has to be locked away, forgotten about.'

'I didn't do anything.'

'You repelled the weather.'

'It wasn't me.'

'Then who was it?'

Benjamin shrugged. He had no idea whether or not it had been he who had repelled the weather. He had felt a sudden white heat emanating from his body, but he had no idea why or what it had done. All he had cared about was Miranda. The creature had pulled her over the edge, and a terrible rage had burst out of him.

'Benjamin … I'm afraid that we have no choice but to impose further sanctions on you. The ghouls were repelled this time, and our deanimation sprays have cleared the land outside the school for the time being, but this can't be allowed to happen again. We will require you to have a companion of our choosing at all times, an older boy to watch over you, because your friends can't be trusted. In fact, I think it would be for the best if you don't see Miss Butterworth or Master Jacobs for the next few days. We will review your sanctions at the end of the week.'

Benjamin tried to speak, but no words would come. He looked from one teacher to another; they all shared the same expression of solemn agreement.

'I'm still waiting,' he said, so quietly that Professor Loane frowned and cocked his head to hear. 'I haven't had my orientation. When will I get to meet the headmaster?'

'Insolent, self-assumptive boy,' Professor Eaves muttered, shaking his head, but Professor Loane silenced him with a sharp narrowing of the eyes before turning back to Benjamin.

'I'm afraid Grand Lord Bastien isn't back yet.'

'I keep getting told that. When will he be? How long have I got to put up with the lies of this horrible place?'

'No supper,' Professor Eaves grunted.

'I think it's time you retired to your room,' Professor Loane said to Benjamin, giving Professor Eaves another long glare. 'I'll have supper brought up to you. You should get some rest after your ordeal today. In the meantime, we shall give some consideration as to whom might make a good shadow companion to keep you out of trouble.'

'And inside locked doors,' Professor Eaves added, before giving a swift shake of his head and turning away.

Captain Roche took Benjamin up to his room. Of all of the teachers, he was the only one for which Benjamin had much of a soft spot. Despite Benjamin's inability to shake the feeling that his eyes had switched to widescreen mode whenever he looked at the captain, he was perhaps more human than any of them. Ms. Ito was awe-inspiringly terrifying, Professor Loane brought back bad memories of automation-like teachers from his Basingstoke school days, and Professor Eaves, he was convinced, wanted him dead, one way or another.

'Where's Grand Lord Bastien gone?' Benjamin asked as they reached the corridor leading to his room.

Captain Roche stared straight ahead, and just as Benjamin began to think he hadn't heard, he said, 'Keep this to yourself, or at least within your little circle of chitchat friends. He's missing.'

'Where?'

'He went north, to the High Mountains. He hasn't returned yet. He was due back a week ago.'

'What's he doing there?'

'That, I'm not privy to.'

'Do you think ghouls got him?'

Captain Roche looked amused. 'Ghouls are of no concern to the Grand Lord,' he said, as though that should have been obvious. 'He went on a consultation mission. He should have returned by now.'

'What kind of consultation mission?'

'Boy, you ask too many questions.'

'Only when there aren't enough answers.'

Captain Roche shrugged. 'Get some sleep. You get no pass from climbing tomorrow morning.'

Though his voice contained no humour, a barely perceptible curl of his lips suggested this was the captain's idea of a joke. Benjamin gave him a polite smile and went inside.

He locked the door, grabbed a pile of old comic books the teachers had brought for him and lay down on the bed. Concentration came poorly, though, and he glanced over the pictures without really taking them in. At first he had found them fascinating. Some dated in the far future, and while their simple stories of war and space adventure gave no clues as to how technology might have advanced, Benjamin was aware he might be holding some antique that, in his time, was yet even to be born.

He was just dozing off when a tap-tap-tap came at the window. Benjamin jumped up and pulled back the drapes to see Wilhelm leaning against the sill, one hand poised for a second knock. Benjamin pulled up the sash and the smaller boy happily climbed through. As Benjamin shut the window again, Wilhelm hopped from foot to foot, rubbing his arms against the cold.

'How is she?'

'She'll be fine,' Wilhelm stuttered. 'She's still in the hospital room, but she'll be discharged in the morning. Nothing broken.'

'She was lucky.'

Wilhelm puffed out his cheeks, letting the air slowly filter out. 'Ms. Ito said that had that ghoul's hook not gotten caught, Miranda could have died. As it was, she was able to climb out and knock it down.'

'Do you think it was Ms. Ito who helped us?'

Wilhelm shrugged. 'I don't know. Seriously, just when I thought I was starting to figure this place out, you come along and make everything go even crazier.'

The sudden grin that bloomed across Wilhelm's face made Benjamin feel a little better. 'I wish I could go to see her,' he said.

'The trellis will probably hold your weight, you know.'

Benjamin shook his head. 'No chance. I can't climb like you can.'

Wilhelm shrugged again, not pressing the issue. Benjamin had seen the terrifying ascent to the overhang of the teachers' tower, and knew he would splat like bird droppings should he even try it. Wilhelm, however, could climb like a squirrel, and even though Benjamin regularly told him to stay away, the smaller boy wouldn't be perturbed. Since Benjamin had been brought there, Wilhelm had shown up almost every night, and even on days when he had nothing much to say, he gave Benjamin the greatest gift he so desperately needed: company.

'Do they know what you did to scare the clouds away?' Wilhelm asked.

Benjamin shrugged and told him what the teachers had said.

'You really think Dusty wants rid of you?' Wilhelm asked when he was finished. 'I know he's a bit of a stickler, but I never saw him as the murderous type.'

'You know what I think? They all say there's no such thing as magic, that it's just unexplained science, and that some people can control it and all that, but that's a load of rubbish. I think there *is* magic. This whole country—or whatever it is—is built out of it, but it's unravelling, and they don't know how to stop it.'

'I guess it would make sense.'

'We've all been brought here for reasons that no one understands, not even the teachers. Half of our classes are about trying to control everything—keep stuff from coming alive, fix stuff that breaks. This place is falling apart, and you know what?'

'What?'

'I think it's been getting worse since I arrived.'

Wilhelm frowned. 'I guess there were no ghouls around the school until you arrived. You've definitely got them riled up a bit, there.'

Benjamin ran to the window and pulled back the curtains. Beyond, a deep twilight covered everything, casting shadows upon shadows until only a few mounds of hills were visible, backed by an expanse of black forestland.

'I need to make a phone call,' he said.

'What?'

'Can you help me? Can you get me to the school lobby without us being caught?'

Wilhelm nodded. 'Of course I can. What do you need to do?'

Benjamin shook his head. He had a theory, of course, though so outlandish it made even Endinfinium seem normal. 'I'm not sure, but I'll tell you as soon as I figure it out.'

25

DAVEY'S ABSENCE

Wilhelm disappeared for a couple of hours, then showed up again around midnight, bringing with him a stolen climbing harness. Benjamin, he explained, didn't have the skills to do the kind of underside climb Wilhelm's small frame and bravado were designed for. Instead, they affixed a pulley rope to the leg of Benjamin's bed and lowered the pulley out through the window. Benjamin went first, with Wilhelm holding the rope secure. With his feet in a brace, Benjamin tugged on a central rope to lower himself to the ground.

Despite the horrors of the afternoon, it proved far quicker to get down to the lobby by going around the school's outer wall to the main entrance, rather than cutting through the school itself. All afternoon, Benjamin had watched cleaners spraying chamomile on the ground outside, but now, while he waited for Wilhelm to descend, the pungent scent of the calming flower thick in his nostrils, Benjamin stood nervously back by the wall, trying not to imagine more ghouls climbing up out of the ground.

Wilhelm hopped down from the rope, making Benjamin jump. His friend was like a mouse—utterly silent. 'Here, wipe this on you. Just a bit on your clothes is enough. I didn't want to do it in the room because the teachers might smell it.'

Benjamin dipped his fingers into a pot of thick grease. 'What is it?' he asked, wrinkling his nose.

'Haulock repellent.'

Benjamin didn't have a chance to ask what it was or who had figured out it repelled the reanimated refuse sacks; Wilhelm was already running along the base of the wall, heading toward the lighter sky that indicated the clifftop. Benjamin glanced warily back toward the area of upland where the ghouls had come from, then hurried to catch up.

By the time he had reached the main doors, Wilhelm was already inside, bent low beside the glass, watching for signs of activity. The lobby, though, was as empty as always. The office, too, was silent and dark.

'I need to get inside,' Benjamin said.

Wilhelm winked. 'I thought you might.'

Since that first night, Benjamin had tried twice to get into the admissions office, but both times he had found the door locked. Mrs. Martin had perhaps wised up that someone had been inside, but Wilhelm, with his seemingly endless inventory of shady skills, had the door open in no time, a wooden knitting needle that had aided him secreted back into a pocket.

'Wait here,' Benjamin said. 'I won't be long.'

The phone was in its old place on the desk. He picked up the receiver and, hearing the dial tone, bent to dial the numbers, when he paused. What was his phone number again? He remembered the code and the first three digits, but the last four....

His father had taught him the number when Benjamin was three. It had never changed, but he had forgotten it completely until his parents had instilled it into his mind in the form of a code.

Zero—that was where everything started, at the bottom of the tree. Seventeen—the number of the house directly across the street. Three—the number of trees in No.17's garden. And then double two—the number of trees in the gardens on either side of theirs.

Four—the number of wheels on Daddy's car. Three—the number of wheels on Benjamin's tricycle. Ninety-two—

grandma's age (he knew now Dad had made it up, but Grandma had forever after been ninety-two and would likely remain that age).

And the last two digits. Which were … thirteen.

Why?

Like the rest, there was a reason, but it was gone now and would likely stay gone. He shook his head as he dialed them, knowing that he would need to write them down or he would forget.

The phone rang. His mother answered.

'Hi.' Putting on a fake child's voice hurt him more than he had anticipated. He grimaced as he said, 'Is Davey there? It's Kyle from Davey's class at school. Can he come over to play?'

Kyle was a made-up name, one he hoped wouldn't make his mother suspicious. His mother was an intensely private person; she wouldn't give out details over the phone to an adult, but perhaps a child might break through her defenses.

'Hey, Kyle. Don't you know what time it is?'

Benjamin nodded against the phone. He sniffed. 'Yep, I do. I just want … Davey to come over.'

Benjamin's mother sighed. 'Kyle … I know, love. I wish I could promise David could go over tomorrow, but I'm afraid David isn't here right now. He's still in the hospital.'

Benjamin gulped. His cheeks flushed, and he had to swallow down a sob.

'When will he come home?'

Again, his mother sighed. 'I don't know, love. He's having a long sleep, but I'm hopeful that he'll wake up soon.'

Part of Benjamin's master plan had been to fake being upset, but now he realised he truly was. And not just because he was stuck in a dark office, speaking to his mother down a phone line that might as well go to another world, but because he knew from his mother's answers that his theory was right.

'I miss Davey,' Benjamin as Kyle whispered.

'I miss David, too,' his mother answered. 'But I haven't given up hope that both of my boys will be back home and playing together before we all know it. You get off to bed now, Kyle. Sweet dreams, honey.'

Mum! Benjamin gritted his teeth to stop himself from crying out for her as the line went dead. He put the phone gently back in its cradle, then wiped away his tears with the sleeve of his nightclothes.

A long sleep.

Benjamin nodded. His mother had used the kind of phrase an adult might on a little kid to hide a serious sickness. Benjamin wasn't stupid, though, he knew what she meant. David was lying in a hospital bed somewhere, in a coma.

Something had happened to him, too.

26

BETWEEN THE WALLS

'Just pass me a pencil, dunce.'

'Choke on it.' Benjamin jabbed the pencil into Godfrey's notebook so hard the nib snapped, but not before it ripped a hole through the top three sheets of paper.

'You little—'

'Is everything all right back there? Godfrey, is Benjamin bothering you?'

Godfrey looked up at the front of the class, putting on his most vomit-inducing expression—mouth flattened, cheeks puffed out, one eyebrow raised, the other pulled into a half-frown.

'No, Professor Eaves. He was just struggling with a question. I think he finds even simple challenges difficult.'

Professor Eaves cast a despairing eye at Benjamin, then turned back to the blackboard. 'See that you try to concentrate, boy. You've caused enough upset around here already.'

Near the front of the classroom, Miranda twisted in her seat to give Benjamin a supportive smile, and Godfrey blew her a kiss. She retorted with a stiff middle finger, which was rapidly pulled back under the desk as Professor Eaves turned around.

'And I think that's all for today. I'll see some of you after lunch for philosophy.'

As the pupils stood up and filed out, Benjamin squeezed

through the desks to Miranda. 'I need to talk to you,' he said. 'Are you going outside during break?'

'Sure—'

'Hey, and what little love affair is going on here?' Godfrey draped an arm around Miranda's shoulder, which she removed with a violent shrug.

'Leave us alone,' she hissed.

'Sorry, can't do that. I've been specifically asked to look after little Benjamin here.'

Benjamin tried to elbow Godfrey in the ribs, but the bigger boy caught his elbow and shoved him toward the classroom door.

'Not so fast, runt.'

Benjamin glared, wishing Godfrey would explode like some of the ghouls had. When Professor Loane had announced the teachers' selection for his chaperone over breakfast, Benjamin thought it was a sick joke. Only when Godfrey showed up at Benjamin's door ready to escort him to class did the horrifying reality set in.

'Why don't you—'

'I have the authority to punish you with up to a hundred cleans,' Godfrey said. 'Per offence. Of course, I'd have to accompany you to the Locker Room, but I'd be prepared to take one for the team to see you suffer. You know, every Tuesday there's a special shipment to the Locker Room for cleaning. Boy's underwear. I hear Snout sometimes does a load in his pants.'

As he had already done multiple times, Benjamin scowled and tried to walk away, but it was no good. For the rest of the day, Godfrey stuck to him like a clinging vine, and contrary to feeling protected, by the end of fifth period chemistry, Benjamin was ready to concoct some chemical monstrosity to end his misery. The best he could do was to slide a note to Miranda asking her to meet him in the science wing after dinner. He hoped that, with the teachers around while they ate, Godfrey's attention span might wane long enough for him to get away.

At dinner, though, Godfrey's crew surrounded Benjamin as they joined him at the back of the line. Despite his protestations, he was ushered to a corner table and forced to sit with Godfrey on one side and Snout on the other, and three of Godfrey's other minions grinning inanely at him from the other side. Two tables over, Miranda and Wilhelm could do nothing but watch.

As the bully poked at Benjamin's food, and then, with a snigger, began to swap out Benjamin's vegetables for less savoury ones in his friends' bowls, nothing would have given Benjamin greater satisfaction than to crash his tray down over Godfrey's head.

'A bit of brown on that one,' Godfrey said. 'You're young and healthy, so it won't hurt, will it?'

Benjamin fumbled with his fork as the urge to thrust it into Godfrey's eye made his fingers shake. He groaned in despair as it dropped under the table.

'Oops, better go pick that up,' Godfrey said. 'I hope the floors were washed last night.'

Benjamin stooped to climb under the wide table, and as the tablecloth fell back down, shutting him into a world with only the legs of Godfrey's friends for company, he felt a momentary sense of freedom. He looked around for his fork just as Snout shifted on his seat, letting rip with a loud guff that brought shudders of laugher from above. On the other side of the table, Derek flapped a hand in Benjamin's direction, and a thick stench filled his nostrils. Eyes watering, Benjamin turned to look for a way out, then realised what table they were sitting at.

Wilhelm's secret door was right underfoot.

In a moment, Benjamin had pushed his fingers into the tiny crack between the boards and pulled it up. As he lowered his legs into the gap, he spotted a clod of congealed custard that had fallen by Snout's feet. He scooped it up with his fork and dropped it on to the little V at the front of Godfrey's shoe, so it would slowly work its way down into his sock over the next few minutes. Then he ducked his head and pulled the secret door back into place.

At first, the sheer dark of the under floor space came as a shock, but as his eyes adjusted to the gloom, lit only by thin slivers of light through loose boards, Benjamin began to acclimatise. The space was barely high enough to crawl on all fours, and with the thudding of feet beating an irregular rhythm and the roar of voices above him, he felt like he was trapped inside someone's ear. Once Godfrey discovered his disappearance, though, they would conduct a search, so he moved quickly, crawling across the floor through dust mites and cobwebs until the slivers of light were gone and the cacophony was behind him.

Then he came to a set of steps heading down, and soon the ceiling opened up, allowing him to stand as he made his way into a wide room with a strange source of natural light—boxes of old light bulbs stacked in the corners gave off a faint glow as they reanimated. They weren't alone, he realised. Dusty tables and chairs reverberated, the faint tapping of their legs like the marching of thousands of ants. Old pictures on the walls creaked from side to side, and a piano in one corner played slow notes in a discordant rhythm.

The room was an old ballroom, and in its abandonment, the place had come alive. How these rooms could exist undetected he had no idea. Surely someone besides Wilhelm, and now himself, knew they were here—

'Welcome.'

He spun. At first he couldn't see who the deep, muffled voice belonged to, until something stepped out of a doorway leading through to an old reception room.

The motorbike was standing on end, infused with human bones, with a skull embedded into its front tire. It moved by rolling forward on its back tire, maintaining balance in a way that Benjamin assumed had come with practice.

'Don't be afraid. I am not one of them. My eyes are blue, look. At least, they can be.'

Benjamin was still too stunned to even consider whether he was afraid, but when the creature's eye sockets filled with an abrupt orange glow, he realised what it meant.

He took a step back. 'Ghoul….'

The orange turned to yellow, then darkened to green before morphing into blue. A revving that could have been laughter came from inside the motorbike's chassis.

'Ghouls are mindless,' the voice said. 'Myself and my fellows are not. Wilhelm told us about you, Benjamin. Welcome to our special place. You are as welcome here as he. Come.'

The motorbike spun round on its balancing wheel and rolled away through the reception room to a door at the far end. A kick-start lever poked out of its chassis and depressed the handle. The door opened out to a balcony promenade encircling a large auditorium. Seats had been removed or adapted and now several dozen other reanimated creatures lazed around, talking, playing cards or games, while another group up on a stage performed some kind of music Benjamin could barely describe. It sounded sharp and dissonant, an attempt to make factory noise rhythmical, and several of the creatures twisted and circled one another in a space cleared below the stage.

'Our common room,' the motorbike said, the kick-start lever gesturing like a tyrannosaur's tiny front paw.

Among the sea of machines and vehicles sat the gatekeeper Benjamin remembered from his first day, holding a hand of playing cards on an outstretched window frame. And there, in front of a television showing an old black-and-white movie, lounged the sin keeper from the locker room.

'Hey!' the motorbike shouted suddenly, accompanying his call with a fierce roar of his motorbike engine, loud enough to make Benjamin jump. A hush fell over the assembled, and representations of heads all turned up toward the balcony.

'We have a visit from young Benjamin Forrest,' he proclaimed. 'See that he's made welcome.'

A series of hellos and unlikely waves followed, and then, as the motorbike turned away from the balcony, music and games began again.

'This place is incredible,' Benjamin said. 'Wilhelm told me nothing of it.'

'We asked him not to, until it was necessary. Too much information at once can be enough to fry a young brain.'

The motorbike rolled away toward another door, where, inside, a comfortable sofa sat against a wall.

'Please relax,' the motorbike said. 'I'm sure you had some pressing reason for coming down here, but you can spare a few minutes of your time, I don't doubt. And I imagine you didn't finish your dinner. Here.'

The kick-start lever expertly scooped something up off of a tabletop and sent it looping through the air. Benjamin caught it just before it struck him in the face. It was soft, and smelt delicious. An apple pie, still warm.

'A small welcome gift,' the motorbike said. 'And I do believe I haven't introduced myself. You can call me Moto. It's rather easy to remember, I'm sure. And once more, welcome, Benjamin Forrest, to the world within the walls, or as we simply like to call it: Underfloor.'

27
___

RESCUE PLANS

'You don't have to worry about Godfrey,' Moto said. 'We are quite well in control of who comes down here and who doesn't. He will find the floor free of any secret doors, and your disappearance will be a mystery.'

'There's so much I don't understand. Why are all these rooms shut off? There must be more rooms here than in the rest of the school.'

Moto's head-wheel spun, his jaw sliding from side to side in what Benjamin assumed was a gesture of amusement. 'More years ago than most can remember, this school was founded by men seeking to create a safe haven for those unfortunates who found themselves marooned here, to nurture and protect them from the ghouls, and worse. This they did to a certain level of success, but there were never enough of them to control as they would like. As always, when humans are involved, wars were fought, alliances formed and broken. Over time, a general truce was struck that survives to this day. We allow them their section of the school, and in turn, they allow us ours.'

'The teachers know you're here?'

Moto's head spun again. 'Of course. Though perhaps those who command here now are a little unfamiliar with us as a whole. We, of course, have the capacity to far outlive them, and quite possibly the world itself, although no one can be sure yet, for obvious reasons.'

Benjamin's head spun worse than Moto's front wheel in his expression of a nod. 'I don't understand anything about this place,' he said. 'All I know is that I'm here, and that back in England something has happened to my brother.'

'Your brother? How would you know?'

Benjamin explained about the phone call, and Moto's eyes flashed with surprise.

'Well, I've never heard anything like that before. Have you spoken to the headmaster about all of this? He alone may have the answers. He is not … how could I say … like other humans.'

Benjamin shook his head. 'He's gone to somewhere called the High Mountains on a consultation mission and he's not back yet.'

Moto did his unique spinning nod again. 'He has gone to seek the Dark Man. Perhaps there is trouble brewing. If he has not returned, that bodes badly for all of us.'

'Can you help me find him?'

Moto's jaw clacked. 'You propose something of great danger. The Dark Man commands all that is evil in Endinfinium—the ghouls, and worse.'

'This man may have done something to the Grand Lord?'

'I did not say it was a man. I am unsure what, if anything, he really is. Perhaps he is no more than thought, but he commands all of the world's evil, and he seeks to claim Endinfinium for himself.'

'How?'

'By destroying all that has been built, and polluting all that can't be destroyed.'

'That's insane. It also makes no sense.'

'Quite. It is no more than a story. No one I have ever met has ever seen the Dark Man, so his existence is believed by many to be no more than a myth. It is true that there are dark forces in Endinfinium, and if the Grand Lord has traveled to the High Mountains, perhaps there is some truth to the rumours after all. There is no doubt, though, that in recent weeks there has been a … stirring.'

'A stirring?'

'Of dark reanimates. Ghouls and others. Since you arrived.'

Benjamin gave a slow nod. So it seemed Wilhelm was right. Perhaps he had no choice in whatever destiny was being laid out before him.

He rubbed his eyes. 'I didn't ask to be part of this.'

'None of us did. But sometimes you can't ask the questions, you can only answer them.'

'I need to find the Grand Lord. Maybe he can tell me why I'm here and what's happened to my brother. It's all connected, I'm sure of it. How can I find him?'

Moto's head-wheel spun. 'You will put yourself in great danger. I cannot advise that this is a good choice.'

'I don't care. How can I find him?'

'You must follow him to the High Mountains.'

Benjamin nodded. He didn't think he'd ever felt so afraid in his whole life. 'How do I get there?'

Moto's head spun again. 'You will find a way.'

'Can you help me?'

This time, Moto's head spun back the way it had come, and his body shook from side to side as though caught in the grip of a sudden earthquake. 'Reanimates do not pick sides. This is your quest, Benjamin.'

In the seamless stone wall beside him, a door began to take shape; at first just a pencil outline slowly sketching itself out, before grooves and protrusions began to appear, and finally it popped open to reveal a dark corridor.

'Good luck, Benjamin,' Moto said, revving his engine for emphasis. 'And remember, you are welcome here any time.'

Before he realised what was happening, Benjamin stepped out into the corridor. He turned back, but the door was already disappearing, and within a few seconds, the wall was featureless again. Not a single mark remained to indicate a door had ever been there.

'Hey!'

He turned. Miranda stood at the end of the corridor, and as she came running over, Benjamin saw her cheeks were flushed with exertion and a fire blazed in her eyes.

'I didn't think you were going to show. Boy, did you cause a stir up in the Dining Room. Everyone's looking for you.'

'I went under the floor.'

'Wilhelm said you might have. He said there's loads of stuff down there.'

'People, too. Kind of.'

Miranda rolled her eyes. 'Why doesn't that surprise me?'

They started into a walk, heading toward the basements. Benjamin wasn't sure where they were going, but nervous energy was eating him up. He told Miranda what had happened, and what Moto had said.

'But he—this motorbike thing—he wouldn't help you?'

Benjamin shook his head. 'After he told me what I needed to do, he seemed to change, like he was afraid. That what I was proposing involved great danger.'

'It's a stupid idea, you know that, don't you?'

'What? Going to find the Grand Lord?'

'Just wait for him to come back.'

'What if he never does? What if this Dark Man guy has kidnapped him?'

'Then what do you think you can do about it?'

Benjamin shrugged. 'I have no idea, but I can't just sit back and do nothing.' He clenched his fists, refusing to cry in front of her. 'I'm a prisoner here. I get followed around, I get told that bad things are happening around me, and that something has happened to my brother back home, yet I'm supposed to show up to bloody trigonometry class and act like I'm in a normal school?' He stamped a foot. 'No. I'm done with all of that rubbish. I want to know what's going on.'

He looked up at Miranda, who stared at him with a raised eyebrow.

'That was quite a tantrum,' she said. 'I'd struggle to do better, myself.'

'I'm fed up with this place. Perhaps the Dark Man will kill me. I don't care. Perhaps if I die, I'll go back home.'

'If it was that easy, no one would still be here,' Miranda said. 'I really don't think you should try to get to the High Mountains. It's like, miles away. And you have to go through the Haunted

Forest. That's where the cleaners come from, you know. People say the moaning of the dead wandering about is louder than the sound of the wind.'

'I'll figure out how to get through there when I get to it.'

'You're really planning to go, aren't you?'

'Yes.'

Miranda put an arm around his shoulders. 'Well, you don't have to do it alone.'

'It's safer that way.'

She smiled, then gave Benjamin a playful punch in the stomach that left him winded. 'We've been friends since literally before I was born. I'm not going to let you do something so dangerous on your own. Got that?'

'Don't hit me so hard,' Benjamin wheezed. 'But yeah, I got it. Thanks, but no way. I'm not letting you get involved in this. The ghouls are after me, not you. If the Grand Lord is the only one who might know why, then I'll find him, alone. I'm not putting you at risk.'

'Too late. I've packed my bag.'

'I don't care—'

'I do. Do you have any idea how hard it is to get to the High Mountains?'

'Do you?'

Miranda shook her head. 'No. But you can't just walk. It'll take forever.'

'I thought of that,' he said. 'Listen, if you really want to come with me, I leave at dawn. Meet me by the back entrance to the school, near the gully, when the red sun passes in front of the other.'

Miranda glared at him. 'I'll be early,' she said. 'So don't try to leave without me.'

'Of course I won't. I need my security, don't I? But we'll need supplies, too. Food, blankets. That kind of thing.'

'I'll tell Wilhelm to pilfer what he can.'

'Wilhelm's not coming.'

'What?'

'Look, this is my quest. I don't want to endanger anyone I don't have to. I can't make anyone fight my battles for me.'

'If you say so.'

'Only me and you. So don't be late.'

After telling Miranda what he wanted her to find, Benjamin made his excuses to leave, not looking back as he walked away.

Guilt immediately weighed on him like a pendulum hanging from his neck. He had no intentions of letting anyone come— Miranda, Wilhelm, or otherwise. As he headed back toward the teachers' apartments, intending to collect his things and leave before anyone else got back from dinner, he wondered whether or not he was making the right decision.

28

TRANSPORTATION

T he cleaners largely ignored Benjamin as he made his way through the kitchens, filling a bag with an assortment of food he hoped would last him a few days —some uncooked vegetables, a bag of mushrooms, a box of dried yellow powder he assumed was the custard sauce that was spooned over everything. Desperation made him brave the store cupboards where the cleaners wiped down surfaces, shifted things around, and stocked items up, but whenever one of the terrifying dead gazes turned in his direction, he just smiled and muttered something about an errand for Professor Loane.

In most cases, the response was a long, slow smile that he was sure would haunt his dreams forevermore.

Soon, he had filled his schoolbag with so much stuff he could barely lift it. He found a safe place to hide it away, then headed down into the bowels of the school to the medical room where he had been patched up by the nurse. As expected, it was quiet and dark, but when he lifted his hand to the door, it began to hum and vibrate, the lock clicking open so he could slip inside.

The scratch on the back of his hand had yet to heal. It had sealed over and no longer bled, but instead of fading away as a scratch from a normal cat would have done, a scar as red and thick as the line from a felt tip pen split the back of his hand from the base of his little finger to the back of his thumb.

During the day, he obscured it with a little soap mixed with flour that he had stolen from the kitchens, and as long as he carried on as normal, it was unnoticeable.

But when he pressed his hand to something and concentrated, it glowed bright enough to illuminate his face in a dark room, and he felt something inside him, like an invisible rope that would do what he wanted if he gripped hard and pulled.

The first time he had tried it had been something of a shock. Lost on his way back to the dorms, he had come up against a locked door and in his frustration wished it would open. He had felt a knot in his stomach and a tingle in his hand, and then the door had slammed back against the wall behind hard enough to break one of the hinges, revealing a stack of cleaning equipment inside.

After that, he had begun a little experimenting, and while he had no idea what he was doing or how it seemed to response to his requests with a certain level of accuracy.

It didn't always do what he wanted, though. It had once made a flower pot explode in his face, and a glass window shatter in the old gym. But after a little experimentation, he'd found he could control it in very small tasks.

One was unlocking doors.

The medical room was dark and silent. Using the glow from the corridor to see by, Benjamin crept across the room to the filing cabinet of medicines and bandages, then held up his hand and concentrated. After a few seconds, he heard the lock click as a prickly sensation ran through his hand. He opened the door and emptied a box of plasters and bandages into his bag, together with a couple of tubes of ointment.

He pulled the medical room door closed but didn't lock it, not wanting to waste the power of his hand when he might not be coming back. After squatting down on the floor outside, he pulled up his leg where he had felt a sudden sharp pain upon entering the room, and dabbed a little cream into a cut that had opened up on his calf muscle. No more than a fingernail's length long, the wound was thin and deep like a paper cut, and it stung right down to the nerve.

The cream made him wince at first, but the pain quickly eased. Then, as if it might help, he rubbed a little cream into the back of his hand.

Nineteen. The first of them had nearly healed, but there would be more if he continued to use the strange power of the scratch from the reanimated cat statue. And what happened if he tried to do something greater than unlock a door? Would he lose a limb? Lose his sight or hearing?

'I have to stop,' he whispered, putting the cream and the plasters back into his bag. A part of him enjoyed the pain, though, a part that actually wondered what it would feel like to use so much of the power it made him truly suffer.

It's trying to control me.

The thought wouldn't leave his mind, but he did his best to ignore it. He collected his bag, then made his way toward the back of the school, to a long corridor that stretched out beneath the outer walls and ran underground in a dead straight line before opening out into a wide, bowl-shaped area that looked like an abandoned quarry. Again he had no choice but to use his power to unlock the door, and this time, he had to dab cream onto a new cut that appeared on the back of his right thigh. This one was barely a hairline crack, though; the door, despite being bulky, had possessed a simpler lock.

He pulled it closed with two hands so as not to make a sound, then looked around as his eyes adjusted to the dark.

Lined up in organised, semi-circular rows were vehicles. Some looked like normal cars, others were small trucks or tractors. Some were carts, designed to be pulled by horses or oxen, while others were wooden, mechanical contraptions that looked like ancient siege machines.

Benjamin couldn't yet drive. Two nights ago, he had sneaked out here and sat in some of the drivers' seats to get a measure of what he might need to do, but it was no good. He was either too short to both see through the windscreen and reach the pedals, or the controls were an unfathomable mystery. Most of the machines needed keys he didn't know how to locate, and even if he did, at some point they would surely need fuel or repairs. It was likely that, within a couple of days, he would find himself back on foot with a heavy bag weighing him down.

He walked along the back line until he came to a small, covered shed. With a smile, he opened the door and peered inside, letting the faint glow of the sky illuminate the treasure lined up against the wall.

Bicycles.

More than a dozen, half of which were in various states of repair, some missing wheels or chains, a couple upended on their handlebars and seats, in the process of being fixed.

Six were in good working order. Two hummed with slight reanimation. Their pedals spun with well-lubricated freedom when he kicked them, and the brakes felt strong and sharp. One looked like a racing bike, but the other was a BMX designed for tricks and off-road, not dissimilar to the one he had at home. It wasn't quick, but it would deal easily with the kind of terrain he expected to encounter. With a satisfied nod, he touched the chain lock until it clicked open, then wheeled the bike outside, trying to ignore a sudden sharp pain on the back of his shoulder.

Using a piece of rope he found at the back of the shed, he tied his bag to the metal shelf behind the seat. Then he pulled the bike to the edge of the little parking area, climbed on and, with one last look back over his shoulder at the towering monument of the school, a black outline against a burnt orange sky, he pushed himself onward into the unknown.

29

HUNTERS

The light of the red sun, which never quite set but moved in a circle low to the horizon, gave Benjamin just enough light to see by as he pedaled along the rocky tracks through the cultivated farmland that provided the school with its food. The ground, lumpy with the occasional protrusion of some great buried man-made object of plastic or steel, was harder to traverse than he had expected, and even hills that appeared shallow were steep enough to force him to dismount and push.

When the true dawn came with the rising of the yellow sun as it passed through the glare of its red counterpart, he was just cresting a long, low rise. Pausing to catch his breath, he looked back at the school perched on its headland a depressingly short distance behind to the southeast. The outline of the clifftop was clearly visible, the school a shadowy cluster of angles and peaks against the grey background of the sky.

A few miles in front lay the undulating expanse of the Haunted Forest, visible between troughs in the hills as a dark green-and-grey blanket. In his way, however, lay the river—a black line meandering gently through the hills from north to south. Even farther south, a tributary broke away, flowing into the gully that became a cavern running beneath the school. The larger part angled west before opening into a wide estuary as it reached the sea.

He had thought long and hard about how he might get across the river, but he hadn't yet seen a single bridge. A couple of miles to the north, however, stood a cluster of buildings with a pontoon protruding out into the water, so he decided to head for that. If there was a ferry, when he reached it he would worry then about how to pay for his crossing.

He was hungry, so he took a snack from his bag and glared forlornly at the carrot his fingers had closed around as if it was the root of all evil in the world, even though it didn't taste that bad. He'd do anything to swap it for a chocolate bar or a piece of his mother's sponge cake.

While he was chewing, something caught his eye, something moving quickly through the hills, following the same rough path that he had taken.

A small truck.

He looked up in dismay at the rising sun. Surely they couldn't have discovered his escape already.

He got back on the bike and headed downhill. At the bottom of the slope, the path reached a crossroads and he turned south, away from the possible ferry dock, making an obvious mark in the dirt to show which way he had gone. Then, as soon as the road had turned rocky a short distance farther on, he climbed off and carried the bike through the grass until he reached the northwest-heading branch a couple of minutes' walk past the crossroads. Not a particularly clever deception, but it might buy him enough time to find a way across the river.

The trail began to rise. Benjamin tried to stay on the bike, but the climb was exhausting, so he jumped off and began to push, glancing back to see if his pursuers had found him.

He was nearly at the crest of the following rise, when the small truck bumped over the hill he had been standing on just twenty minutes before. He couldn't see who was driving, but he recognised the boy standing up in the open back, holding onto a rail on top of the cab.

Godfrey.

How had they found him?

With a muted cry of exasperation, Benjamin jumped back onto the bike and pedaled downhill as fast as he could. He listened for the sound of an engine, but the wind whistling through the gullies and crevasses that crisscrossed the rocky hills masked everything. As he neared the bottom of the slope he risked a glance back.

He caught a momentary glimpse of wheels rising up over the hilltop, the front of the vehicle glittering in the sun, then everything was turned over and over, the world spinning, as he sailed through the air to land in the grasses beside the path. He hadn't seen the rock that had hit his front tire to throw him from the bike, but he felt the one that crashed into his forehead, turning everything black.

'What shall we do with him? Do you think there'll be a reward?'

'We might get a pass from the Locker Room for a couple of weeks, but that'll be about it.'

Benjamin's head pounded. His eyelids felt stuffed with glue as he forced his eyes open. He was lying on a patch of grass, facing away from whoever was talking. His arms were tied behind his back with what felt like garden string, the fibres making his skin itch. His ankles were also tied. His left side felt numb from how he was lying but if he moved they would know he was awake. Instead, he lay still, listening.

'He's nothing but trouble, but he's the teachers' favourite. I say we dump him in the river and let him take his chances. He'll come back as a cleaner in a couple of months most likely.'

The voice was vaguely familiar, one he had heard around the dining hall.

'He's still knocked out. If he wakes up and sees us, we'll get into trouble. If we just untie him and go back, no one will know.'

The second voice belonged to Snout.

'Shut up, you pansy. Let's take him over the river and tie him to a tree outside the Haunted Forest, see what comes for him.'

'Yeah, and us, too. I say we go back.'

'Just because you've got the hots for that girl he runs around with. As if she'd be interested in you anyway.'

Benjamin placed the voice now. Derek, one of Godfrey's crew. One of the nastier ones, but not a boy to act alone. He was a member of the construction club so had likely been driving the truck. Even so, he wouldn't have come out here unless—

'Shut up, you idiots. Listen.' The voice belonged to Godfrey. His tone was dark, conspiratorial. Benjamin felt a tingle of fear. Despite the strange happening in the gym, he had always considered Godfrey a bully and a fool, but now … he wasn't so sure.

'There's a place down by the river,' Godfrey said. 'Someone I know is waiting for him. We'll be rewarded for handing him over.'

'With what?'

Godfrey gave a sinister laugh. 'What do you miss the most? Whatever you want, my friend can get it. Chocolate? Cookies?'

'Video games?'

'Boiled sweets?'

'You want it, it's yours. He can get anything.'

'Ah, man.'

'Let's go, then.'

'But what about—'

A short cry of pain was accompanied by a tired, 'Shut up, Snout,' then, strong hands pulled Benjamin up. He squeezed his eyes shut and then opened them, pretending to have just woken up.

'Well, look who it is, and his teddy bear's picnic club friends,' Benjamin said to Godfrey. 'You're as ugly in the morning as you are the rest of the day.'

Godfrey scowled, then punched Benjamin in the face. Not a hard blow, but it took Benjamin by surprise and left his ears ringing.

'Perhaps the river's the best option after all,' Godfrey said, glancing back at the other gang members sitting behind him. As well as Snout and Derek, there were three other boys Benjamin had seen around but couldn't recall their names.

'The sharks and crocs will eat him,' Derek said.

'They'll spit me out,' Benjamin answered, trying to sound convincing.

'We'll chop you up first so they just think you're food.' Godfrey turned to Snout and Derek. 'Load him up.'

They tied the bonds on his hands and feet together, pulling the rope so tight Benjamin was bent almost double, then carried him to where the van was parked and tossed him into the back. Derek, Snout, and another boy climbed into the front, while Godfrey and the others got into the open back. Godfrey stood beside where Benjamin lay, always ready with a sharp kick if Benjamin offered up a token insult. They didn't gag him because Godfrey seemed to enjoy the verbal trade, plus no one would hear if he cried out for help.

The van bumped along for about an hour, then came to a stop atop a small rise. Snout untied the rope linking Benjamin's hands and feet, then the others pulled him out of the van and stood him up. Godfrey tied a third piece of rope around Benjamin's neck like a leash.

'You lot stay here. I'll be back soon.'

Taking a hard piece of bamboo fencing cane from the back of the van, Godfrey herded Benjamin down a path that angled around the rise, then down to the black waters of the river.

Benjamin had never seen the river close up before, and now that he did, he realised there could be none quite like it. It wasn't that there was rubbish floating in the water; it was that there was so much rubbish, he could imagine every city on Earth having decided to drop their waste into this particular river. TVs and refrigerators bobbed in the slow-moving current near the riverbank alongside plastic watering cans, wooden picture frames, old shoes, and all manner of other discarded objects both large and small. Just off the near bank, a red-and-white soccer ball bobbed among bottles and juice cartons, while halfway across, the stern of an upended fishing trawler eased past as the river laboured its way toward the coast.

The path steepened. Benjamin had no intention of going near the water, but every time he paused, Godfrey jabbed him in the back so he had little choice. They descended through bushes and small trees, past areas of bare earth having been dug out by rises in the water. The rocks underfoot became slick, and Benjamin worried he would slip and tumble face-first into the water.

'This way,' Godfrey snapped, poking Benjamin down a set of stone steps leading into a gully carved out of the riverbank. At the bottom, Benjamin found himself at the entrance to a cave cut into an overhang. Water lapped around his feet.

In the gloom below was a ceiling of mud, roots, and the occasional glimmer of plastic or glass shards, where a small wooden shrine hummed with reanimation, shaking from side to side as though trying to break free from wooden fittings embedded into the mud. Set into a frame on a little altar was a bleached human skull which looked like any other human skull except for one distinct difference: the metal circles in the eye sockets.

Godfrey pushed Benjamin into the sludge, shoving and berating him until he lay flat on the mucky ground where the point of Godfrey's makeshift spear poked into his back. As Benjamin lay still, Godfrey began to chant in a language Benjamin had never heard before. He turned his head, looking toward the shrine with its metal-eyed skull, then let out a gasp of horror.

The eyes had begun to glow orange, flickering like the bulbs of a wind-up flashlight. The jawbone lowered, and out of a crackle of radio static, a reedy voice said, 'Why have you come?'

'I have a gift for the Dark Man,' Godfrey said. 'The troublemaker, Benjamin Forrest. Tell him to come, and I'll bring Forrest to him.'

'The Dark Man will not be commanded,' the voice said. 'But your folly will be overlooked this time.'

Before Godfrey could speak again, a grinding filled the air, a sound so loud Benjamin's ears began to ring. Unable to clamp his hands over them to keep the sound out, Benjamin pushed one side of his face, and then the other, into the muck, hoping to fill his ears with enough silt to stop him from going deaf.

'He's coming!'

The point of Godfrey's spear lifted and Benjamin rolled onto his side to look back at the river.

'Godfrey … what have you done?'

The water was drawing back from the river's edge to reveal a dry mud path down toward its centre. Benjamin stared, openmouthed, as the waters parted, creating two immense walls of rubbish and gunge with a thin passageway leading between them.

Benjamin stared down the path toward the centre. The far side of the river was a grey haze, but dark tendrils of smoke rose up out of the ground to form themselves into a shape.

A tickle of dread ran down Benjamin's neck. 'Please, Godfrey, no. Please don't take me to him.'

Godfrey ignored him as he stared at the distant figure. 'There you are,' he whispered. 'You came, like you said you would.'

'Godfrey, no! Turn away from him!'

The rope jerked, pulling Benjamin forward. He tried to resist, but Godfrey jabbed the point of his spear into Benjamin's ribs until Benjamin climbed to his feet. Then he tried to break away, but Godfrey grabbed his arms and swung him around.

At the very centre of the river stood a black-cloaked figure, unmoving, face hidden in shadow. Despite the walls of water that loomed like townhouses over his head, light spread out from him, illuminating the path, casting Godfrey and Benjamin in a sepia glow.

Come to me. Let us be united.

Benjamin spun around. The figure hadn't moved. Godfrey was still dragging him, eyes fixed upon the Dark Man up ahead.

You hear me, Benjamin. Come to me. Let us be united.

'Who's speaking to me? Who are you?'

You know my name. You know me as well as you know yourself.

'No! Get out of my head!'

Benjamin threw himself at the floor, but Godfrey planted a heavy kick to his stomach and dragged him back upright, holding on to his shoulders to march him forward. Benjamin started to struggle, and Godfrey threw his spear aside to clamp his arms around Benjamin's chest and lift him off the ground.

The Dark Man was just a stones' throw from them now. A hand lifted to push back the hood. Benjamin jerked out of Godfrey's grasp, twisting away just long enough to catch sight of something huge and long and metallic turning in to the end of the path between the rubbish walls, when Godfrey swung him back around to look into the calming, all-knowing face of a man older than his father, dark-haired, blue-eyed, a smile breaking out on his lips—

'No!'

Benjamin clenched every muscle, feeling a uncanny connection with the world around him, as though he could touch anything behind his body that he chose, and he reached for the walls of water, drawing them forward. The world filled with a rumble as spray soaked him and rubbish bouncing in the water jostled together like the clacking teeth of a giant, then, in the instant before the two walls crashed together, the Dark Man's smile vanished, replaced by a momentary look of hatred. He scowled at Benjamin once, then faded away into nothing.

Godfrey screamed as the walls began to topple. He let go of Benjamin and bolted for the far riverbank, even as the water crashed down. Benjamin turned back the way they had come, where something monstrous bore down on him, a huge metallic maw opening to scoop him up an instant before he would have been crushed into nothing by a thousand tons of water. He bumped down a ramp into blackness and crashed into something metal, then heard Godfrey's scream as the other boy was also sucked up by the giant, slithering beast.

Then everything turned on end. Benjamin rolled backward, and for the second time in as many hours, he found something heavy connecting with the side of his head.

30

LAWRENCE

W hen he woke up, something hard was at his back. His head hurt too much to open his eyes, so he reached around—his bonds were gone, even though his sore wrists were a reminder of where they had been—and felt the rough, crusty bark of a tree.

'Benjamin?'

The voice was familiar. He searched for the name: 'Miranda?'

'You're awake! Thank heaven!'

He groaned. 'It looks like it.'

She sat on the grass in front of him, her crimson red hair framing her face. 'Wow, that was quite something. Another second and you were gone. Are you all right?'

'What happened?'

'Look.'

Benjamin shook his head to clear away some of the grogginess, then turned to take in his surroundings. They sat on the edge of a meadow surrounded on all sides by trees. The meadow gently sloped downhill, and there, amongst the long grass lay a giant, red snake.

He frowned. But it had windows, and appeared to be made of metal.

'Great, isn't it? Edgar's snake-train. When we told him you

had gone missing he called it and it promised to bring you to safety. I mean, I've read about rollercoasters in books, but that was incredible. I can't believe any ride could be better than that.'

'Edgar?'

'He's here, and so is Wilhelm. We rescued you.' She glanced back over her shoulder, where another boy sat in the shade of a nearby tree, sleeping quietly. His hands were tied behind his back.

'Is that who I think it is?'

Miranda nodded. 'We also rescued Godfrey. I suggested we throw him into the river, but Edgar wouldn't think of it. Said he was too valuable. Maybe only for the thousands of cleans he deserves as punishment for kidnapping you, but I'd happily see him disappear into that sludge.'

'I remember … he took me down to the river and called for the…' Benjamin looked up. 'I saw his face, Miranda.'

'Whose face?'

'The Dark Man. I looked into his eyes.'

Miranda shook her head. 'No you didn't, so don't worry. Edgar says that was a projection. For some reason, the Dark Man can't leave the High Mountains.'

'We're all in danger, I know it.'

She smiled. 'Then why did you run off on your crazy quest? You didn't even manage to get across the river.'

'I was working up to it.'

Miranda's smile dropped. 'Look. We saved you this time, but if you ever, ever, *ever* run off again without telling anyone, I swear I'll pull out your teeth one by one. Really slowly, no anesthetic. None. Not even over-the-counter stuff.'

'Okay, it's a deal.'

'Good.'

A shadow fell over them and Benjamin looked up. Edgar stood there, carrying a basket of wild mushrooms. Wilhelm stood beside him, his hair all ruffled as though he had enjoyed the ride with his head out of a window.

'Welcome back to the land of the living. And welcome, also, to the Haunted Forest.'

Benjamin looked around at the pleasant meadow. 'It doesn't look very haunted.'

'Not during daytime, but you don't want to be wandering around in here by night.'

'Godfrey does,' Miranda said. 'Godfrey wants to stay here on his own and get eaten by ghouls. I heard they have really small teeth so it takes ages and ages.'

'Don't be rude, Miranda,' Edgar scolded. 'It wouldn't be right to leave him behind. But, alas, the yellow sun is setting, so it's time to get back on board. I'll call Lawrence.'

Benjamin frowned. 'Lawrence?'

'My snake-train.' Edgar gestured behind him. 'The fastest mode of transport in the whole of Endinfinium.'

'It's incredible.'

'It's a "he." And yes, he is. You're from when, 2010?'

Benjamin shook his head. 'I'm from … well, *was* from 2015.'

Edgar stroked his pointed beard. 'Well, Lawrence is a reanimated AGV Italo, an eleven-car Italian train that at your point in history is the third fastest train in the world. You know where Rome is?'

'Of course. Italy. We studied it in school.'

'Lawrence ran along the Rome-Milan line, enjoying some of the most spectacular views of that fine country, no doubt.' Edgar sighed. 'Alas, I've only ever seen pictures in books, but Lawrence has assured me it was quite the picturesque journey. Unfortunately, everything comes to an end—at least, in some places—and Lawrence was eventually scrapped in 2032. Some time after, he awoke here in Endinfinium.'

'That's amazing. How do you know all that?'

'We talked, of course. He's not the easiest of creatures to converse with, but from time to time he finds something to say.'

'Oh.'

Edgar led them aboard. Godfrey, a little surprisingly, perhaps, offered no resistance to being led back onto the train. Lawrence's interior was very much like a posh version of Benjamin's father's trains, but the walls, floor, and ceiling were infused with thick scales to give Lawrence a flexible mobility that no regular train had. The locomotive part had developed a very animalesque mind of its own, its sleek front becoming a huge mouth, and the windows massive, all-seeing eyes that glowed enough to illuminate the terrain a carriage's length in front of them.

Edgar told them to strap in. Godfrey was secured to a chair near the back of the carriage and warned that if he ran his mouth, he would have to wear a gag for the rest of the journey. Benjamin strapped in next to a window that opened and closed as the great creature breathed. Beside him, Wilhelm looked like a nervous kid about to fly for the first time.

'It doesn't run on rails,' Wilhelm muttered. 'Sometimes it goes straight up.'

'Where are we going?' Benjamin asked. 'Not back to the school, I hope.'

From his seat at the front, Edgar turned around. Beside him stood a huge, blinking screen that was one of Lawrence's eyes. At the moment, it showed only an area of forest at the edge of the meadow.

'The High Mountains,' Edgar said. 'I have heard you desire to speak with the Grand Lord concerning personal matters. I would like to speak with him, too. I'm rather interested in the reason for Grand Lord Bastien's failure to return. While I might no longer be part of the school's affairs, I also have none of the duties of the other teachers, making myself the perfect person to go and find him.'

The snake-train jerked, throwing them against the seat straps, and Benjamin winced as pain shot through his legs. Several new cuts had appeared on the backs of his thighs. He eased back into the seat, wishing he didn't have to sit down.

Lawrence jerked again, and then the forest was rushing toward them. Benjamin and the others whooped with excitement as trees whipped past, the snake-train dodging back and forth to miraculously miss every single one.

Miranda hadn't been joking about a rollercoaster ride. Lawrence both thrilled and terrified as he tore first through the forest, then skimmed across the surface of a lake, before rushing up the side of a steep, rocky hillside in motions that reminded Benjamin of a cat climbing a tree.

The ride lasted several hours and Benjamin found himself dozing off at one point, only to be awakened by Miranda's screams as Lawrence leapt off the top of a high cliff, then splashed down into a lake's inky depths, before surfacing in a rush and landing with a dancer's delicacy on a pebbly shoreline. The snake-train barely paused for a breath, and then he was off again, rushing into yet another forest, dozens of wheels that had reanimated into metal feet pulling him swiftly over the ground.

Finally, as the yellow sun began to set, dipping behind the red sun as it began its own circuit across the sky, Lawrence clambered up the side of a steep valley and came to a stop on a rocky crest that overlooked a vast, sweeping floodplain.

Edgar turned back in his seat. 'Behold,' he said. 'The High Mountains.'

Several miles distant, the floodplain rose again into a row of jagged peaks that spanned the horizon. Behind an initial wall of snowcapped teeth, lightning flashed, and the sky glowed where volcanic eruptions sent red-and-yellow fireworks pluming into the air.

They climbed stiffly out of their seats and went outside. Like a wingless dragon, Lawrence had curled around a large, granite outcrop, his metallic locomotive head nodding slowly in the direction of the High Mountains like an apprentice acknowledging an old master.

A terrible sense of foreboding hung about the place. It wasn't especially cold, yet Benjamin shivered. Miranda's hand slipped into his, and he felt Wilhelm standing close on his other side.

'Down there,' Edgar said. 'Those foothills mark the entrance into the Dark Man's domain.'

'What's beyond the mountains?' Benjamin asked.

'The beginning of everything, maybe.' Edgar shrugged. 'The truth is, I do not know.'

'How far have we come from the school?'

'Many hundreds of miles, depending on how you count them.'

Benjamin wasn't sure what to say to this, so he pointed at the valley floor. 'We have to go down there and find the Grand Lord. If we stick together, we'll be safe.'

Edgar shook his head. 'No. It's too dangerous. The ghouls will smell us before we even get close. They can smell purity, and all of us together … it would be overwhelming.'

'How then?'

Edgar looked uncomfortable. 'You must go, you and Miranda. Wilhelm and I must stay here.'

Miranda stared. 'You're going to let us go down there without you? I trusted you—'

'Calm your tongue and your blood,' Edgar snapped. 'One day that temper of yours will get you into trouble.'

'But you said—'

Edgar lifted a hand, and Miranda's mouth snapped shut. She glared as her cheeks puffed out, then she let out a long gasp and sagged, catching herself with her hands on her knees.

'As you can see, I have significantly better control of the magic of reanimation than you, my dear,' Edgar said, somewhat sadly. 'With a cloaking spell, you and Benjamin could get into the Dark Man's camp and search for the Grand Lord without your presence being known. However, it is not easy, and it will require all of my concentration.'

'So you have to stay here?'

Edgar nodded. 'Where I am safe from detection.'

'What about Wilhelm?'

Wilhelm gave them a brave grin. 'While I appreciate that this Dark Man guy might be a little more dangerous than anything we've encountered so far, and my gut instinct tells me to stay behind and wash Lawrence's windows … there's no way I can let you go down there without me.'

Miranda beamed, but Edgar shook his head. 'No, I need you to stay with me, I'm afraid.'

'Why?'

'I need you to help me. With your magic.'

'What magic?' Wilhelm put up his hands. 'Look, these two, they might be able to make things explode and stop it from raining, but I can't do any of that stuff.' He looked at each of them in turn. 'And to be honest, I'm quite glad.'

Edgar smiled. 'Oh, but you can. In certain circumstances.' At Miranda's look of surprise, he shook his head. 'I think it's time I explained a few things about the nature of what we're all calling magic.' He turned to Miranda. 'My dear, we have only ever focused on your abilities; however, there are others. Both Benjamin and Wilhelm possess skills of their own.'

Wilhelm gave a sharp shake of his head. 'I don't think—'

Edgar put a hand on his shoulder. 'The power that you find here works in two basic ways,' he said. 'Reanimation, or creation; and deanimation, or destruction. Like most things in life, however, there is rarely just black-and-white, but a whole spectrum of grey. With the right practice, it is possible to achieve all manner of things. If, for example, I cause the dust particles around me to reanimate, I can give the appearance of levitation.'

Benjamin nodded. 'Like when I met you for the first time?'

Edgar nodded. 'In a vacuum, it wouldn't work. But even the smallest particles can be manipulated.'

'Why can't I do that?' Miranda asked.

'Because you haven't learned how. It takes time. And it is not possible for all of us to do everything. That is something I have learned over the years. Back in the days before the Oath and the restriction of its use, the magic of Endinfinium came to its users in three distinct ways, and everyone who woke up here possessed one of those three abilities.'

Benjamin listened but said nothing. He hoped no one had paid too much attention to the cuts on his arms and legs, but when Miranda had mentioned one particularly sore one on his forearm, he had shrugged it off as a fall from his stolen bike.

'Miranda.' The girl looked up, and Edgar smiled. 'You, my dear, are a channeler. You can use small amounts of power at will, with no adverse effects to you. Your skills are raw, but they can be refined.'

'A channeler? Why don't the teachers tell us any of this?'

Edgar shrugged. 'Too many accidents. I opposed the sanction to restrict all use, which is one of the reasons I left. They were trying to protect you, I know that. But lying about it? Making people swear an oath that there's no such thing? Ridiculous. It's caused more deaths than it's saved, I'm sure. That was why, when I encountered you, I did my best to teach you.'

'That's awesome,' Wilhelm said. He stuck out his arms and made a blasting sound in the direction of the nearest rocks. 'Am I a channeler, too?'

Edgar shook his head. 'Wilhelm, you are what we refer to as a weaver. Alone, you have no power, but when linked to a powerful channeler, great things can be done. You amplify the power in the same way that a microphone amplifies sound.'

Wilhelm smiled. 'So I do most of the heavy lifting?'

'Something like that.'

Wilhelm looked at Miranda. 'Typical.'

Miranda glared at him, then turned to Edgar. 'You're a channeler, too?'

Edgar nodded. 'My power is no greater than yours, my dear; perhaps even less. The difference is, I've learned how to use it.'

'And Benjamin? Is he a channeler or a weaver?'

Benjamin pulled his hand out of hers. 'I'm neither,' he said. 'I don't have any magic. I told you, I'm here by mistake.'

Edgar watched him, nodding slowly. 'Don't be afraid,' he said.

'I'm not afraid—'

Edgar reached out a hand and Benjamin flinched, making Edgar cry out as an invisible force threw him backward. As Edgar climbed stiffly back to his feet, Benjamin winced at a sharp, needle-like pain that had appeared in his side, bringing with it a tingle that ran up his back and his neck, making his hair itch. His cheeks burned and he wanted to run, run run—

'Benjamin!'

He lifted a hand. 'Keep back!'

'Be calm,' Edgar said. 'I can teach you how to control it. You pulled down the water walls in the river, didn't you? You broke a spell of the Dark Man himself. That takes greater power than I can imagine.'

'No! It had nothing to do with me!'

'We both know it did.'

Words meant nothing. All Benjamin felt was the damnation in Edgar's eyes. The wizard was looking down on him, almost mocking him, and Benjamin felt his anger building. It would be so easy to force them away. He could crush Edgar in an instant.

He could crush all of them, disperse their pieces to every corner of the known world.

He stepped back, and something caught his foot. The sky spun anticlockwise and he landed heavily on a clump of lush grass, rolling sideways. Something soft yet sour pressed into his mouth, something that tasted like washing up liquid. Gagging, he spat it out.

A flower shaped like a kitchen sponge lay on the ground. Similar ones in green, yellow, and purple bobbed nearby in the breeze. Benjamin looked up, his anger raging … and saw tears of laughter running down Wilhelm's face.

'Oh, that made my day. That kitchen-flower went right in your mouth. How did it taste?'

Edgar was smiling. As Miranda ran to help Benjamin up, he felt his fading anger being replaced by a deep, dark sadness, like the water at the bottom of a lake that never sees the light. He wiped a tear from his cheek and let out a long breath. 'What's happening to me?' he whispered.

Edgar sat on the ground beside him. 'You, Benjamin, are a summoner,' he said, 'capable of using great bursts of power. Uncontrolled, it will destroy you. I knew it as soon as I met you, then when Miranda and Wilhelm came to me, it was easy to follow your trail. The magic you control is like a scent, if you have the nose for it.'

Benjamin pulled up his sleeves. Several cuts had broken open, and blood oozed through the fine hairs on his skin.

Miranda and Wilhelm stared.

'Every time,' Benjamin said, lifting up his arms as though he had never seen them before. 'How do I stop it?'

Edgar frowned. 'There are ways, but none of them are here, in the shadow of the Dark Man, whom some say is the greatest summoner of them all. It would be prudent to return you to the school. You should have told me of this before. The magic's backlash is harming you. If you can't control it—'

Benjamin shook his head. 'Not until I've found the Grand Lord and discovered what happened to my brother.'

'It's foolhardy.'

'I don't care.'

173

Edgar sighed. 'Then we must do as I suggested. Wilhelm and I will prepare a cloak for you and Miranda, but I can't hold it for longer than a couple of hours. You have to be back by the time the red sun completes a circuit of the world. Even if you can't find the Grand Lord, you mustn't linger long. When the mask wears off, the ghouls and the Dark Man will feel your presence, and believe me, they will come for you.'

Benjamin looked up at Lawrence's huge spiraling form, curled around the rocky outcrop. The snake-train seemed to be humming, his huge, metallic maw opening and closing like the mouth of a panting dog. 'He's afraid, isn't he?' he said.

Edgar laughed. 'He's terrified. Lawrence isn't known for his bravery, but this close to the Dark Man, few are. Are you ready?'

Benjamin glanced at Miranda. 'Are you?'

The girl pouted. 'Of course I'm not. But if you think I'm letting you go down there alone…' She punched him on the shoulder, making him wince. 'Let's get on with it.'

Benjamin turned back to Edgar. 'I'm sorry for being such a pain in the butt,' he said. 'I can't begin to tell you how thankful I am that you got me this far.' He paused and looked around at Miranda and Wilhelm. 'And you guys, too. You're the best friends I could want. But this isn't over. I still don't understand much about Endinfinium, and I'm tired of it. I want answers. Edgar, do what you have to do.'

Edgar nodded. 'Let's go hunting,' he said.

31

THE BAGGERS

O nly from a distance did Benjamin realise how Lawrence had camouflaged himself. Looking back up the hill toward the rocky crest, he told himself over and over that the grey-red protrusion was their mode of transport and not a granite tor sticking out of the earth, and only when he squinted could he see the occasional movement as Lawrence's great bulk shifted, detect how the chameleon-like snake-train altered his colour to blend in with his surroundings.

Miranda punched him on the arm. 'Stop slacking. We're going forward, not back.'

'I'm scared.'

'Me, too. Come on.'

She broke into a run down the slope, dodging boulders and shrubs like a dancing deer. Benjamin, more of a lumbering bear in contrast, picked his way carefully through the strewn obstacles while trying to keep her in sight.

Their target was an area a couple of miles ahead where undulating foothills rose and then split apart to form a mountain pass. Sparks of light and rumbles in the earth seemed to be coming from there, so it was a suitable place to look for the Dark Man's lair, yet close enough for them to return to Edgar before the cloaking spell wore off.

It had been an interesting sight: watching Edgar sitting cross-legged on the ground, humming in a trance-like state with one hand on Wilhelm's shoulder; the small boy also with his eyes closed, brow furrowed in deep concentration. When Edgar at last opened his eyes long enough to tell them to hurry, Benjamin at first felt like nothing had happened, until he looked at Miranda and saw how her hair had taken on an orange tint as though she had been wrapped in a plastic sheet. And from the way she looked at him, he knew he appeared the same.

Up ahead, a spiny forest closed in, with leafless trees that bent low to the ground as if battered by a raging wind long ago. Miranda plowed straight in among them, ducking and dodging through the thickets. If not for her ragged breathing just ahead, Benjamin would have lost her, and she had been out of sight for several minutes before he ducked under a gnarled branch to come up right behind her, so close that he slipped and fell on his bum to avoid a collision.

'Shh!' she hissed, grabbing his arms and pulling him close.

'What's the matter?'

She didn't need to answer. They had come out of the trees by the edge of a gentle forest stream with bubbling water that looked fresh and drinkable, though the creatures standing in its shallows made Benjamin want to turn and run.

'Wraith-hounds,' Miranda breathed, voice filled with both horror and wonder. 'I read about them in a storybook. I didn't think they were real.'

The creatures—nine of them, all standing in the river—were the size and shape of big dogs with something definitely doglike in their physical makeup: a patch of fur here, a paw or an ear there. The remainder of each hound, however, was a homage to a school art room's display window: bodies and heads and tails and teeth and legs all made from what humanity had tossed away—cans and bottles, cups and plates, broken glass—and everything was covered with a fine layer of recycled paper slicked against the bodies of each wet hound as they drank from the water swirling around their feet.

'Are they dangerous?' Benjamin whispered.

'Deadly,' she answered. 'We go around before they figure out Edgar's trick.'

They gave the wraith-hounds a wide berth, moving upriver until they could cross in safety. From time to time, though, wraith-hounds were visible moving through the trees, and once, Benjamin saw a pack of ten or twenty running at full pelt, thankfully heading westward, away from them.

Other creatures began to appear, too. Orange-eyed, part human, part metallic, sometimes lying inert beneath the trees, some only half out of the ground, arms or tentacles or other protrusions waving about in the breeze or lying uselessly on the mossy soil.

'Ghouls,' Miranda said as they passed a cluster that looked near humanoid. 'I'd guess they're either sleeping, or they didn't reanimate properly.'

'Let's hope they stay that way.'

Soon, the trees began to thin out, the ground to rise, and both Benjamin and Miranda became desperate for a rest and some of the food Edgar had given them. Miranda pointed to the hilltop and suggested they stop there.

They were both puffing when they reached it, but a flat rock offered a view into the following valley, and the prospect of a short rest had gotten Benjamin excited. At the flat rock, they witnessed the sight below for the first time, and it removed all thought of food.

'Oh, my,' Miranda gasped, gripping Benjamin's arm.

The hill overlooked a vast strip mine that had been dug into the floodplain. From where Lawrence had stopped it had been invisible, hidden by the ridge of foothills. The strip mine was at least the size of two football grounds set end to end. At the end nearest, hundreds of tiny shapes rushed back and forth, climbing scaffolding, working pulleys and cranes, fanning fires, smelting steel. At the other gathered what could only be a war host: dozens of machines lined up in rows, some of which Benjamin recognised—cars and buses, trucks, even a couple of airplanes— and some he didn't—bubble shapes and elongated things like mobile spears.

Alone, the war host would have been fearsome, terrifying even. But compared to the two monstrosities that sat in the middle like captured grubs in the midst of an ant colony, it was an insignificant nothing.

'What are they?' Miranda said.

The immense vehicles were the size of ocean liners. Running on massive caterpillar treads—each wheel the size of a suburban house—at one end hung a huge, weighted mechanism to balance out the massive excavator wheel at the other, sticking out like the head of Goliath's chainsaw. Teeth the size of cars glistened in the fires' glow and the volcanic eruptions lighting up the sky.

Benjamin had always loved construction vehicles. As a little kid, he had collected them: dump trucks and bulldozers, cranes and JCBs. Even in secondary school he had sometimes slid the plastic box of them out from under his bed and relived the games of his childhood with his favourite toys.

There were some great ones, like the giant, Saudi Arabian dump trucks each the size of a house, or the massive cranes used to build the skyscrapers of New York. All, however, paled in comparison to the undisputed king of all construction vehicles, the don, the boss, the main event.

'They're Bagger 300s,' Benjamin said. 'A Bagger 300 is the largest self-mobile machine ever built. It's a mining excavator, but it looks like there have been some … modifications.'

'What are they going to use them for?'

Benjamin gulped. Where car-sized excavator buckets should have been, shone the shiny teeth of two dozen cutting saws.

'Judging by the size of those saws, I'd say to smash something up pretty bad.'

'The school?'

Benjamin shook his head. 'No way. While a Bagger 300 can technically move on its own, they're really slow, like a few metres per hour. They weigh hundreds of tons. You can't just drive one like a car—'

Almost as if they had heard him, one of the excavators lurched forward, and its chainsaw head swung around to carve a huge gash into the hillside. As lumps of solid rock the size of cars and trucks bounced down, only one thought came to Benjamin's mind.

'We have to stop them,' he said.

32

CAPSULES

Benjamin wanted a closer look, so they followed the ridgeline until they were right above the excavators, where they could see that one end of the strip mine had a long, upward-leading slope. Maneuvering like two castles trying to joust, one Bagger succeeded in turning around and began to roll up the ramp, while hundreds of cheering ghouls swarmed around it like ants.

'There's something unusual about them,' Miranda said. 'I can't quite figure it out.'

Benjamin frowned. 'I think I know what you mean,' he said. 'They don't seem … natural.'

They followed the ridge a little farther until they could get no closer without climbing down into the pit.

'How's it possible for something that big to reanimate?' Miranda said. 'Yet, there's something odd….'

'They're not,' Benjamin said.

'What?'

'Back home in Basingstoke, I used to love these things. I watched Internet videos about them, bought magazines with articles on them, watched TV documentaries, and you know what? They're exactly like I imagined.'

'So?'

Benjamin grabbed her shoulder, gave it a little shake. 'Don't you see? That's the whole point. They haven't reanimated, at least not much. They look just like regular Bagger 300s, but modified to be even more awesome and destructive.'

'Which means what?'

'Which means, they have to have someone operating them, and they have to have a regular fuel source. Come on, let's go down and take a closer look. If we can figure out how they're running, perhaps we can find a way to stop them.'

From where they stood, the ground dropped away sharply into the pit, but a little farther along was an access road that wound down into the centre.

'We can go that way,' Benjamin said.

'They'll see us!'

Benjamin grinned. 'Don't worry. We're ghouls now, remember? They won't notice us.'

'I'm glad one of us has confidence.'

'Come on,' he said, hoping he sounded more confident than he felt.

They hurried down the road that jagged back and forth across the sides of the strip mine, which had collapsed in places, and they had a few nervous moments before they reached the bottom, a trickle of fallen rocks settling around their feet.

In front of them loomed one Bagger 300 like a giant, metal dragon, the extending arm of its excavator-turned-chainsaw stretching over their heads like a steel-framed bridge. Benjamin had always dreamed of seeing one up close, but now that he did, he felt nothing but terror. The whole machine hummed with electricity, like a giant, live fuse. The arm lifted and descended, its chainsaw blade whirring so loudly Benjamin and Miranda both clamped hands over their ears.

'What now?' Miranda shouted.

'I want to see who's driving it.'

Soon, they walked in the midst of the war host, dozens of smaller reanimated machines staffed and tended by hundreds of ghouls of all shapes and sizes, who all wandered around them, unaware of their presence.

'Up there,' Benjamin said, pointing to a box-shape in the

centre of the vehicle. 'That's the control cab, but I can't see anyone. Perhaps it's got an autopilot.'

'What about fuel? It must use something,' Miranda said. 'Does it have petrol tanks?'

They ran to the back of the vehicle, dodging ghouls going about their work, ducking under protruding spikes and rails. Something glowed with a flickering light from between the spider's web of struts. As they emerged out from between two tall caterpillar treads, Benjamin saw a huge, oval-shaped orb suspended above them like the egg sack of a giant spider. About the size of a car, it glowed a deep ochre blue and sparkled with an electricity that made the surrounding steel support struts hum with life.

'What is it?' Miranda said. The chainsaw at the front had shut off, but the engine's grumble was still loud enough to make Benjamin's ears hurt.

The glowing capsule hung from one of the rear balancing struts that was itself the size of a footbridge, suspended in a net of thick cables and wires.

'I'll climb up and take a look,' he said.

'No! You're not going up there!'

He pushed away Miranda's hand. 'Look, it's an easy climb. No harder than a tree. I need to see what's inside.'

Miranda's expression was a mixture of fear and anger. 'It's too dangerous.'

'We've come this far, and that's the key to stopping this thing, I know it.'

Miranda started to protest, but Benjamin shook his head. 'Look, you can drag me back to Edgar, or you can let me climb.'

'You're as stubborn as Captain Roche is wide.' Miranda punched Benjamin on the arm. 'Don't think I'll catch you if you fall. I'll just stand here and watch.'

'Can't you reanimate me a mattress or something?'

Miranda glared, but finally nodded. 'I'll think about it. Hurry up,' she said. 'I think Edgar's spell is wearing off. You're not looking so … orange as before.'

'I'll be quick.' Before he could stop himself, Benjamin grabbed her arm, pulled her close, and gave her a light peck on the cheek. Then he grinned as Miranda blushed the same crimson colour as her hair and shoved him away.

'Hurry up!'

With a cheeky salute, Benjamin climbed up onto the nearest struts and pulled himself up the side of the Bagger 300, targeting the balancing arm overhead. It was a steep but easy climb; the machine's complex body offered hundreds of hand- and foot-holds, and the balancing arm was just an oversized set of monkey bars. Soon, the glowing capsule was right ahead.

As he neared it, his temples abruptly began to pound, like someone repeatedly hitting him on the side of the head. The capsule was translucent but opaque, like a cloudy river. Something lay inside, suspended in a solution that shimmered and sparked with electrical pulses of every possible colour.

Free me.

Benjamin stopped and looked around. Who had spoken? The headache was nauseating now, and he feared losing his balance and falling off. Adjusting his grip, he crawled a few inches closer until he was right over the top of the capsule.

A man lay inside. Tall, older than anyone he had yet seen in Endinfinium, and wearing a dark green robe. A beard of wispy grey. Bald. His body shone with an otherworldly luminescence, as though he wasn't quite part of this world, still lingering somewhere else, too.

Benjamin sensed great power, more than any power in the world—in any world.

'Grand Lord Bastien…?'

Eyes snapped open, then narrowed as Benjamin met the old man's gaze.

Free me!

The machine lurched forward, knocking Benjamin off balance. His feet slipped, and he grabbed the nearest support strut. He hung loose, two storeys from the ground.

Benjamin Forrest. You have come. I knew you would. Free me and save the school.

'Benjamin!'

Miranda stood below him, looking up, terror on her face.

'I'm all right. Miranda, quick, the capsule … I think the

Grand Lord is inside. Use your magic to break it open!'

'How?'

'I don't know! Just concentrate!'

The orb was just ahead of him. If he swung himself he might be able to jump down on top of it. Perhaps it had a lock somewhere that would enable him to free the trapped man.

He started to swing himself just as a tiny voice called: *Bennie? That you, Bennie?*

Pausing, Benjamin caught hold of a second strut, then looked around.

A short distance ahead of them stood the second enormous Bagger, halfway up the access slope. Its fuel orb glowed bright like a giant light bulb.

If the first uses the Grand Lord's power to move it, then who does the second use?

Miranda was screaming at him from the ground now, too. Benjamin reached for another strut, just as the very fabric of the world erased itself beneath a thundering shard of black light.

Benjamin screamed as he fell, trying to refocus on what had for an instant been erased from existence. The glowing capsule and its suspended passenger flashed past him, then he landed on something soft and cushioning.

He stuck out a hand and felt nothing, then rolled and bumped another foot to the ground. He sat up and, rubbing his eyes, wondered what on earth had just happened.

Miranda was beside him. 'Are you all right?'

'I don't know.' The Bagger 300 still loomed above him, engines humming. 'What happened?'

She gave him a bashful smile. 'I caught you. I know what I said, but .... quick, something's shooting at us. Did you see—did you *not* see that?'

A squeal filled the air again, and Miranda hauled Benjamin backward as a shard of the world in front of him erased then reappeared. Black light, stripping everything away, and leaving a hole in the ground that might just go on forever.

'It's coming from that mountaintop,' Miranda shouted, pointing up at the pass. 'Quick, get behind the wheels. He won't destroy his own war machine.'

'Who won't?'

'I'm guessing that might be the Dark Man up there.'

They ducked in behind the caterpillar treads, Miranda pulling Benjamin along, fingers clenched so tight around his, he worried bones would break. They dodged around scurrying ghouls as they ran for the road back up to the forest, but the creatures paused and turned to watch them like waking statues.

They had just reached the bottom of the road when an unearthly howl rose up behind them, like a million hungry souls catching sight of their prey.

'Don't slow down!' Miranda screamed, tears in her eyes. 'We have to move faster, or they'll catch us!'

Within a couple of turns of the road, Benjamin was gasping for air, but the sight of hundreds of rushing ghouls, all scrabbling up the sides of the strip mine like rats trying to escape from a trap, put another burst of fire into his legs. He took the lead, pulling a sobbing Miranda after him, reaching the top just as the first of the ghouls scrambled up over the edge beside them.

'Shoot it!'

Miranda screamed, throwing her hands haphazardly up into the air, and the ghoul's chest exploded in a crackle of electricity. The creature fell back into the pit, pieces of it bouncing past hundreds more climbing up.

'Come on!'

They raced through the grass toward the relative cover of the spiny forest, while ghouls climbed up over the edge of the pit, though many looked to be already dropping off the pace. Benjamin wondered, now that they were out in full view of the mountaintop, what had happened to the black thunderbolts. He prayed that the Dark Man had lost them, and he closed his eyes, recalling the voice he had heard calling his name.

Bennie? That you, Bennie?

They had never told anyone their secret. It sounded ridiculous anyway, they'd only ever used it for fun, and it got fainter over distance, but on many nights, they'd both lain awake in their bedrooms and held conversations through the walls, conversations no one else could hear.

He'd always thought himself a freak, but he'd clearly heard

the voice of the other man, too. Could it be David and he weren't alone? That there were others?

'What is it?' Miranda gasped as they ran. 'What did you see in that thing?'

Benjamin shook himself back into the present. 'The Grand Lord,' he said. 'I know it was him.'

'What did he look like?'

'Older than Edgar. Bald, grey beard, a green robe.'

Miranda nodded. 'That sounds like him. I met him once. I didn't get to see him clearly because there was only a single light in his room and he stood in the shadows. I remember staring at his cloak and thinking it was too shiny to be black.'

'What do we do now? We can't go back down there.'

'We have to go back to the school and warn the teachers. They'll know what to do. Despite what they say, they know all about the magic. They'll be able to save him.'

Benjamin wasn't so sure, but he wasn't in any mood to argue. Unable to run any longer, he stopped, bending double, gasping for air.

'Come on,' Miranda said, even though she looked about to collapse herself. 'We don't have much time.'

Benjamin tried to speak, but only a dry heaving of his chest came, and then he was crying, with Miranda pulling him close against her, his tears mixing with her own.

'Benjamin, we have to move.'

'I know, I know, I just can't stand this place any longer.'

Miranda drew away from him. She cupped his cheek, and with the same strength he remembered from the first day she'd met him down on the beach, she turned his face toward her.

'What did you see down there?'

Tears filled Benjamin's eyes as he shook his head. 'The other capsule—'

'What? What about it?'

'I know who was inside.'

'Who?'

'My brother.'

33

EDGAR'S STAND

To their right, a roar rose up out of the forest.

'The wraith-hounds,' Miranda said. 'They've got our scent. We have to run.'

Emotions swirled as Benjamin raced through the trees, his brother's mind-voice seeping like poison through him. The scratch on the back of his hand stung worse than ever, and the latent power inside him stirred, wanting release.

David. I'll come back for you, I promise.

Flickers of movement appeared to either side. They had splashed through the river some minutes before, and now the land rose steadily toward the hilltop upon which Edgar, Wilhelm, and Lawrence waited for them. They had seen other ghouls, though the creatures had made no move toward them as if aware that there would be no escape from the savage, rushing wraith-hounds.

They burst into the clearing they had entered on the way into the valley, and Miranda took a few steps forward, then fell to her knees with a cry.

'What is it?'

'I turned it,' she gasped, clutching her ankle. 'I turned it!'

'Come on, get up!'

The surrounding trees were full of shapes, bounding and

skipping. Benjamin pulled Miranda to her feet, and she limped a couple of steps before stumbling again.

'I can't. I can't! Leave me!'

'Never.' He gripped her hand. 'Come on, you can hold them off, and if you can't, maybe I can.'

A growl rose up from the trees, and the undergrowth rustled. Then, hundreds of the beasts broke out from the forest in a long, disorderly line. Jaws made from broken cans and glass and bent nails snapped and snarled. Benjamin gritted his teeth as the hounds slowly advanced, aware that their prey was crippled, ready for the kill.

'There're too many,' Miranda cried. 'I can't hold them all off. I don't have enough power.'

Benjamin stared at the oncoming creatures, anger rising. Deep down he felt a knot like a muscle waiting to clench.

'I do,' he said, pulling Miranda up beside him. 'I can turn them back.'

'No, you mustn't,' she gasped. 'You can't control it. It'll destroy you.'

Benjamin smiled. 'I don't care. For all I know, this could be a dream. And if it's not ... make sure they save David. Make sure they save my brother.'

As the hounds roared and rushed forward, Benjamin stepped in front of Miranda, lifting his hands, hoping something would happen. As he sought for the power within, trying to clench the knot in his stomach that would unleash it, a sudden wind caught him from behind and he stumbled to his knees, falling over in the long grass. Jaws rushed toward him, then the ground split apart, drawing him away from the hounds as they leapt for him, many plummeting into the dark before they realised what had happened. Hands gripped his shoulders and pulled him back. He looked up, expecting to see Miranda. Instead, Wilhelm stood there, Edgar beside him, arms aloft and face set like stone as he stared down their pursuers.

'Back, you ugly scoundrels!' Edgar shouted, and the ground shuddered, knocking more of the hounds into the chasm, sending them tumbling into the dark. Then, to Benjamin he said, 'Get to Lawrence. He'll know what to do. I'll hold them off.'

Benjamin lifted Miranda on one side, Wilhelm on the other. The girl screamed and shouted at them to wait for Edgar, but the old wizard waved them away as brave hounds continued to throw themselves to their deaths. As they reached the edge of the clearing, Benjamin took one last look back to where Edgar was kicking away the first of the wraith-hounds to make it across.

Lawrence, still curled around the outcropping, pulsed with colour in greeting as they approached, then lowered his huge maw to allow them to carry Miranda inside. Wilhelm helped to seat her in front of Godfrey, still tied up in the back, then Benjamin returned outside to wait for Edgar.

A line of wraith-hounds raced up the grassy hillside, a handful of lumbering ghouls at their backs, but of Edgar, there was no sign. Benjamin looked up at Lawrence's huge head, hoping for some instruction.

'Go,' the snake-train mumbled in a booming hoot.

Benjamin ran inside, and Miranda started screaming again as the maw closed, sealing them off. Through Lawrence's massive eyes, they saw the rushing army of wraith-hounds, when a swish of Lawrence's massive tail sent hundreds flying back into the trees.

With a bellowing roar, Lawrence raced down the hillside, building up speed through trees and clearings, over outcroppings and through rivers, taking them away, away, away from the High Mountains, the war host, and the eyes of the Dark Man.

'We left him behind.' Wilhelm ran a hand through his hair. 'He sacrificed himself for us.'

Beside him, Miranda was inconsolable, face in hands.

'Then let's not let it be in vain,' Benjamin said, cheeks burning, shame and guilt gripping his skull like a monkey's paw. 'We have tell the teachers what's going on, that the Dark Man's army is coming. Then we have to be ready when they come.' He took a deep breath, suppressing the urge to cry. 'We have to be ready for a war.'

PART III

THE BATTLE FOR THE END OF THE WORLD

34

MIRANDA'S SECRET

For the first couple of hours of the journey, no one spoke. Lawrence was a like a giant homing pigeon—he knew the way back by memory, but for his passengers, the thrill of the outward rollercoaster ride was gone. Edgar's sacrifice hung over all of them, and Benjamin's mind was filled with memories of those glass-and-metal teeth.

'How long do you think the school has?' Miranda said at last. 'I mean, before that war host arrives?'

'A week at most,' Wilhelm said. 'Do you think they'll have to evacuate?'

'And go where?' Miranda snapped. 'Over the edge of the world?'

'Well, what then?'

'He'll crush you all,' Godfrey said, piping up for the first time. 'He'll smash the school to pieces and blow up all of those horrid monsters that hide in the walls. He'll build a new school in its place, one where we can learn real skills rather than stupid stuff like how to tie ropes together.'

Miranda turned to glare at him. 'Shut up.'

'Oh, look at you, all weepy-weepy because your idiot friend didn't come back. You fools. The Dark Man is the rightful lord of Endinfinium. He's the only one who cares about its people.'

Miranda stood up and started back toward Godfrey, fists clenched.

'No!'

She stopped. Benjamin shook his head. 'Let him speak. What people?'

'The ones who can't stay dead.'

'The ghouls?'

'Call them what you want, runt.'

'What do you know about ghouls?'

'Only that they were once people, just like you and me. People who came here and died here. People whose souls were forgotten by the teachers and those idiots who built everything, who ended up twisted around by the taint of this place and fused with the rubbish millions of people tossed away.'

'He doesn't know what he's talking about,' Wilhelm said.

'Don't I? The teachers won't tell you anything, and do you know why? Because they want to control you. They want to use your powers for their own benefit. They know the truth. The cleaners are the bodies of the dead, but the dark people—the ones you call ghouls—they're the souls.'

'They've been reanimated!' Miranda shouted. 'They should have stayed dead.'

'Like you should have?'

Miranda jumped out of her seat, ran up to Godfrey, and started hitting him round the head. She had landed a couple of solid blows before Wilhelm and Benjamin managed to pull her off.

With Miranda smoldering, the others decided it might be better to move Godfrey a bit farther back down the train. After asking Lawrence to slow for a couple of minutes, they took Godfrey a couple of carriages closer to the rear, and as Benjamin secured his bonds, Godfrey scowled at him with unbridled hatred.

'Go ask your girlfriend what I'm talking about,' he said. 'Go on. You should have left her back there with those wraith-hounds. She'd have fitted in really well.'

When they returned, Miranda was moping in a side seat, her head leaning against a window that was part glass, part scales. She looked up with a resentful glare, then looked away again.

Wilhelm and Benjamin exchanged a glance before the smaller boy pulled Benjamin close. 'Look, I'll just go and, you know, have a quick look outside,' he said. 'See if Lawrence needs anything. You talk to her.'

Benjamin shifted from foot to foot, unsure of what to say while Miranda glowered in a seat near the front, arms crossed.

'Look,' he said, finally plucking up the courage to sit down beside her. 'What happened to Edgar—'

'Don't talk about Edgar,' she snapped, not looking up. 'I don't want to think about it.'

Putting a hand on her arm was akin to putting his head into a pond filled with hungry sharks, so he didn't. 'I'm your friend, aren't I?'

'Yes.'

'Do you trust me?'

'I trust you to get into trouble, and that I'll have to get you out of it.'

Benjamin rolled his eyes, assuming the answer was a yes. 'Then tell me what's wrong.'

She lifted her head and turned toward him. 'I'm not sure you can understand,' she said. 'The world I know is not the world you know. Edgar … he was like a father to me. I never had a father before. I never knew what it was like.'

'What do you mean?'

'Tell me about your family,' she said.

Benjamin frowned. 'Like what?'

She punched him on the arm, then looked bashful and muttered an apology. 'Like anything.'

Benjamin took a deep breath. 'Well, my dad is a train driver. My mum works in a bank. And David, he's just six.'

'More.'

Benjamin smiled. 'All right … my mum does this thing if she's cooking and she gets angry—she pulls off her apron, rolls it up into a ball, then unrolls it and does it again. When the anger's gone, she puts it back on and gets on with things as if nothing has happened. And my dad, he's a complete bookworm. He never watches TV, just reads all the time. He likes really thick fantasy books, stuff like *The Wheel of Time* or *The Kingkiller Chronicles*. He has them all in hardback, and they must weigh a ton. Mum likes to watch reality TV shows, but Dad will just sit there in a chair and read.'

'Are they kind to you?'

'Of course. They're just normal. If I'm dicking about, they'll tell me off, but they always come in to say goodnight and I can tell Mum makes a real effort with my packed lunch because even though the plastic tub is really small, she always arranges it so the apple doesn't crush the edge of the sandwiches like my mates' apples always do.'

Miranda lifted a hand to stifle a cough, but it came out watery, like a sob. She glared at him, daring him to mention the sheen in her eyes.

'They sound wonderful.'

Benjamin, too, felt like crying. 'Yeah, they're not bad, as parents go.'

Miranda nodded and pulled up her sleeve. 'Touch my skin,' she said.

'Um, okay.'

He laid a hand onto her arm, and ran two fingertips up and down. Just like his own skin, but even softer. It was covered in fine, almost invisible hairs, and the colour was a completely even off-white, blemish free.

'Feels normal, doesn't it?' she said. 'Like anyone else's?'

He nodded.

'I don't have any parents,' she said. 'Not in the way you do. I was born in a laboratory. I grew up in a home with forty-nine other girls who looked exactly like me. We ate the same, and did the same things. My name was Red-37.'

'I thought—'

'When I woke up here in Endinfinium and was asked my name, I picked the name of a girl in a storybook I liked to read at night back in the Growth Centre where I grew up. It sounded so much nicer.'

'You're an um, a…'

'I'm a clone.' She shrugged. 'It might sound strange for you to hear it, but in five hundred years … not so much.'

'But, what, I mean—'

The door opened, and Wilhelm came running in. 'We have to hurry,' he said. 'I think we have less time than we thought.'

'Lawrence, can you open your eyes?'

The front screen blinked on. Lawrence had come to rest on a hilltop, looking back over the top of a vast forest toward the yellow sun hanging low in the sky.

'Face west, please, Lawrence,' Wilhelm said. The train-snake turned around. A line of black covered the horizon, a mass of churning greys and blacks, completely obscuring the red sun.

'What's that?' Benjamin asked.

'That's the storm,' Wilhelm answered. 'The storm that's bringing the war.'

35

THE WAVE

They sat across three seats with Benjamin in the middle and Wilhelm and Miranda on either side, hanging on for dear life as Lawrence raced at top speed through the Haunted Forest. The looming thunderclouds were almost on top of them, and while the Baggers and the other machines might take a couple of days to arrive, already ghouls were rising up out of the ground like toadstools blooming after a heavy spell of rain.

The snake-train broke through the last trees of the Haunted Forest, and the river appeared below, high with flood water.

'Lawrence!' Benjamin shouted. 'Can you make it across?'

'Swim,' rumbled the foghorn-like voice.

'I think it might be best to close our eyes,' Wilhelm said, as the snake-train leapt out toward the river. They hung over the churning water for a few seconds, before an explosion from somewhere behind sent Lawrence flipping sideways, and the snake-train roared as he hit the water, side-on. They dipped under, the view turning dark, then they reemerged, bobbing in the languid shallows near the riverbank. Slowly, they twisted around as the current took hold, pulling them out into the faster-moving channel.

Benjamin unbuckled his seatbelt and fell heavily to the new floor. The others struggled with theirs, but he didn't have time to wait. He jumped up and ran for the door leading into the next carriage, wrestling it open and climbing through.

Godfrey had been one carriage farther back, but as Benjamin ran across the windows that now made the floor, the carriage dipped into the water as the current caught it. He reached the end, pushed up the door, and climbed through … and stared at only half a carriage. Across a churning black mass of water, Lawrence's back half lay against the riverbank, and Godfrey, a vicious scar now cutting across his face, stood unsteadily at the end of his half of destroyed carriage, holding on to a luggage rack now at shoulder height.

'Godfrey! What have you done?'

Godfrey scowled, eyes glowing orange. 'You're not the only summoner, Forrest. But you are the weakest.'

Benjamin gritted his teeth. The way the snake-train's walls shivered revealed Lawrence's pain, and attacking Godfrey might harm him, but Benjamin didn't care. The scratch on the back of his hand began to itch.

Godfrey's hands came up at the same time as Benjamin's, and there was a flash of light. Then he was falling back, the remaining half of the carriage tipping over, brackish water sloshing over him. He grabbed hold of the nearest seatback for support while the river rushed past as they gained speed. Behind him, the door slid open and Miranda peered through, Wilhelm behind her.

'Where's the rest of the train?'

'Godfrey blew it up.'

They stared at him. 'How?' Miranda said.

'He's a summoner, too.'

Miranda scowled, and Benjamin sensed her holding back a tirade of colourful insults. In the end, though, all she said was, 'That pig. What do we do now?'

Benjamin put a hand on the floor. 'Lawrence, can you hear me? Are you all right?'

'No tail … no swim,' boomed the foghorn voice.

Lawrence's heavy locomotive front kept them low in the water, but as the current strengthened, it pulled them faster and faster.

'Lawrence has no more control,' Benjamin said. 'We're going to slowly drift out into the sea. We have to use magic; it's our only choice.'

Miranda nodded. 'Not you, it's too dangerous. I'll do it. Me and Wilhelm.' She turned to the smaller boy. 'How does that weaver stuff work?'

'I just had to hold Edgar's shoulder. That was all. He said he could draw the power out of me.'

The river was rushing now, wide enough to barely see the banks on either side. In the distance to the left stood a promontory poking up into the sky. The school. They were so close, but it was now falling away behind them. If they didn't turn around soon they'd be out in the open sea and then….

The edge of the world. Benjamin squeezed his eyes shut, not wanting to think about it. When he opened them again, something huge and white was approaching from the horizon, pushing up a bore of black water in its wake.

'Look!' he shouted, pointing. 'There's some kind of ship. It's massive. Perhaps we can flag it down and they can throw us a rope or something.'

Miranda and Wilhelm exchanged a glance. 'Um, it might have once been a ship,' Miranda said, 'but I don't think it's a ship any more than those wraith-hounds were pots and pans.'

'Cruise-shark,' Lawrence hooted.

'It must be hungry,' Wilhelm added. 'It's coming right at us.'

As the cruise-shark approached, its huge front end opened like the bow of a whaling ship, revealing an open maw and serrated metallic teeth. The current took them toward it, and they were as helpless as a scrap of plankton in the sights of a hungry whale.

'Shore,' moaned Lawrence.

'Look!' Miranda shouted. 'We're coming out of the river mouth. The current will be weakest here where it's got the most resistance. We need something to push us in to the coast where the water's shallower.'

The massive reanimated cruise ship now blotted out the yellow sun hanging low in the sky.

'We need a wave,' Wilhelm said. 'Can you make that wave in its wake a little bigger? Perhaps make it push us into the shore?'

Miranda frowned. 'Grab hold of me,' she said. 'I'll try.'

She threw open a side window, blasting them with chilly, salty sea air. Wilhelm ran up behind her and gripped her shoulders with both hands. Miranda began to growl under her breath, and as Benjamin watched, the black wave grew larger, rising up in front of the reanimated cruise ship like a giant foreshadow.

'Come on,' Miranda muttered under her breath. 'Bigger, bigger....'

A long, blaring sound came from Lawrence as they rose up toward the ship's black maw, so huge it blotted out the sky.

'A little more, Miranda!'

Something slammed into them from the side, and Lawrence groaned again, rolling sideways. Miranda lost her grip on the window ledge, and the three of them tumbled across the floor, colliding with the far windows, then rolling back again as Lawrence righted himself. Through a window, Benjamin saw a massive, swinging anchor headed right for them. They sat on the crest of the wave; this time, it would knock them straight into the huge ship's mouth.

'Dive, Lawrence!' he screamed. 'Now!'

The snake-train dipped into the water. Miranda and Wilhelm screamed. Benjamin hooked his feet over a chair's armrest and grabbed one of them with each hand. Through Lawrence's eyes, he saw a colossal drop open up in front of them, a steep hillside of silvery, shining water.

Lawrence let out a groan, then they flew down the front of the wave as it barreled over them. For a few seconds, Lawrence seemed in command, angling right, away from the roar of the crushing whitewater, when the wave broke over their heads and everything became a black, tumbling apocalypse. Benjamin, thrown across the floor, floundered in the darkness for anything to hold on to. His fingers closed over a table edge before it was twisted out from under him and he landed hard on his back.

Just when he began to feel like a soccer ball caught in a rolling metal drum, they bobbed down into the water, crunched over sand and rocks, then came to a slow halt.

Benjamin rubbed twenty different bruises as he climbed to his feet. Miranda had a nasty welt around her right eye, and Wilhelm's shirt had been ripped clean off by a metal armrest.

Only sand and rocks were visible through Lawrence's huge eyes. Benjamin opened a side door and, one by one, they climbed out.

All around, the beach was strewn with fresh debris.

'Benjamin … oh, look what's happened to him.'

Miranda took Benjamin's hand and turned him around. On her other side, Wilhelm was rubbing his eyes.

'He saved us,' he said.

Lawrence opened his mouth to let out a low, dying groan. With only two and a half carriages left, both battered and crunched, he was just a wreck lying among other wrecks.

'Thank you, Lawrence.' Benjamin placed a hand on the snake-train's side. 'We can't thank you enough.'

Lawrence's mouth opened and closed. A foghorn blared. 'Save … school,' it sounded like. 'Edgar … love … school.'

'Lawrence—'

The snake-train's eyes closed like curtains being drawn on a theatre production, and with a great moan like an expulsion of breath, Lawrence lay still.

Far out to sea, the huge cruise-shark had vanished back beneath the water. The yellow sun was visible once more, hanging low over the horizon, but above the looming cliffs, the sky was filling with dark clouds.

'Come on,' Benjamin said. 'Let's go.'

He took their hands in his, and together they headed for a path leading up the cliff. Just as they climbed out of sight, Benjamin took one last look at Lawrence's still form lying on the beach, and drew in a deep breath.

Too many had fallen already. The Dark Man had to be stopped.

36

FALLENWOOD

When they reached the top of the cliff, they were exhausted, and collapsed to the springy turf, sitting back to back, none of them really wanting to speak. Miranda faced outward to the sea, Benjamin back inland, and Wilhelm up-coast in the direction of the school.

'What do we do now?' Miranda said at last.

Benjamin turned to look out to the sea, which was calmer now and lit up by the brilliance of the yellow sun that hung above a truncated horizon, the edge of the world a thick, golden line of crayon. No more than an hour remained before the yellow sun sank beyond the edge. The red sun, making its way around the world to the west, would soon disappear into the mass of approaching cloud. The darkest night Benjamin had yet known in Endinfinium was nearly upon them.

'I can't see the school,' Wilhelm said. 'We must be ten or fifteen miles south of it. We'll never get there in the dark.'

'What about a cave?' Miranda said.

Wilhelm groaned. 'Ah, come on. Scatlocks roost in caves.'

Miranda shoved him in the back so he rolled away into the springy grass. 'Well, come up with a better option, then!'

'Stop it!'

Wilhelm sat up and flung a clump of sod at Miranda, who ducked, and it hit Benjamin in the chest with a soft *splat*. He looked at the brown stain on his shirt, then couldn't help grinning. After a moment, the other two started smiling too.

'We're kind of screwed, aren't we?'

Miranda shrugged. 'We still have each other.'

'It could be worse,' Wilhelm said. 'Godfrey could still be with us.'

'We have an hour before full dark,' Benjamin said. 'Let's not waste that time bickering, shall we?'

At Miranda's suggestion, they walked inland, up a rise away from the cliff edge until they could see the lay of the land. From the hill's crest the land dipped and rose in a series of forested valleys and bald hilltops before reaching the edge of the river estuary a couple of miles farther south. The wave had taken them further north than they had expected, but they were still out of sight of the school. A coastal path followed the clifftop, but after dark, the many steep descents into river valleys and secretive coves would be treacherous.

'Look, over there,' Miranda said. 'What's that dome shape poking out of the trees?'

Deep green and barely taller than the trees around it, the dome looked made of glass and steel.

'Looks like an old observatory,' Wilhelm said.

'That's our sleeping place,' Benjamin said. 'Let's get moving.'

The dome was three valleys away. Down in the forest, the gloom had already set in, hampering progress, and by the time they emerged on the last ridge before the dome's valley, they could barely see anything at all through the trees.

Just down from the ridge, an overgrown trail led into the woods. Wilhelm suggested they gather some dry wood on the way and make a fire when they arrived, so they collected bundles of twigs and a few bigger logs and carried them under their arms.

The dome was farther than it appeared from the ridge where they had first seen it, and Benjamin was beginning to think they had taken a wrong path, when they emerged into a clearing to find a tall building standing in front of them.

'It's an old glasshouse,' Wilhelm said. 'It looks like it's been abandoned.'

At a couple of storeys high, the glasshouse had probably once been magnificent, but creeping plants had turned its glass walls green, while its steel frame had rusted, and in some places, broken away.

'Do you think this place has anything to do with the school?' Wilhelm said as they went through an opening where double doors had once stood. 'It's been abandoned for years by the look of it, but I can't believe it just appeared here. Someone must have built it.'

Miranda pulled creepers away from a sign beside the door. '*Endinfinium High Horticultural Society: Biosphere One.* I guess that's your answer. Looks like the school used to have a gardening club.'

Wilhelm laid a hand on her shoulder as she made to step inside. 'And the second question, possibly the more important one, is why was it abandoned?'

Benjamin pressed a hand to the glass. 'It's stone cold,' he said. 'Could that be it? Everything else I've seen has reanimated, but this looks just, you know, normal. Perhaps that's why. They wanted it to reanimate and it wouldn't, so they went somewhere else?'

'In any case,' Miranda said, 'I'd feel safer inside than out. Who knows what lives in these forests?'

Benjamin shivered at the thought of the wraith-hounds finding them sleeping. 'Come on, let's take our chances,' he said.

The others followed him inside. In the gloom, it was nearly impossible to see anything, but once-ordered rows of raised flowerbeds now burgeoned with oversized plants, many of which had overturned their pots and grown new sets of roots in the thick humus on the floor.

Everywhere was damp and pungent, the air kept moist by the glass roof that, despite having been punctured in several places by overgrown trees, still maintained the glasshouse in a semi-tropical state.

'Look,' Wilhelm said. 'Over there in the middle. Is that a cave?'

A large, black shape about took up the centre of the main room. At first Benjamin thought it was a rockery feature, like he had seen in botanical gardens back home, perhaps once adorned by a variety of tropical climbing plants. When he reached up to touch it, however, he found it dry and rough, though cool like wood rather than cold like stone.

'It's a tree stump,' he said. 'Perhaps they found it in the forest and dragged it here.'

Wilhelm walked around the outside. 'It's massive. The tree must been enormous. It's all split at the top so it looks like it got destroyed by lightning.'

'There's a kind of hollow in the middle,' Benjamin said. 'It's the best shelter we've found.'

Miranda stared up at the tree. 'I don't know. This place creeps me out. Perhaps we should move on.'

'And go where?' Wilhelm said. 'It's getting dark.'

Miranda reluctantly agreed.

They climbed in through the loose stones and dirt until all three were nestled into the hollow beneath the stump. The concave shape naturally collected heat, so they were soon warm, even before Wilhelm suggested they build a fire.

Holding up a handful of green things, he said, 'I found these turnip-tops growing in a flowerbed around the back of the stump. The turnips themselves were all shriveled and dry, but we can eat the leaves.'

'I hate turnips,' Miranda said. 'I used to eat a lot of them in my ... old life.'

'If we warm them by a fire, they might taste better,' Wilhelm said.

He cleared a space, then broke up twigs and arranged them into a conical shape. In the deepening gloom, Benjamin glanced at Miranda, and while he couldn't see her face, he felt her body tense.

'What's the matter?'

She gave a little shake of her head. 'I can't do it,' she said. 'I don't know how. The magic ... I can push and pull stuff, but making heat ... turning something into fire ... I haven't got a clue. I might burn the whole forest down, or make the three of us combust.'

Wilhelm gave a little chuckle. 'Why such a lack of faith?'

Miranda punched his leg. 'If it's so easy, why don't you do it, then?'

Wilhelm grinned, pulled something out of his pocket, and held it up. With a flick of his fingers, a little flame appeared.

'Didn't you learn anything during orienteering class?' he said, waving the match back and forth in front of them. 'Captain Roche's first rule was never to go anywhere without carrying a source of fire.'

'But all our stuff got lost when Godfrey blew up Lawrence!'

Wilhelm shrugged. 'I have trouser pockets.'

His smug look made Benjamin smile. Even Miranda, despite her scowl and the extra punch she gave his leg, looked suitably impressed.

'Just give me a minute,' Wilhelm said, touching the flame to a bundle of dry grass. 'Perhaps, if we can find some water, I can cook us some turnip leaf soup.'

'Oh joy to end all joys,' Miranda said, but the keenness in her eyes told Benjamin she wouldn't turn down a bowl if offered.

As the twigs began to catch fire, the warmth started sinking into Benjamin's bones. He gave a contented sigh and leaned back against the dry stump, just as it shifted with a hideous shriek, and thick, bony branches bent over their heads, trapping them like animals in a cage.

'Oh, alchemy!' boomed a thunderous voice, and a gust of freezing wind blew out the fire.

'My arm's stuck!' Wilhelm shouted.

'Stop moving around,' Miranda said, pushing him as he tried to back into her.

'I can't get my arm out!'

Benjamin turned back to the wooden stump and put his hands out. It was warm. The stump had reanimated right in front of them and, under his palms, he could feel it pulsing like a living thing.

'It's alive,' he said. 'Stop struggling or it might crush us.'

'I can't see anything!'

'Intruders, are you?' came the booming voice again, which reminded Benjamin of Lawrence's foghorn voice, though more organic, like wind being pulled through an entire orchestra of woodwind instruments and slowly molded into a coherent sound.

Miranda grabbed Benjamin's arm. 'It's a talking tree,' she hissed.

'I'm no such thing!' boomed the voice again.

'Then what are you?' Miranda shouted back.

The branches trapping them suddenly pulled up. Wilhelm screamed and dashed off into gloom, but Benjamin took hold of Miranda's arm, and together, they turned back toward the stump.

Two football-sized eyes watched them out of the crusty, ancient wood. Both were a deep, forest green with black pupils and their glow was bright enough for Benjamin to make out Miranda's face as the girl stared openmouthed.

'And who are you?' the voice boomed. 'Aside from being intruders who come into Fallenwood to light your fires? Don't you understand the meaning of respect?'

Branches snaked out and encircled their ankles and wrists, holding them tight. From the gloom behind came an unusual crackling sound, like a basket full of hundreds of twigs being slowly upended.

'I'm Miranda Butterworth,' Miranda said. 'My friends are Wilhelm Jacobs and Benjamin—'

'Help me!'

Wilhelm's scream had cut her off, and the rumble of a large object rolling along the floor made them turn around. In the gloom, it was difficult to see what was going on, but Wilhelm appeared caught in the middle of a huge ball of twigs, his arms and legs held outstretched.

'You bring your fire here, little man,' boomed the voice. 'Let me show you the nature of fire.'

High above, glass and metal shrieked and shifted, and then the gloom became light as the roof shook free from years of accumulated grime and dirt. Mirrors and windows shifted, reflecting and refracting the light until a dull red glow filled every space.

The brightest dot was centred on Wilhelm's chest, and a thin wisp of smoke began to rise from the third button of his school uniform's jacket.

'Let him go!' Miranda screamed. She jerked one hand free, clenched a fist and, with a crackle of breaking wood, all of the twigs shifted and collapsed to the ground in a heap. From somewhere underneath came Wilhelm's muffled cry for help.

'Channeler,' murmured the stump. 'How interesting.'

The heap of twigs shifted, and then up from the huge tinder pile rose humanoid shapes—strange, wooden creatures, some with multiple arms and legs. Wilhelm, cowering on the ground, was lifted up and held with his hands at his sides.

'Look, we're sorry,' Benjamin said, turning to the stump. 'We didn't know anyone lived here. We're just trying to escape from the Dark Man and his army, which, by the way, is marching toward Endinfinium High as we speak, intent on wiping it off the face of the, um … wherever the hell we are.'

The stump shifted back and forth as if nodding. 'Finally, a few manners. What you say is of disputed interest. Your name is?'

'Benjamin Forrest, sir.'

'Forrest!'

A wave of *ahhs* came from the assembled twig creatures, and the two nearest to him rustled with excitement, Wilhelm was forced to dance a little jig.

'With a name like that, one must share a love for trees,' the stump said.

'There was a wood at the end of my street,' Benjamin said. 'I used to go down there with my little brother, David, and we used to climb the trees and fish in the river, and ride our bikes on the dirt track someone had made. I'm sorry we tried to start a fire. We were just cold, that's all.'

The stump gave a sound that could only have been a chuckle. 'Well, no harm done. At least not much. We're all friends here. Welcome, Forrest, Firestarter, and Firehair. Welcome to the Kingdom of Fallenwood. I imagine you're hungry? Let me see what my Fallenwoodsmen can find for you.'

37

VIEWING PLATFORM

Much to Benjamin's surprise, the huge talking stump was able to move, if slowly, shuffling from side to side like a lame hippopotamus, and as they walked, he introduced himself as Fallenwood, Lord of all of Fallenwood.

'Don't you have another name?' Benjamin asked.

'We have no need of names,' Fallenwood said. 'I have assumed something for you to call me. We have no names for each other, because we are all one and the same.'

'Like ants?' Wilhelm said.

Fallenwood shook from side to side. 'Another scourge,' he muttered, then said under his breath, but just loud enough for them to hear, 'All truces have failed....'

'Were there once people from the school here?' Miranda asked.

'Yes, yes. People from the school built this crumbling place. We are not best fans of humans and the rest, but the rain can be so terribly cruel.'

All around followed bundles of twigs and branches, continuously connecting and intertwining to form wheels and rollers and globes, like a magically animated wicker basket factory.

'Can they speak? Do they have minds?' Benjamin asked Fallenwood.

'Oh, yes,' the great stump said. 'Just no way to communicate by themselves. If enough of them get together, anything can happen. One by one, however, they're simple creatures. They have no need for conversation or philosophy or the understanding of existentialism. They're content with idle play.'

Fallenwood led them through another door and into a wider auditorium room where Benjamin exchanged surprised glances with Wilhelm and Miranda at the lights glowing in fittings on the wall and in strips along the ceiling. The floor was piled with woodchips and other dry plant matter that had long ago run out of moisture, and the Fallenwoodsmen tumbled and danced among it like organic fairies. For Benjamin, watching them was as close as he had come to watching television since his arrival, as they played out dances and mimicry and dramas like a constantly evolving theatre troupe.

'Where did you get the lights?' Wilhelm asked.

'Something the humans left behind,' Fallenwood said. 'On the roof. Things that collect sun.'

'Solar panels,' Benjamin said. 'Wouldn't they have fallen into disrepair by now?'

'Oh, they did,' Fallenwood said. 'And then they fixed themselves.'

'It doesn't bother you?' Wilhelm asked. 'The lights?'

Fallenwood chuckled. 'Oh, forget the eyes,' he said. 'They're for your benefit. They see nothing, and the Fallenwoodsmen see nothing, either.'

'Then how do you—'

'We *feel* you. The air, as it swirls around, paints a picture of you that I can see as clearly as I could with any eyes.'

Wilhelm lifted a hand in front of Fallenwood's huge, blinking —and now revealed to be fake—eyes. 'How many fingers am I holding up?'

'How many do you have?'

'Ten.'

'Then somewhere between that and zero. Am I right?'

'I guess.'

'You are hungry?' Fallenwood said, apparently tiring of the subject. 'Please, sit and eat.'

A maelstrom of Fallenwoodsmen intertwined to form three woven chairs and a trellis table, upon which bowls of green leaves and coloured fruit were placed.

'Gifts from the forest,' Fallenwood said. 'Our finest cuisine.'

The food looked and tasted almost exactly like the school's food, but all three were starving and ate like it was the last meal on Earth. Fallenwood stood motionless beside them, so still that Benjamin often forgot the stump was there.

After dinner was over, Fallenwood suggested they get some rest. None had the strength to argue, so the Fallenwoodsmen again interwove, this time into three comfortable beds. Covered by a layer of soft moss and leaves, Benjamin was asleep almost before his head had touched the bundle of dried grass provided as a pillow.

When he woke, the room was filled with the grey light of a reluctant dawn. His body ached all over, but his mind felt more rested than it had in weeks. Miranda and Wilhelm still slept peacefully in their beds, but Fallenwood stood behind them like a sentry and, upon seeing Benjamin was up, asked if he would take a morning stroll.

They didn't go far. From what Benjamin could gather, the entire Fallenwood kingdom extended only up to the boundaries of the old botanical society building, and even a couple of rooms inside were off limits due to the collapsed roof.

'You are new to Endinfinium, one gathers,' Fallenwood said as Benjamin walked alongside the huge, lumbering stump. 'Your outlook is not so jaded as one might expect of a long-term resident.'

'At times,' Benjamin said, 'I feel like I'm drowning in the mysteries of this place. I've given up trying to understand.'

'In time, answers will reveal themselves,' Fallenwood said.

'Do you know? Do you know what Endinfinium is, and why we're here?'

'I only know what I have discovered with my own senses, that it is a place in which the concept of death that many of you outsiders understand is no longer relevant. There are different rules here.'

'But why? How can plastic bags fly, and motorbikes walk like men, and twigs dance?'

'How can something that is eighty percent water care to wonder about such things?' Fallenwood said. 'Your understanding of sentience is archaic. Surely if you can have powers of thought and reason and emotion, is it not possible that other objects can?'

'But plastic bags and other rubbish … they aren't alive. We made them.'

'And who made you? Complexity is overrated.'

Benjamin shrugged. 'Nothing makes any sense.'

'Not where you're from, no. But remember, the rules here are different.'

Aware he was starting to sound like a petulant child though unable to stop himself, Benjamin said, 'But why? And if this is a place with different rules, then why am I here? Why any people at all?'

Fallenwood appeared to let out a long sigh. 'Because you all have something in common.'

'What?'

'I'm not sure. But if you continue to ask questions of your surroundings, eventually you'll figure it out. Don't give up, Forrest.'

Benjamin felt like giving up, yet he forced himself to think about David. 'We have to leave today,' he said. 'A great army is approaching the school. I think the Dark Man is using Grand Lord Bastien and my brother, David, to power his machines.'

'Even here in Fallenwood, we have heard of the Dark Man … and his power. It would be useful if he were stopped.'

'Just "useful"?'

'The Dark Man is a human, like you,' Fallenwood said. 'His battle is with other humans. The Kingdom of Fallenwood is not his concern.'

'But if he destroys the school, it might be.'

'We are of no threat to him. My Fallenwoodsmen dance only for themselves, not for others. You and your friends … you were privileged.'

'How can you know?' Benjamin said. 'What if he decides to raze the forests, burn them all down?'

Fallenwood gave another trumpeting laugh. 'But why would he? Everyone needs wood.'

Benjamin opened his mouth to argue, but instead he said, 'If all the peoples of Endinfinium join against the Dark Man, we can banish him. We can push him back behind the High Mountains and put an end to the ghouls and other horrible creatures.'

'Do you really want to see him banished?' Fallenwood said. 'Wouldn't you like to know who this Dark Man really is?'

Benjamin shivered at the ethereal face he had seen at the river's parting.

'No,' he snapped. Then, before Fallenwood could respond, he added, 'I'd better go and wake the others. We have a battle to fight.'

Fallenwood refused any requests to join their fledgling army, though he did offer to have his Fallenwoodsmen provide a little assistance. First, he had Benjamin, Miranda, and Wilhelm assemble in one of the roofless rooms, to stand on a wooden board that had once been part of a cupboard. Then, before they had a chance to back out, the Fallenwoodsmen bound and wove beneath them, lifting them up off the floor. They held on to each other in sheer terror as they became the unwitting pinnacle at the top of a rapidly growing tower that rose up out of the ruined botanical society building, past the towering trees, until they were marooned on a tiny, shaky platform as high as an electricity pylon.

'We're going to die,' Wilhelm stated. 'I mean, we should have died about thirty times already. At some point our luck's going to run out.'

'Stop moving about!' Miranda shrieked as Wilhelm took a couple of steps from one side to the other, while she lay immobile on top of it, white-knuckled from gripping the wood. 'Can't you just sit down?'

'Look! You can see the school!' Wilhelm shouted, pointing off to the south as a gust of wind caused the platform to lurch precariously, only to sway back level as the immense wicker frame below moved to counter it.

'And over there you can see the people coming to destroy it,' Benjamin said.

'Where? Oh … there.'

Even Miranda stopped her terrified mumblings to look. Far to the northwest and beyond the river, the Haunted Forest lay like a black smear on the land, except for one lighter swath that ran from the foothills almost to the water's edge.

'Tell me that's not…'

Benjamin nodded. 'They're cutting their way through. I wondered how the Baggers would get here.' He looked around at the others. 'There's still a chance. We can hold them at the river.'

Wilhelm gave a bitter laugh. 'Right. With our army of three. Who wants to stand in the middle?'

38

THE LIGHTHOUSE

Despite a few scares, the Fallenwoodsmen brought them back to the ground without harm, and even though Fallenwood invited them to stay for lunch, Benjamin told him about what they had seen and insisted they be on their way. Fallenwood wished he could have been of more help, but with the threat of rain, he was sorry he couldn't offer them an escort to the edge of the woods. He did fill their pockets with food, however, and wish them good luck.

None of them spoke until they were out of the woods and up on the high lands near the cliff. Then, when the distant grey of the Haunted Forest came back into view beyond the river valley, they stopped for a council meeting.

'Okay, what now?' Wilhelm said. 'I'd guess we're twenty miles from the school, or twenty from that river. We have no transport, so it's a hard day's walk. If they're already at the river, then we'll get to the school at the same time they will, which means there'll be no warning.'

Miranda nodded. 'Or, we head out to cut off the Dark Man's army and we somehow make a stand while one of us goes to warn the school.'

'Hmm. You're a channeler and I'm a weaver, so perhaps we can do something. Benjamin should go to the school.'

'No.' Benjamin shook his head. 'They've got my brother. And

I'm a summoner. I can call on much more power than either of you.'

'Power you don't know how to use,' Miranda said. 'At best, you'll make an unholy mess while destroying yourself. Great idea.' She punched him on the arm. 'And at worst, nothing at all will happen and you'll just look like an idiot.'

'Well, what do you suggest? How can we warn the school in time?'

'There's an old watchtower a couple of hours' walk north of us,' Wilhelm said. 'I saw it when we were on that hideous stick platform. It might have a radio or some kind of signaling device.'

Benjamin nodded. 'It's the best plan we've got.'

'But still not much of a plan,' Miranda muttered.

'Well…'

She looked ready to punch him again, but held her hands stiffly by her sides instead. Around her, the grass gave an artificial tremble. 'Let's get going,' she said through gritted teeth, then turned to march north along the coast path.

'She's got spirit,' Wilhelm whispered as he and Benjamin started after her. 'I like that.'

'Spirit's what we're going to need against that ghoul army and those Baggers,' Benjamin said. 'It might not be enough, though.'

By midmorning, the tower had come into sight—a stone structure as tall as a couple of houses stood on end, pointed like a needle with a thicker top part that had an outdoor walkway, and with its eroded paintwork and large cracks in the walls looked in about as good a repair as the botanical society.

'That's not a tower, that's a lighthouse,' Miranda said as they crested the last rise before the headland on which the whitewashed building stood.

'What do I know?' Wilhelm said. 'I grew up in the city.'

'It's for guiding ships,' Benjamin said. 'I wonder when it was built.'

'One way to find out. Hurry up.' Miranda marched off into

the lead again. Wilhelm, who was sweating despite the chilly sea wind, gave Benjamin a tired glance.

'I hope it has seats inside,' he said.

'Come on.' Benjamin gave him a pat on the shoulder for luck. 'Hopefully, she'll have found a kettle and put it on.'

A little stony path led to a door around the back. Miranda had already gone inside, though Wilhelm hung back, looking a little sheepish.

'What's the matter?'

'Just a bad feeling, that's all. You go first.'

'Thanks.'

Benjamin called out for Miranda as he pushed the door open to reveal a dark lobby with cracked tiles and chipped paint. Though there was no sign of the girl, a staircase in one corner wound up around the walls, pausing at a landing on each loop. Benjamin followed it with his eyes as it twisted up to the high ceiling.

'What's that?'

Wilhelm looked at him.

'What?'

'That thing hanging from the ceiling. It looks like a giant spider's nest.'

Wilhelm took a couple of steps back toward the door. 'No way. I draw the line at giant spiders.'

'Wait! It's moving. It's … Miranda?'

The bag jerked. 'Help!' came a muffled cry.

'She's caught in a trap.' Wilhelm pointed at a lever on the wall by the stairs, one that neither had noticed before. A rope led up to a pulley system occasionally visible behind the jerking bag. 'Someone maybe left it here to catch animals. Let's go cut her down.'

They dashed up the stairs. Despite the ordeals over the last few days, Benjamin still hadn't quite adjusted to heights, and his head spun as they wound up and up.

Wilhelm, smaller and lighter, had run on ahead, and as Benjamin reached a midway landing, Wilhelm pulled up a crusty blind to reveal a window overlooking the sea. Light flooded in, its glow revealing a brown sack hanging from a chain with something shifting about inside it.

'Miranda!' Benjamin shouted again.

'Get me out!'

'It's attached to the wall,' Wilhelm said. 'I saw a lever. Shall I go back down and release it?'

'No!' screamed Miranda. 'Do you want to kill me, you idiot?'

'We have to cut her free,' Benjamin said. But just as he started to look around for something to cut with, voices floated up from the floor below.

'Sir! We've caught something!'

'What is it?'

'Look, sir!'

A group of kids from the school rushed into the lighthouse, and Benjamin groaned. He recognised several, and among them was Godfrey's friend, Snout. But it was the burly shape coming sideways through the door that made his heart race.

Captain Roche looked up. Even in the gloom on the lighthouse floor, the shock on his unnaturally wide face was apparent. He flicked a wall switch, and the inside of the lighthouse lit up in dazzling white light.

'Well, well, well. Forrest. Jacobs. And let me guess: Ms Butterworth is currently messing about in our animal trap. Would one of you clowns like to tell me first, what the hell you're doing here, and secondly, where the hell you've been?'

39

MUTINY

'Yes sir,' Wilhelm said. 'I will gladly go and wait outside with the others. As I just explained, I had nothing to do with anything. It was all Benjamin and Miranda. I just want to go back to the school and finish my homework.'

'You little sneak,' Miranda snapped.

'Go on then, boy,' Captain Roche said. 'Don't think you're getting off with no cleans, though. It takes more than a little butt kissing to get out of this one.'

Wilhelm gave the captain a sweet smile and ran off outside to where the other students waited in a group. Benjamin stared after him. Had Wilhelm really gone turncoat or was he just trying to avoid a lengthy spell in the Locker Room? Beside him, Miranda glowered at the floor.

'And you, Forrest,' Captain Roche said. 'What's this rubbish about an army?'

'I'm not making it up. If you go up to the top of the lighthouse and take a look, you can see for yourself.'

Captain Roche turned his imposing gaze from one to the other. 'I was up there a short while ago, and all I saw was the Haunted Forest. Lots of unpleasant trees. No one likes to go in there unless they have to, do they?'

'There's an army of ghouls and other nasty things coming to destroy the school! You have to warn the other teachers!'

Captain Roche planted his huge hands on his hips. 'You know what happens to kids who don't follow the rules,' he said, 'if all the cleans down in the Locker Room don't make any difference?'

Benjamin sighed. 'No, sir, I don't.'

'Two choices: you get cast out to the Haunted Forest, or you get set adrift on the ocean and you take your chances. You like either of those options, Forrest? Both can be arranged.'

'How can you be so cruel?' Miranda shouted.

Captain Roche just shook his head. 'You think that's cruel, Butterworth? You've been here, what, three months? I told Loane there had to be a better choice for prefect, but the fool wouldn't listen. And you, Forrest, not even a month yet, is it? You don't understand the sacrifice so many have made so you could grow up here in safety. We can't send you back to where you came from; we don't know how. We could let you wander until something nasty comes up out of the ground to swallow you. Instead, we try to give you a life, but for the safety of everyone, there are rules to follow.'

'And one of them is that there is no magic, is that right?'

Captain Roche scowled at Benjamin. 'Don't you speak such a dirty word in my presence, boy. I'd have the hide flogged off of your back if it was my choice, but as it is, I'll have to settle for five thousand cleans. I hope you have a comfortable sleeping bag.'

Benjamin exchanged glances with Miranda. Arguing with the captain was useless. 'Okay, sir, you can take us back,' he said. 'I'll do a million cleans, if that's what it takes, but just go up to the top of the lighthouse and tell me what you see. It's important.'

'I told you, I saw nothing but lies and bad children playing petulant games.'

'It's not a game!'

'Your little cohort, Jacobs, has already accepted his punishment, why won't you?' Captain Roche looked from one to the other. 'You're making fools out of yourselves.'

'You have to go and look!'

Captain Roche ignored him. 'And you, Butterworth? Are you

willing to accept your folly and return to the school, or do I have to take matters into my own hands and declare you both outcasts from this moment forth?'

Miranda glanced at Benjamin. *She's making it my decision,* he thought. And they were wasting time. Getting back to the school was paramount, even if they had to go in manacles and stocks.

He gave her a short nod.

'Yes.' She let out a long sigh of feigned defeat. 'I have a good sleeping bag. Captain, *sir.*'

'Good. Let's get going, then.'

Captain Roche lumbered toward the door, with Benjamin and Miranda following behind. As they went outside, the other pupils fell silent. Where they had been standing in a group, they now moved out into a semi-circle around the entrance, offering no way through. Only a brave few glanced at Captain Roche, but as he stopped and stared, they all reached out and joined hands. Wilhelm, far from the self-made outsider he had always been before, stood in the middle with the others fanned out around him.

'What's this?' Captain Roche said.

Wilhelm stepped forward and glanced at Snout, who stood on the edge of the line to Wilhelm's right. 'Tell him, Simon,' he said.

Snout took a step forward. He looked about to cry. 'Godfrey showed me how to do it. I didn't know what it meant, or what I was doing, but…'

He lifted his hands in front of him, palms down. The air shimmered and, like a veil covering the lower part of his body, the ground lost its distinction, turning into a wash of colours, becoming fluid, like a bowl of mixed paints. Slowly at first, and then with increasing speed, the colours swirled into a whirlpool out of which something spindly and grey but with an orange hue began to climb.

'Enough!' cried Captain Roche, lifting one huge hand and the whirlpool of colour exploded with an electrical crackle. Snout jumped back with a look of shock. The air cleared, the ground became solid, and the creature, whatever it was, was gone.

Gasps came from the other pupils. Captain Roche glared at them in turn, as if daring any of them to mention what they had just seen. Snout, sniveling, shrank back into the ranks, his gaze on the ground. Others appeared unsure of where to look. Only Wilhelm looked defiant.

'You're a channeler, sir. There's no use in denying it.'

'I don't—'

'We all just witnessed you banish the ghoul Simon here had summoned. Can you explain it in any other way?'

'You will pay for this humiliation,' the captain growled. 'You'll clean until your hands are raw.'

'Everyone saw it,' Wilhelm continued. 'And Simon's not the only one who can do something he can't understand. Miranda and Benjamin can. Billy here, and Alina. And what of the others who are weavers, like me? They might not even know it. It's time you stopped hiding this magic from us and started teaching us how to use it, so we can protect both ourselves and the school.'

Captain Roche sighed, and his huge head swung from side to side. 'It was for your own safety,' he said slowly, turning to look at all of them. 'Few can draw on the power unless they know what it is they're drawing and how to do it. And the loss of a few is worth the survival of the many.'

Benjamin glanced at Wilhelm, and his friend gave a little wink, which made Benjamin smile. 'Are you prepared to believe us yet?' he asked Captain Roche. 'About the Dark Man's army?'

The captain turned to him, and something in his eyes suggested that, correct or not, Benjamin and his friend would still be punished for their insolence, but he gave a slow nod.

'We will return to the school with haste, and there we will decide what needs to be done.'

As the captain led the boys toward a machine that looked like a horse trailer with the front halves of two robotic horses sticking out of one end, Benjamin and Miranda closed ranks around Wilhelm.

'I guess I need to start trusting you,' Benjamin said. 'I don't know how you got the other boys on your side, but that was awesome.'

'I knew I could convince them. I didn't expect Snout to be able to call a ghoul, though. That's a bit worrying.'

Miranda punched him on the arm. 'That was to say sorry,' she said, 'for calling you a sneak. You had me convinced.'

'Um, thanks.'

'Welcome.' Miranda took hold of one of Wilhelm's arms and one of Benjamin's and quickened her pace, pulling them toward the robotic horse-trailer. 'Round one to us,' she said. 'Hopefully, the other teachers will be easier to convince.'

'Uh-oh,' Benjamin said, looking up.

'What?'

He held out his other hand and a little drop of water landed on his palm. 'It's starting to rain.'

40

DRESSING DOWN

M rs. Martin made them chamomile tea in the lobby while Captain Roche went off to confer with the other teachers. Benjamin had to admit, it felt good to be back. Not quite homely, but within the confines of the warm walls and with a comfortable leather seat underneath him, it was certainly close.

As she brought the tray out and set it down onto a low coffee table, Mrs. Martin said in a quiet voice, 'My sister's name is Margerie. I'm Madeline. Endinfinium took me but left her. I often wondered what happened to her. We were identical.'

'She's the secretary at my secondary school,' Benjamin said, feeling like a mystery had been solved yet another door to freedom had been slammed shut. 'She looks like you. She looks exactly like you.'

Mrs. Martin smiled. 'Even our parents couldn't tell us apart.' She started to get up, then paused. 'If you ever find a way … back … I'd be interested in knowing about it.'

Benjamin, Miranda, and Wilhelm looked at each other as she retreated into the office. 'Doesn't explain the phone line,' Benjamin said. When he saw their blank stares, he realised he hadn't mentioned it to the others.

He was about to explain, when Snout came running up the hall, stopping just short of them. He gave a curt nod, wiped his sniffling nose with the back of his sleeve, and then said, 'Ms. Ito will see you now.'

Wilhelm was like a tittering bird as they followed Snout toward the teachers' apartments. 'She's going to murder us,' he said, gaze unsure where to rest. 'Captain Roche might look scary, but he's a pussycat compared to her. I've heard rumours, you know. She doesn't get tired. She can scream until your eardrums pop, even if it takes days.'

Miranda and Benjamin shared a glance. Miranda looked flustered, but Benjamin took a certain level of comfort in being balled out by an angry teacher.

Ms. Ito waited in the library with Professor Loane. With a sweep of her hand, she dismissed Snout, who was running almost before he'd turned around. Professor Loane closed the door, then stepped off to the side and stood patiently like a butler while Ms. Ito stumped back and forth. Stump, stump, stump in one direction, a long, lazy sweep as her cast swung around, and then stump, stump, stump back in the other direction, eyes holding them with a cruel stare.

After the ninth lap, she finally stopped and turned to face them. 'Should we get the scolding out of the way first, or should we save that for later?'

None dared to speak. Benjamin started to open his mouth, though his tongue felt thick and useless, so he closed it again with a sharp snap.

'Unfortunately,' Ms. Ito continued, 'we are unable to select pupils in the same way that a regular school does. Ours are delivered to us; we do not get a choice. And quite often, we end up with all manner of riffraff gracing our rather divine corridors. Do you have anything to say?'

All three stayed silent. Ms. Ito nodded. 'Good, good. I should hope not. Foolish is the upstart who believes they can talk over the wise. Isn't that right, Loane?'

By the door, Professor Loane snapped to attention like a pupil caught napping. 'Yes, of course, Ms. Ito. Quite right.'

Ms. Ito narrowed her eyes. Benjamin waited for a curl of her lips, a wink, or perhaps even a slight wrinkling of the nose, anything to suggest an element of humour, but none came. She turned back to the others.

'Certain things I am about to talk about will never leave this room, is that clear? Not even in the event of capture and torture.'

Three heads shook vehemently.

'No.'

'Nope.'

'Of course not.'

'Good.' Ms. Ito spun on her cast, then did a couple more laps of the room. 'More years ago than you could count—and we're not quite sure how many, so don't ask; the tomes of Endinfinium's history are slow to reveal their secrets— Endinfinium was created out of some kind of evolutionary disturbance, and like any common parasite, began to grow and spread. East—or what became considered east—to the edge of the world, west to the High Mountains and beyond, south and north to regions yet unexplored. Like fleas on the back of a diseased horse, people began appearing all over the place. While no one is quite sure, one can assume those days were terribly dangerous, with one's chances of survival slight in the least. None of you, with your cavalier attitude and remarkable disrespect for rules, would have stood a chance.'

Benjamin risked a glance across the top of Wilhelm's head at Miranda, who stared at Ms. Ito like she was some kind of sorceress.

'Then,' Ms. Ito continued, 'a group of those early settlers decided to found a school to help others like them, since there seemed to be no likelihood of an end for these strange appearances. They created the building you now stand inside, designed everything you see, and created all of the rules that keep those ghastly phantoms and other hideous things at bay. It is likely this process took many hundreds of years to complete, and even now, those among us who choose at our triangulation to stay, continue to keep and respect those traditions. Am I clear so far?'

Benjamin nodded along with the others. He really wanted to

ask what a triangulation was, but Ms. Ito's tone was not inviting questions.

'So you see, this school is quite something to be treasured. Every one of those poor, mindless fools you see wandering the corridors—the cleaners, I mean, not the pupils; although at times there appears to be little difference—came here from someplace else, but didn't have the knowledge or the knowhow to survive.' Ms. Ito tapped the side of her head hard enough to make a sound. 'So … think. Think about how lucky you are to have this support network. And yes, we are fully aware that some of you have realised you have the ability to do certain unusual things—everyone who comes here does, that's a prerequisite of attendance, it seems—but we have taken steps to reduce their effectiveness until you are ready for proper instruction.'

Ms. Ito paused, slowly looking from one to the other, holding each gaze for several seconds. 'And that is why you are in trouble. Not just for sneaking around, failing to show up to classes, running off with certain … outsiders, and putting your lives into incredible danger, but the presumption that, when it comes to this ability you like to call magic, you know best.'

Ms. Ito began to pace up and down again. They watched her in silence for several minutes, until the tension was so great Benjamin wanted to scream. Finally, Ms. Ito stopped.

'However. I am sure it has been noted by all of you, that myself, Professor Loane, and Captain Roche, and a number of others, are teachers'—finally, a tiny smirk suggested Ms. Ito had a sense of humour after all—'and that makes us less human than pretty much anything kids of your age can imagine. We are also human beings, however, and the human part of me—the non-teacher part—says to all three of you with as much feeling as my black, black, *black* heart can muster … thank you.'

Benjamin started, certain he had misheard.

'What you did was incredibly stupid, but it might have given us a chance to save the school. Some days ago, Grand Lord Bastien, the most powerful among us and the least influenced by the Dark Man's eternal taint, decided to journey to the High Mountains to seek an audience with the Dark Man. He has yet to return. Captain Roche told us what you told him, but I think it would be best if you started from the beginning and told it all again.' She turned and executed an ankle sweep on a metal chair behind her. It flipped over, then landed directly behind Ms. Ito, who sat down with a soft thud.

'I'm waiting,' she said. 'Leave nothing out.'

41

THE CAVERN

Ll three were allowed back to the dorms to sleep. Benjamin couldn't believe how happy he was just to see Gubbledon, and he gave the reanimated horse a big hug when he met them at the door after their dash across the precipice. The school and the dorms, Gubbledon said, had been on indefinite lockdown due to the poor weather. Benjamin didn't know whether Gubbledon knew more or not, but he honoured what he had promised Ms. Ito and said nothing.

The other pupils had already eaten their evening meal, so Gubbledon prepared them something from the kitchens, and the three of them, together with the reanimated horse, sat at a corner table of the common room while a few other groups played or studied around them.

'We were all quite worried,' Gubbledon said. 'The official word was that you'd gone out on an orientation trip and had gotten lost. It must have been terribly dark out on those hills at night. Did you run into any ghouls?'

Wilhelm nodded. 'Millions of them,' he said. 'Miranda gave them one look, though, and they just melted away.'

As Miranda glowered, Gubbledon snorted with amusement. 'If it was anything like that, I'm not surprised.'

After dinner, they retired to their rooms. Benjamin was delighted to change his clothes after so long, even if only into a pair of school pajamas that looked like a less complicated version of his school uniform. As he climbed up onto his bunk and lay down, he suddenly realised how tired he was.

'What do you think they're going to do?' Wilhelm said. After listening to everything Benjamin and the others had told them about what happened in the High Mountains, the teachers had called an emergency meeting. They were at turns thrilled, angered, and upset over the deaths of Edgar and Lawrence, the monstrous Baggers with their captured "fuel," and the huge army approaching the school. Godfrey's apparent defection to the Dark Man's forces disappointed them, while they were fascinated by the mention of Fallenwood, at which point Ms. Ito's eyes went starry and faraway as if she had known the reanimated stump some time long ago.

An assembly had been called for the morning, and Benjamin felt sure he was so tired he would sleep right through it unless someone dragged him awake.

He was just wishing Wilhelm goodnight when a knock came on the door and, without waiting to be asked, Snout entered. Like before, he looked sheepish, face downcast as he stood in the doorway, as though awaiting further instruction.

'I wanted to say … sorry,' he muttered.

'What for?'

'For being part of Godfrey's crew when they tried to sell you to the Dark Man. I was just going along with, you know, the ride.'

From the top bunk, Benjamin couldn't tell what Wilhelm, sitting on the bottom, thought, so he just said, 'We all make mistakes, Snout. It's all good.'

'And one other thing,' Snout continued. 'Godfrey … I don't think he was himself. I think he was … possessed.'

'By the Dark Man?'

'Yeah. Something like that.'

Snout didn't wait for another comment; he nodded reverentially, then went out.

'Do you think he was right?' Benjamin said. He sat up in bed, waiting for Wilhelm to answer, and he was just about to ask the question again, when he heard soft snoring from the lower bunk.

With a sigh, he figured it was about time to catch up on some of his own sleep.

The next morning, before breakfast, everyone in the school assembled in the Great Hall, and it was only when he could see everyone together did Benjamin realise how few of the building's residents were actually members of the school.

Perhaps eighty pupils stood in ordered lines, faced by ten teachers on the stage. Professor Loane stood at a podium in the centre, with Ms. Ito, Captain Roche and Professor Eaves behind him. Six others stood at the rear, while three more teachers patrolled behind the pupils. Off to the side stood Mrs. Martin beside Gubbledon, the sin keeper, and the gatekeeper, as well as a couple of the human staff from the kitchens. At a rate of fifteen graduates per year, Benjamin wondered where they'd all gone, though he wasn't sure he wanted to find out.

'I have some bad news,' Professor Loane said. 'A very bad storm is coming and with it, a grave threat to our school. In the continued absence of the wise Grand Lord Bastien, those of us on the teachers' council have decided the best course of action is for all pupils to be moved out of the school until the threat has passed. Fifteen miles north lies an old study centre affiliated with our school. It is still maintained by a housemaster, Doctor Bernard Cage, who has promised us you will be well looked after.' Professor Loane glanced behind him. 'Professor Eaves has volunteered to lead this expedition, and he will be accompanied by housemaster Gubbledon.'

'It's a trap!' Benjamin hissed to Miranda louder than he had anticipated. A couple of other pupils around them told him to shut up.

'Do you have something to say, Master Forrest?'

Benjamin's cheeks flushed. 'No, sir. I just … sneezed.'

'Good. Professor Eaves, if you please.'

Professor Eaves lumbered up to the podium. 'Today, we will

eat breakfast in the Dining Hall together, and we will leave right after,' he said. 'Everyone is permitted one small bag. Be sure you take only essential items. We will be going on foot, and it is imperative we reach the study centre by nightfall. Is that clear?'

There were mutters of agreement, and a couple of pupils gave military salutes that brought sniggers. From the smiles around him, Benjamin could tell that Loane's proffered threat hadn't been taken seriously. For most pupils, the trip was a day or two off regular classes.

'What are we going to do?' Benjamin said to Wilhelm and Miranda as they filed out of the hall. 'You can't tell me there's no connection with Eaves locking us outside for the ghouls and now volunteering to take the pupils out of the school. He's up to something. Do you think he's working for the Dark Man?'

Wilhelm glared. 'Dusty? No way. He's not bright enough. He probably volunteered because he's scared.'

Benjamin nodded, still unconvinced that Dusty Eaves didn't have it in for him. The old professor, however, didn't come across as the type who might be a spy. Either way, no chance was he getting dragged off to some out-of-the-way study camp if his brother was trapped in one of those machines.

'I'll meet you in the Dining Hall,' he said. 'I left something in the dorm.'

Without giving them a chance to reply, Benjamin ran off, but as soon as he was out of sight, he doubled back toward the teachers' apartments. Outside the entrance, he bumped into Professor Loane, arms laden with books from the library.

'Sir … I want permission to stay behind,' he said. 'I told you my brother might be a prisoner of the Dark Man. I can't leave him.'

Loane sighed. 'You know, Benjamin, what's in that machine might not be your brother at all. You said you didn't see him, you just heard his voice? No one doubts what you heard, but Endinfinium doesn't follow the rules of the world you knew before.'

'People keep telling me that.'

'It's true. What you might have heard could have just been a memory.'

Benjamin shook his head. 'No, my brother is in that machine, I'm sure of it.'

'Let's just say it is your brother. We will do everything we can for him, as we will for the Grand Lord, but our priority is to destroy this army. Each of us has sworn to protect this school and everything it stands for. Without it, there is no hope for people like yourself who arrive in Endinfinium with no knowledge of how to survive. You understand that, don't you?'

Benjamin sighed and nodded. 'But … he's my brother.'

Professor Loane patted Benjamin's shoulder. 'We will do everything we can. Grand Lord Bastien is the wisest and most powerful of all of us, and if we can save him, we will. But this school meant everything to him. He would rather die than see it destroyed, and we will honour that if need be.'

Benjamin lifted a hand to protest, but Professor Loane shook his head. 'No, Benjamin. You will go with Professor Eaves to the study camp where you will be safe. We can handle this, but not with interference.'

'I can help. I'm a summoner!'

He stared at one of Professor Loane's books and concentrated, trying to make it do something—burst into flame or break into pieces. All the cuts and scars on his body began to ache at once, in particular the scratch on the back of his hand, yet nothing happened.

Professor Loane sighed. 'You are the recipient of one of Edgar Caspian's labels,' he said. 'Little more than that. I can feel you have great power, though no understanding of it. You're like a river surging blindly ahead. What do you do when you come up against a sinkhole? How do you cross it?'

Benjamin gave a confused shake of his head.

'We'll talk when this is done,' Professor Loane said. 'We will teach you everything we can, but at the moment, you are as good as blind.'

'Why won't it work?'

'I created that sinkhole. Knowledge is the greatest power, and I have far more than you.' The professor's expression was almost smug. 'Run along now. You'll need a decent breakfast for the journey. And don't even think about trying to sneak off. If need be, we can bind you to a little cart and have it trail along after Professor Eaves like an obedient puppy.'

When Benjamin got to the Dining Hall, he was seething. The back of his hand still ached as he slumped down into a seat between Wilhelm and Miranda.

'I got you extra pineapple,' Wilhelm said, passing over a bowl. 'Looks like they happened upon a tin of fruit somewhere.'

'Thanks.'

'He won't let you stay?'

'How did you…?'

Wilhelm lifted an eyebrow, then turned to Miranda and smirked. 'I didn't, but I do now. You owe me a slice of apple.'

Miranda stabbed a slice of apple and dumped it into Wilhelm's bowl hard enough to splash custard over the tabletop. When he scraped it up with his finger, she punched him on the arm. 'Disgusting boy.' Turning back to Benjamin, she said, 'What are you going to do?'

'I don't care what anyone thinks. The Dark Man has my brother, I'm sure of it. I have to save him somehow. Once we get to this study place, I'm going to run away. Professor Loane has put some kind of blocker on me so I can't use my power, but perhaps if I can get outside, it'll work again.' He gave a hopeless shrug. 'To be honest, I have no idea.'

'Professor Loane has covered the whole school,' Miranda said. 'Nothing I try works, either. If you run off, though, I'm coming with you. So is Wilhelm.'

'What? I've had quite enough of—'

'—boring school life,' Miranda finished for him. 'Don't you want to be a hero?'

'Well, make sure that after I'm torn apart by the Dark Man's wraith-hounds, they build a statue for me out front there.'

'Don't worry, I'll make sure it has three eyes, just so it's accurate.'

Around them, pupils were putting away their breakfast things and heading back to the dormitory to pack their bags. Benjamin, Wilhelm, and Miranda joined the back of the group, waiting to put their plates into the washing-up pile.

'It's a shame we can't get them to help,' Wilhelm said,

pointing at the lurching cleaners as they cleared plates and dishes. 'After all, it's not like any harm can come to them. They're already dead.'

Benjamin looked up. 'Where is it they're supposed to come from?'

'The Haunted Forest.'

Benjamin clapped Wilhelm on the shoulder. 'You're a genius. Come on, let's go.'

'Where?'

'We have to find Snout. He can raise ghouls, can't he? If he can raise ghouls, then surely he can raise cleaners?'

'He said Godfrey taught him how to do it, that all he seems to be able to do is to bring nasty stuff back to life.'

'Perfect. Let's go get him.'

Benjamin talked them through his plan, and even though Miranda and Wilhelm looked unconvinced, they agreed it was worth a try, so they nodded, agreeing to his proposals. As Miranda ran off for the basement levels, Benjamin and Wilhelm went up toward the dormitory, ready to ambush Snout.

In the end, they didn't even need to. Snout came huffing along with his rucksack on his back, shoulders slumped and eyes downcast as if watching his pet dog die on an endless loop reel.

Wilhelm stepped out in front of him. 'Hey! Are you busy?'

'Do I look it?'

'Can I ask a favour?'

'What?'

'We need someone for a special mission.'

Snout frowned. 'What are you talking about?'

'You don't have to go outside; you can stay in here.'

Snout gave a slow nod. 'Sure, whatever.'

He was happy enough to follow Benjamin and Wilhelm down a few flights and into the basements where it was at least warm and dry.

When they reached the basement level with the door that exited out onto the gully heading inland, they stopped.

'We've found Godfrey,' Benjamin said. 'But he's gone a bit crazy. We were just wondering if you could talk some sense into him.'

'What's in it for me?'

'Well, I heard from Professor Loane that calling up a ghoul is worth five thousand cleans in the Locker Room. Captain Roche hasn't told him what you did by the lighthouse, but, um, it's possible that someone else might.'

'What? Who? You told me to do it!' He jabbed a finger at Wilhelm.

'I didn't exactly ask you to call up a ghoul,' Wilhelm said. 'I just said, "Please show them your powers." There's a big difference.'

'You tricked me!'

'But, my dear Snout,' Benjamin said and clapped a hand onto Snout's shoulder, 'don't tell me you didn't enjoy showing what you could do. Especially since everyone always talks about Godfrey. Wasn't it nice to be out from under his shadow?'

Snout shrugged. 'He couldn't have done that.'

Benjamin might have disagreed, but he said nothing. Instead, he waited as Wilhelm said, 'Of course he couldn't. You control the dead. That makes you a … necromancer?'

'Is that good?'

Wilhelm nodded. 'It's the best,' he said.

'So what do you want me to say to Godfrey?'

'It's not really about what we want you to say….'

'What do you mean?'

'Look,' Benjamin said, 'let's just get going and we'll show you.'

Miranda waited for them just outside the door. Pattering rain fell into the gully, and the twisting path looked slippery and treacherous. After taking one look at the route leading ahead, Snout started backing up. For a few minutes' walk it was open to the air above, steep gully sides patched with clumps of green and brown where vegetation fought to cling to crumbling rock. After that, though, the sides closed in until it became a full cave.

'I'm not going in there.'

'Don't worry, it comes out again in the hills surrounding the river. It's a shortcut so we don't get wet.'

'Where exactly is Godfrey?'

'Um, he's in the Haunted Forest.'

'You've got to be joking. That's miles! I'm not going out there. Find someone else for your stupid mission. He probably won't listen to me anyway.'

Snout started to turn back, but Miranda slammed the door shut. 'Oh, sorry about that,' she said. 'Perish this wind! Now the door is locked from the inside. Either we go this way, or you walk back through the rain to the front entrance of the school. And since we're going this way, you'll have to go alone. You know that ghouls come out in the rain, don't you? Have you figured out how to send them back yet?'

Snout glared at her, then gave a short shake of his head. 'Okay, let's get this over with. But I'm definitely telling the teachers on all of you if I get my uniform wet.'

Miranda had found a lantern back in a store cupboard inside the door, but they tried to hold off using its limited supply of oil for as long as possible. The rain was getting heavier, though most of the path was covered by steep overhangs so they were able to keep dry. Snout scowled as a couple of drops fell onto his shirt, but he said nothing.

Soon, the rock walls closed in overhead to form a cave, and even Wilhelm began to get nervous as the rock creaked and groaned like a giant's unsettled stomach. Miranda, though, took Wilhelm's lantern and marched ahead of the group, seemingly unperturbed.

'Don't worry,' she called back, 'Captain Roche took us this way on an orientation trip a month or so ago. It's perfectly safe. In a few minutes we'll come to a huge cavern with a hole in the roof where there'll be some natural light. On the other side of the cavern, the path begins to rise, and it comes out on a hill not far from the river. If we can find something big enough that floats, I'm pretty sure I can get us across to the forest.'

Snout shook his head. 'You're crazy. Why would Godfrey be over there?'

'Perhaps he doesn't know how to get back across. We can help him.'

They continued along the path. From all around came the sound of dripping water, but beneath their feet it was louder, as though a river ran through the rock below.

'What's that sound?' Benjamin asked.

'It's a tributary of the river,' Miranda said. She turned and grinned. 'It goes right under the school. If the ground feels a little soft, don't put your weight on it. You might fall right through.'

Wilhelm jumped, grabbing hold of Snout's arm for support. Snout brushed him away like a stray bogey.

'Come on,' Benjamin said. 'Let's stop slacking off.'

Up ahead, the path began to widen, and Miranda quickened her step, eager to show them the cavern as though it were something of her own creation. As the path opened out, the air filled with a grey light, and Benjamin heard a soft pattering that could have been rain, over a light rustling, like brittle leaves caught in a breeze.

'Is that it?' he said. 'Is that the underwater river?'

'Don't be silly,' Miranda said, glancing back over her shoulder. 'It's below us.'

'Then what's that noise?'

'The rain.'

'No, that shu-sha-shu-sha sound.'

Miranda stopped, the others halting behind her. They had emerged into the cavern, and far above, a circular grey blot gave them a view of clouds so dark it might as well have been night. A light rain fell, making a growing puddle in the centre of the cavern floor, water slowly eating up the dust as it spread out toward their feet.

'I hear two noises as well,' Wilhelm said. 'What's the other one?'

Benjamin looked around. The walls of the cavern were dark and filled with blots of shadow, though they all seemed to be shimmering like something alive. Miranda gulped. Very slowly she lifted the lid off the lantern so that the light pushed the shadows away from the nearest section of wall.

Huge, black haulocks hung from the rock, their canvas bodies shifting like the wings of roosting bats.

'There are loads of them!' Wilhelm hissed.

'Godfrey said they don't like rain,' Snout muttered. 'He said it stuck to their wings and made it hard for them to fly. I don't know how he knew that. I thought he was making it up.' He sighed. 'I can't believe I let you idiots talk me into this.'

'They're sleeping,' Benjamin whispered. 'I think we need to get out of here real quick, before they wake up.'

'Turn off the lantern,' Wilhelm said.

'They don't have eyes,' Miranda answered.

'Yeah, but the heat or the sound of the burner might startle them. If one wakes up, they all will, and we'll likely end up as a late morning snack.'

They took hold of each other's hands in a line, with Miranda going first. Unsure of where the path was, she edged forward, one step at a time, feeling with her feet for the most trodden part of the ground. Inch by inch, they made their way across to the other side.

The cavern's exit announced itself as a deeper section of black. Miranda made to turn the lamp back on, when Wilhelm tugged at Benjamin's wrist and pointed at the ceiling.

'Look!'

A light had appeared above and was slowly descending into the cave along with the whoosh of beating wings—a light held out in front of a human shape backed by billowing black sheets, a light that, as it descended, illuminated the stern, sour face of Professor Eaves.

'Dusty!' Wilhelm gasped, a moment before Benjamin clapped a hand over his mouth. Then he whispered: 'He's half ghoul!'

Like a geriatric prince of darkness, Professor Eaves came to rest in the centre of the cavern, head and shoulders bent forward, one hand outstretched to steady himself while the other held the lantern aloft. As his huge wings folded up behind him, he lifted his head and rose to stand straight, still holding the lantern over his head like a slave making an offering to a god.

As his jacket slipped back up over his wings, disguising them as the slight hunchback the pupils poked fun at when the old man was out of earshot, the lantern flared, filling the room with light. Thousands of haulocks rustled in greeting, while nestled beneath their wings like clusters of kittens, tens of thousands of scatlocks all began to stir as one. The cavern shook with their rustling. Benjamin and his friends all clapped their hands over their ears.

Professor Eaves' face was twisted like a fairytale demon's as he spoke in a screeching, scratchy language that none of them could understand. The haulocks, though, shuddered and rustled, bodies clapping together in nightmarish applause. Then, almost as one, they took to flight, filling the cavern with black, beating wings.

'Where are they going?' Miranda whispered into Benjamin's ear.

'I don't know, but I think we'd better get out of here, too,' he hissed back. He stood up, pulling Wilhelm and Snout up with him. 'Quick, into the tunnel.'

Wilhelm gasped. 'Too late.'

A spotlight illuminated them from behind, casting long shadows ahead into the mouth of the cave. Professor Eaves stood there, part crouched, hands bent into claws and lips curled back in an expression of utter hatred. All around, black shapes fluttered and shifted.

'Spies!' Professor Eaves shrieked, voice still retaining the hideous scraping tone with which he had spoken to the haulocks. 'Take them!'

'Run!' Wilhelm hollered, and they took off into the passage lit up by Professor Eaves' light as the beating of wings rushed in pursuit. Screaming with terror, they blundered into the darkness, the chasing haulocks blocking off the light. While Miranda fumbled with the lantern as they ran, Benjamin was thrown against the passage wall, sharp rocks cutting into his back.

'Help me!' Wilhelm screamed.

Miranda's light came on, illuminating the tunnel. A maelstrom of flickering blackness had engulfed both Wilhelm and Snout, dragging them back down the tunnel.

Benjamin felt the pull of Miranda's magic as one haulock was dashed against the passage wall and another broke into pieces, but it wasn't enough. More filled the space, and black canvas wrapped around Benjamin's ankles, dragging him back.

'No!' he screamed, reaching out, drawing on everything he could. Pain surged, igniting under his skin like a thousand tiny fires. He squeezed his eyes closed, clenched his fists, and pulled tight every muscle in his body.

'Leave … us … *alone!*'

The rock gave a deafening rumble, and Benjamin opened his eyes, only to be blinded by a cloud of dust as the ceiling shattered and huge rocks crashed down to block the way back. Darkness enveloped him, but as the shifting rock fell still, so came a welcome sense of calm.

Benjamin lay still until the groaning tunnel had fallen quiet, then he rolled over and sat up. His body screamed at him, but as the seconds passed, the tingle of pain began to ease. He thought he was going to pass out, when two warm hands pressed against his cheeks. He opened his eyes. Miranda leaned over him, the lamplight making her hair like fire.

'Are you all right?'

'I'm fine. Wilhelm … where is he?'

Miranda shook her head. 'He's not here.'

Benjamin stared into Miranda's face, feeling more hopeless than ever. 'They took him,' he said. 'Professor Eaves and his haulocks. They got Wilhelm.'

42

PLANS

Rain was falling steadily when Miranda dragged Benjamin out of the tunnel onto the hilltop overlooking the river, where they both fell in a heap in the wet grass, gasping for air, breathing in the sweet scent of fresh vegetation.

'Benjamin!' Miranda gasped after recovering her breath, eyes shining with tears. 'What happened to you?'

He touched his face where the pain was worst and felt the sting of a vicious burn from above his ear to below his jaw. Part of his hair seemed to have been singed off, and a cut ran across his cheek, dripping blood.

'The power,' he said. 'I called it. I trapped Wilhelm and Snout in the tunnel with the haulocks and Professor Eaves. It's my fault.'

Miranda slapped him hard across the least injured side of his face, then immediately began to apologise. Benjamin scowled. 'What on Earth was that for?'

'Don't say it was your fault. I'm tired of hearing it. Professor Eaves is one of them. He turned the haulocks on us.'

'We have to rescue Wilhelm.'

'How?' Benjamin slammed his fists into the ground. 'How can we do anything? Everything we try fails … it's useless.'

Miranda squatted beside him. 'Look. What else can we do? We can't just give up.'

Benjamin ignored her, crawling through the grass to where the open hillcrest overlooked the river valley and the dark expanse of the Haunted Forest.

'The Dark Man's army … where is it?'

He squinted. Behind them, the school was a black smudge, perched on the clifftop a couple of miles distant. In front, the river had risen with the rain, sloshing rubbish and junk onto the banks as it dragged its relentless load down to the sea.

The rain was heaviest near the river, a slanting grey sheet that covered the world in a funeral veil.

Miranda frowned. 'It's not there.'

'It must be. There were thousands of ghouls, not to mention the machines. Where have they gone?'

'There's no way they can cross the river in this weather, unless the Dark Man parts it again like he did before.'

Benjamin shook his head. 'I doubt he can. If his power was that strong, he wouldn't need those machines to attack the school. He could just kind of … smash it with magic.'

'Unless it's protected against his magic by other magic.'

'Maybe. But whatever the reason, he's chosen to send actual machines. So where are they?'

'Those … what did you call them? Baggers? They were—'

'Bucket excavators. Mining machines modified with giant chainsaws to chew through the school's outer walls.'

'There's no bridge, and even if there was, there's no bridge that could hold one.'

'And they don't float. So that means—'

Both of them looked at the ground. 'That sound we heard … it wasn't a river, was it?'

Miranda shook her head. 'There's a tributary, but it passes the school to the south, and we shouldn't have been able to hear it. There are tunnels, though. The ground below us is like Swiss cheese, with caverns all over the place.'

'I was wrong,' Benjamin said. 'They're not going to cut through the walls. They're going to cut through the foundations, collapse the school down in on itself.'

Miranda stared out at the river in thoughtful contemplation, while Benjamin looked past her at the swollen, bloated channel of rubbish drifting past like God's own dump. He felt like his hopes and dreams were out there somewhere, slowly floating away among the rest of the rubbish, headed for the edge of the world.

'Where does it all come from?' Benjamin said, letting his thoughts voice themselves. 'It's insane. Look at it. There's more junk in that river than water.'

'No one's been to the source,' Miranda said. 'Not that I know, or that anyone will say. But that rubbish, it's getting in there somehow.'

Benjamin tried to stand, and his left leg screamed at him, so he squatted back down, pulling his trouser leg up for inspection. Another vicious burn ran all the way to his knee.

'If we could collapse it,' Benjamin said, wincing as he gave the burn a tentative prod, 'we could trap them underground. The ghouls and wraith-hounds are already dead, so it's not like we'd be killing anyone. We just need a way to free David and Grand Lord Bastien.'

Miranda shook her head. 'Look at the state of you from just pulling the roof of that tunnel down. There's no way you can collapse those tunnels enough to block the Dark Man's army. It would kill you.'

Benjamin tried to stand and this time he made it shakily to his feet. He closed his eyes, felt for the power, but instead of that destructive rope waiting to be pulled, nothing but a weak thread, like a string about to break, was in its place.

'I think I'm about out of magic,' he said.

Miranda came over to stand beside him. 'We need a plan. Any ideas?'

Benjamin looked at the black smudge of the school, then again at the river. All around, the rain continued to fall, and the river grew wider and wider, slowly overflowing its banks. From where they stood, it arched up around to the north, skirting the line of hills, before disappearing into the haze on the horizon.

'It's so simple,' Benjamin said quietly. 'We divert the flow of the river and flood the tunnels under the school.'

Miranda snorted. 'Oh, right. So simple. Me and you? How on Earth do we do that?'

Benjamin limped a few steps downhill. 'It's a long shot, but it might be our best chance. First of all, we need an entrance to those tunnels a bit closer to the river. Do you know of one?'

Miranda rolled her eyes. 'Just for the record, I think this is a stupid idea that has no chance of working. But since we don't have any other ideas, I'll play along. You want a tunnel, I'm pretty sure we can find one.'

She stood up, reached out for his hand.

'Ready?'

'Ready when you are.'

Miranda nodded. 'Then let's go.'

43

STOLEN BOAT

The wooden runners of the toboggan skimmed across the grass, taking Benjamin's full weight with ease. Miranda part ran, part rode it, jumped off to push it to a faster speed, then jumped back on as it raced down the next hillside, slowly making its way to the bay to the immediate south of the school. The toboggan Miranda had found in the same vehicle store Benjamin had stolen his bicycle from worked partly due to the slick grass and partly due to little touches of Miranda's magic to give it a kick whenever it slowed.

Finally, they found themselves at the top of a steep cliff path leading down to a beach too dangerous for the toboggan, so they started down on foot, Miranda supporting a hobbling Benjamin.

'It's an ocean,' she said again. 'It might be full of crazy hybrid creatures, but it still follows ocean rules, and there are people who still fish in it.'

'Let's hope so,' Benjamin said. 'Though I don't remember ever eating fish for school lunch.'

'I'm not sure it's fish they're trying to catch,' she said.

The cliff path steepened, turning back on itself so sharply that at times it didn't even look like a path at all but a series of ledges all sliding off of each other. Benjamin did his best to walk unaided, using his hands to offset the ache in his burned leg.

The last section of the path was a set of carved steps, and

Benjamin breathed a sigh of relief as Miranda helped him down onto the rocky backshore sloping away toward a layer of sand.

He had never been down here before. The cliffs rose up in a tight ring to either side, almost enclosing the bay except for the opening spanned by the rocking rope bridge he had crossed on his first day. To the right rose the headland where he had emerged from the tunnels with the gatekeeper; to their left was the back wall of the school—an uneven tower of stone and concrete built into the cliff face that rose sheer out of the water.

Waves lapped at the shore. The rain had eased, but they were still soaked through. Benjamin pressed his sleeve against his face to ease the pain of the burn.

'There,' Miranda said. 'A boat.'

It looked like a real boat. Others, too, had been pulled up against the beachhead and secured to mooring poles poking up out of the sand. More bobbed not far out in the bay. The shallows and the bay's narrow entrance kept them safe from the giant cruise-sharks. Who they belonged to was anyone's guess.

'Don't worry,' Miranda said, thinking she could read Benjamin's thoughts as they hurried along the shore. 'We'll bring it back.' She grinned. 'Eventually.'

'Are you sure you weren't cloned from a criminal?' Benjamin asked, then immediately regretted his attempt at a joke when Miranda gave him a sour look.

'I hope not.'

'I'm sorry.'

'Don't worry. Come on.'

The boat she chose was a small motorboat with a little cabin and a large outboard motor resting on the sand. Part of the wood had infused with plastic as though it had reanimated to include pieces of ocean waste, but it was thin and sleek and hopefully fast enough to avoid the cruise-sharks.

'We're going to get in trouble again,' Benjamin muttered as they pushed the boat out into the gentle surf and climbed in. 'They might as well move our dorms into the Locker Room.'

Miranda shrugged. 'Perhaps they'll give us a double cubicle, so at least we can complain about the teachers while we clean.'

Benjamin smiled. The idea had a certain twisted romanticism to it. Then, almost as if becoming suddenly self-aware, he tried to shake off the feeling. *This isn't my home,* he thought. *I'm going back to Basingstoke somehow, and I'm taking David with me.*

'Wow, that must hurt,' Miranda said. Benjamin looked down, thinking she was referring to his burned leg, but she was staring at the back of his hand. The scratch from the reanimated cat statue glowed a bright orange, its light pulsing as if something lived under his skin. 'Is that the same one?'

He nodded. 'It's getting worse. I think I'm falling apart, piece by little piece.'

Miranda gave him a grim smile. 'I'm pretty sure Mrs. Martin will have some duct tape in the admissions office somewhere. Hang in there, we'll fix you up. I'd like to give you a punch for good luck, but you know.'

'Yeah, hold that one. Save it for Wilhelm.'

Miranda laughed. 'His account's already full.'

'Hey!'

A figure ran out of a dark tunnel entrance at the base of the cliff. It looked like a man, but he was bare-chested and wore only the ragged remains of trousers.

'That's my boat!'

'I think that's our cue,' Benjamin said. 'Have you given any thought as to how you're going to start this thing?'

Miranda stared at the outboard motor. 'Push and pull,' she whispered, frowning.

The engine burst into life, and the boat swung around in a tight circle. Benjamin grabbed the side with one hand just before he was tossed out and stretched for the wheel with his other, pulling the boat back into a straight line. As the man shouted at them from the beach, they headed for the break between the cliffs.

A few minutes later they passed under the thin, swinging rope bridge. 'It seems like months ago,' Benjamin said. 'But it was barely a couple of weeks.'

Miranda smiled. 'You've certainly stirred things up.'

'And I don't think I'm done yet.'

Shouting rose up from behind. Several other men had appeared and were jumping into boats to come in pursuit.

'Can you make it go faster?' Benjamin asked.

Miranda wiped sweat and spray from the water off of her brow. 'I'm doing my best!'

The cliffs rose over the top of them, and Benjamin stared up at the rope bridge hanging across the gap that made the entrance to the bay. The memory of that terrifying crossing still brought him out in cold sweats.

They were just passing between the headlands when Miranda gasped and fell back into the bottom of the boat.

'I … can't….'

'You have to!'

'I'm exhausted!'

Three boats came in pursuit, and they would catch up in less than a minute. Benjamin climbed past Miranda to the outboard motor and tried to start it manually, but it was out of oil. In desperation, he stared at the approaching boats, then began searching around the bottom of their own boat for something that might help.

A couple of oars had been fitted into a rack beneath a seat. He pulled the first one out, but when he glanced back at their pursuers, he blinked in surprise. The boats had given up their chase and turned back.

'What happened?'

Miranda climbed up and staggered back to the motor. The water had become choppier, and the current was spinning them around in a circle. Half a mile out to sea, something huge rose and then dived again.

'We left the safety of the bay,' she said.

44

MEMORIES

As the huge cliffs drifted away behind, Benjamin poked an oar into the water and turned them south, while Miranda sat in the back and got the motor started again. Every couple of minutes, though, she had to stop for a break to recover her strength, and each period of motion was shorter than the last as she began to tire.

'We didn't think this through,' Benjamin said.

Miranda aimed a weak punch at his arm. 'What else could we have done? I hoped the motor might have worked on its own.'

'Can you make the water push us? Maybe that's easier.'

Miranda nodded. 'I'll give it a go.'

A few minutes later, they were moving south at the head of a little bow of water Miranda lifted up as they passed. Slow progress, and Benjamin wondered what would happen when they finally encountered the cruise-shark, but at least they were moving. They were far off the coast now, and the cliffs moved slowly past them—a rugged undulation of crags, headlands, valleys, and caves, all fronted by bright yellow sand that looked rather inviting. They passed the small inlet where Benjamin had woken up, where lumps shifting in the sand hid the turtle-cars that had tried to eat him.

'I'll figure out what this place is one day,' he said, more to himself than to Miranda, who was still crouched by the back of the boat, concentrating on her makeshift propulsion system. 'Nothing exists without a reason for existing. It's basic science.'

'Well, if you figure out a way to get this motor to move without oil, I'm all for it,' Miranda gasped. 'Priorities, please.'

Benjamin glanced out at the horizon. From this low to the water, the edge of the world wasn't visible, but it was out there somewhere, just a handful of miles distant.

Another mystery to be solved, he thought. *What lies over the edge? Is it the end of everything?*

The clouds had begun to clear a little, and although the red sun was still lost behind the black bank of storm clouds that covered the school, the yellow sun was making its way toward the horizon. Benjamin was squinting up at it, when something shiny red jumped out of the water and dived in again.

'That thing,' he said, turning to Miranda. 'It's coming closer.'

'What is it?'

'Looks like some kind of snake. The way it jumps like that … it makes me think of sea monsters.'

'We haven't seen the cruise-shark yet. Is that thing big enough to divert the river?'

Benjamin shook his head. 'No way. But it's fast. Way faster than we can go.'

Miranda turned to glare at him. 'Perhaps you'd like to use the oars for a while? I appreciate you acting as lookout, but if we don't get a shift on, we'll drift right over the edge.'

Benjamin grinned, then winced as it stretched the burn on his face. 'Sorry. Why don't you take another break?'

Miranda sat up as Benjamin prodded the oars tentatively over the side, merely keeping them pointed inland.

'What's that?' Miranda said, pointing to the south. 'The water looks all different.'

The grey-blue of the sea had turned white and choppy, as though a million fish all flapped at the surface at once. As they reached the edge of the whitewater area, lumps of rubbish bumped off the side of the boat, spinning them around. Benjamin righted them, and nodded in understanding.

'This is the river estuary,' he said. 'The river must still be high, and of all this junk is the result.' He turned and pointed at the farther cliffs. 'That's where we must have landed.' He frowned. 'That's strange—'

Miranda dived for the back of the boat and leaned over the edge, making a blowing motion with her lips. A swell of water lifted them up, pushing them through the rubbish and toward the river mouth.

'No … time … to … mess about…. It's coming.'

A shiver ran across Benjamin's shoulders, and he looked at the setting yellow sun, where a line of black funnels poked up out of the water, slowly rising as they moved directly toward the immense discharge of rubbish.

'The cruise-shark….'

Miranda had tears in her eyes. 'Benjamin, you're an idiot. This was a stupid idea. We have no chance of outrunning that thing.'

He joined her at the back, prodding the oars into the water, trying to shovel them forward even as lumps of rubbish struck the bow and jerked them back and forth, spinning them around with the current.

'Maybe I can use my power,' he said. 'There must be a way to make it work—'

'Just keep rowing!'

The cruise-shark's massive bow rose out of the water, and an endless stream of rubbish poured like plankton into its open maw. Within a few seconds, it had obscured the sun to become a massive black shadow bearing down on them.

'We got away once,' Miranda gasped. 'It won't … let us … escape … again.'

Benjamin looked up at it. The monster was perfect for his plan. If only he could get it up the river. He closed his eyes, felt for the rope, and it was there again, powerful and strong, ready to do his bidding … and to take its share of his lifeblood as its reward.

He reached out as something broke the surface midway between their boat and the cruise-shark, appearing for just a few seconds, before ducking down under the water.

Benjamin let go of the rope and turned back to the beach.

'Did you see that?' he screamed at Miranda, scanning the coastline. 'I thought so! I looked, but I couldn't see—'

The maw of the cruise-shark was right in front of them, and the monster began to lower itself to scoop them up among its next mouthful of rubbish. As it began to rise again, Miranda screamed and clutched hold of Benjamin, pulling him close.

'If we're about to die, I just wanted to say—' she began, until something else pushed out of the water beneath them and steered them away from the cruise-shark. It surfed down the front of the bow wave, pushing them in amongst the flotilla of rubbish as the cruise-shark's maw crunched down.

'Lawrence!'

The snake-train's head poked up out of the water, and Miranda gave an excited yelp, leaning over the back of the boat, rocking it so much Benjamin fell over.

'Edgar! You're alive!'

When Benjamin climbed up again, Edgar—looking a little bit disheveled, but otherwise the same as Benjamin remembered —opened up a side door and beckoned for them to jump down onto Lawrence's nose and climb in. A few daring seconds later, they were sitting inside Lawrence's locomotive head, soaking wet but strapped into comfortable reclining chairs with a view through the front and side windows.

'You died!' Miranda exclaimed, as soon as she got her breath back. 'Both of you.'

'I did nothing of the sort,' Edgar said. 'I simply gave you the best chance I could to make it back to Lawrence, then I made a tactical retreat.'

'Where?'

'I climbed a tree,' he said, lifting an eyebrow as if letting them in on one of the great secrets of mankind. 'I climbed the biggest one I could reach, then cast a little spell to keep the wraith-hounds from finding me. Of course, you were long gone, and it was a long journey back from the High Mountains. I managed to hitch a rather secret ride on a ghoul train, though.'

'And what about Lawrence? Godfrey blew him up.'

'He reanimated.'

Benjamin stared. 'So quickly? We thought he was dead.'

'It took a while to track down the rest of him, and he's still a little sore, but he'll live. Aren't you learning yet? Things don't live or die here in the same ways they do where you're from.'

'I guess not.'

Edgar's expression turned grave. 'It doesn't mean they can't, though. And I'd suggest that from the size of the army I sneaked along behind, the Dark Man has a few ways to make people proper dead. So now, how about you tell me what you've been up to since we last met? And why on Earth were you floating around out there?'

Benjamin told Edgar their plan, and Edgar gave a thoughtful nod.

'Lawrence can do a far better job of leading that cruise-shark than you could have done.' He shouted some instructions to Lawrence, and the snake-train slowed right down, the sloshing water calmingagainst the windows. From their vantage point, it was impossible to see if the cruise-shark was still behind them, but Lawrence suddenly lifted his head and gave a high-pitched whistle.

'He's taunting it,' Edgar said. 'Don't ask me what he's saying, but I've been around long enough to understand how many of these creatures think.'

Lawrence bolted forward, throwing them all back in their seats, and the sea rushed past the windows. Then they were under the surface, encased in an aquamarine tank.

'Most of the rubbish floats,' Edgar said. 'We need to get under it so Lawrence doesn't get slowed down.'

'Where does it all come from?' Benjamin asked. 'It's like the most polluted river of all time, times a hundred. Whoever's dumping all this must be so wasteful. I bet even the rivers in India aren't this bad!'

Edgar smiled. 'That's a mystery for you to solve another day, Master Forrest. For now, we have more pressing engagements.'

Lawrence broke the surface and let out another high-pitched whistle. This time, he turned back toward the open ocean and through the front of the train, they saw the cruise-shark lumbering in pursuit.

Lawrence picked up speed as he headed up the river estuary,

ducking under the water for a while, then resurfacing, checking that the cruise-shark was following, then swimming through the surface rubbish for a while, making sure the sea monster could follow. The ride through the water, as Lawrence swung his mighty body back and forth to propel them, was far more comfortable than the journey over land, and Benjamin actually enjoyed the journey upriver. He closed his eyes and thought of home, trying to remember what had happened to bring him here, but the memory of that day in the forest was getting vaguer and vaguer…

David's voice, calling out to him, something about needing to run—

Benjamin sits up. Pain races up his leg from his ankle, caught on a protruding root by the side of the potholed forest road. He can't run any farther, he knows it. Whatever was behind him will catch up now. The race is over.

He has come out of the forest not far from a tight corner. A rumbling comes from through the trees, and lights flicker against the undergrowth.

A truck.

A truck is coming.

'Bennie!'

His brother's voice is right behind him. Benjamin turns but instead is confronted by something grey-and-orange that glows as it appears through the trees. It has hold of his brother and is dragging him toward the road. From farther back among the trees, other orange lights flicker like candles.

Like eyes.

The creature is an abomination of metal and flesh, crouched like a wildcat waiting to spring, but with human arms protruding from a metallic body. A black hood doesn't quite cover a bare human skull.

'No! Leave Bennie alone!'

It is now that he realises it is his brother who has hold of the creature, his podgy, under-exercised arms wrapped around its waist as he tries to pull it back.

'Run, Bennie!'

And then something happens. A light flashes, and the creature wails and falls away, hands like metal straws clutching at its face. David crawls toward him as others burst from the trees.

'They want you, Bennie. I can't let them have you.'

'David….?'

There is a tearing like nothing Benjamin has ever heard, as though the fabric of the world is parting.

'Bennie! I'm sorry!'

Lights illuminate them as a horn blasts. Benjamin is tumbling into the dark, and he looks up to see his brother's face looking down on him, as though he has fallen into a deep, dark well. Then there is a thump, the squeal of tires, and a scream that can only have come from his brother—

'Benjamin?'

Miranda stared at him. 'Are you all right? You were moaning in your sleep.'

He shook off the dream like an unwanted coat and nodded. 'I think so. I just had a … strange dream. About my brother, and about how I came here.'

'Everyone's journey is different,' Edgar said. 'Some remember well. Others never do.'

'He protected me from ghouls. They were after me for some reason, but he knew about them. Then there was a truck and … I think … part of him … came with me.'

Edgar nodded. 'The spirit disassociated from the body is a powerful thing,' he said. 'It's almost like atomic energy. That could be why the Dark Man is using him.'

'And Grand Lord Bastien?'

Edgar looked from one to the other. 'Has no one ever told you?'

'Told us what?'

Edgar rolled his eyes, sighed, then nodded. 'Of course. The Grand Lord left for the High Mountains before you arrived. No one ever liked to talk about it. The elephant in the room and all that.'

'What are you talking about?'

'The Grand Lord isn't … human.'

255

45

PARTING

'The official name we had for him, back in my days at the school, was "disassociated soul,"' Edgar said. 'You might prefer to simply call him a ghost.'

'Like, you can see through him?'

Edgar gave them a pained look. 'Not … exactly. It's more complicated than that.'

Benjamin wanted to ask another of the many questions queuing up in his mind when Lawrence suddenly dipped under the water, headed straight for the bottom of the river. Huge headlights blinked on to illuminate a drifting mess of junk, from TVs to bicycles and the tatty, water-ruined remains of old books and magazines, jerking and tossing in the current like dying fish.

'Hang on,' Edgar said. 'Lawrence? Are you all right?'

'Seek deep place,' Lawrence boomed.

Edgar frowned, then nodded. 'Most of the river is too shallow for the cruise-shark to follow,' he said. 'Lawrence is looking for the deepest part of the channel.'

The snake-train's headlights revealed an otherworldly landscape. In places, whole buildings poked out of the riverbed; in others, jumbles of half-crushed cars had become ecosystems for thousands of darting fish. Occasionally, the riverbed even resembled the kind of regular river Benjamin had seen on television nature programs—great sweeps of seaweed covering silt beds, with fish of all shapes and sizes darting among the swaying blue-green arms.

Satisfied, Lawrence began to head for the surface. He twisted as he broke, the cruise-shark lumbering along close behind, the river churning around it as it scooped up hundreds of tons of water up into its maw.

As Lawrence splashed back down into the water, Benjamin let out a cry and pointed out through the side window.

'There!' he shouted. 'Right there! That's where the tunnels are!'

Lawrence executed a sharp dive that left them all gasping against their straining seatbelts. He made a tight underwater loop, then resurfaced so close to the cruise-shark's maw that they were covered by its shadow.

'He's a lot braver than I remember,' Benjamin gasped.

Edgar, pale-faced and seemingly on the verge of throwing up, gave a weak shrug. 'They don't always reanimate quite the same way,' he said. 'I think he's enjoying taunting it. A week ago, he wouldn't have gotten into the same river.'

Lawrence cut to the right, headed straight toward the riverbank. Though they couldn't see the cruise-shark behind them, great waves crashed up the slope down to the riverside, leaving a tide line of rubbish stretching back from the bank.

Miranda's hand closed over Benjamin's, squeezing hard enough to make him wince. 'Here we go,' she said. 'Let's hope this works.'

Lawrence raced up through the shallows, then burst out of the water and onto the riverbank before cutting back and spinning around, letting out another high-pitched whistle. Through the front windows they saw the cruise-shark rushing at the shore, maw snapping. It was almost on them when it abruptly veered left, its prow embedding in the silt clinging to the riverbank. A sudden rush of water sloshed over them, lumps of rusty junk bouncing off of Lawrence's side.

With a satisfied hoot, the snake-train moved farther up the hillside, then turned to reveal the results through the windows. The cruise-shark listed in the shallows, its maw snapping over nothing as water surged around it, looking for a way through.

Already the water was carving a channel out of the hillside's soft topsoil, and a river of junk went pouring into the nearest cave entrance.

'That's some plan you had there,' Edgar said. 'Now what?'

'We free my brother and the Grand Lord,' he said.

'How?' Edgar asked.

Benjamin shrugged and grinned. 'I haven't figured that out yet, but I will. Something has finally gone the way I wanted it to.' He pointed out the window at the increasing flood of diverted water. 'That's got to be a good sign, right?'

Lawrence took them up to the highest of the nearby hills so they could see the school. It appeared nothing had changed. The school perched like an old bird on the edge of the clifftop, the grass on the hills around it glistening with fresh rainfall. When Lawrence cut his engines, a faint sound was audible over the rushing water: the hum of machinery.

'It's getting louder,' Benjamin said as they climbed out of the snake-train.

'It's them,' Miranda said. 'The Dark Man's army. They're coming up to the surface.'

Benjamin opened his mouth to reply, though there was nothing he could say. A half-mile ahead, the ground subsided in a sudden rush, then a chainsaw blade as wide as a house appeared out of the ground to fill the air with a buzzing noise so loud Benjamin felt his skull reverberating.

From all around it came a rushing, howling army of ghouls and wraith-hounds.

'My word,' Edgar gasped, steadying himself against Lawrence's metallic hide. 'We have no chance.'

The monstrous Bagger, flexing and twisting like nothing metal should, squeezed out of the hole and crunched down onto the ground. Around it, earth began to crumble, collapsing the caves under its immense weight. The chainsaw blade lifted up to the sky, and the Bagger's engines roared in challenge, then it moved off toward the school's outer wall, the massive caterpillar treads leaving muddy rents in the ground big enough to bury a car.

At the vast machine's rear, a silvery bubble gleamed in the

sunlight.

'David—'

Benjamin began to move forward, but Edgar put a hand out to stop him. 'No. That's the Grand Lord.'

'How do you know?'

Edgar gave a grim smile. 'Something else you'll learn when you can control it. You can feel others, and in time, you learn how their respective personalities are reflected in their power. How do you think I knew where to find you?'

Benjamin stuck out a hand. 'I owe you big time, Edgar. I won't forget. Good luck.' When Lawrence gave a low growl, Benjamin smiled and patted the side of the snake-train. 'And you, too, Lawrence.'

'You're not coming with us?' Miranda said, turning to glare at Edgar.

Benjamin smiled. 'You don't need magic to know that,' he said.

'He's right,' Edgar said. 'I need to go to defend the walls. The more of us there are, the more of a chance we have. I hope to see you again.'

Miranda turned to stare at Benjamin. 'And where do you think you're going?'

'I have to find my brother.'

Miranda marched past him. 'Let's get moving, then,' she said. 'David isn't going to rescue himself.'

'You can't come with me! It's too dangerous.'

'Yeah, and look how well you've done at dealing with danger. You'd be in pieces if it wasn't for me bailing you out all the time.'

Benjamin opened his mouth to answer, but nothing came out. He looked at Edgar for support, but the wizard just shrugged. Even Lawrence gave a low grunt that could have been laughter.

'I guess you're coming with me, then,' Benjamin said, though Miranda had already started off down the hill. Edgar gave him a thumbs-up, then climbed back into Lawrence.

'Good luck!' he shouted from the doorway as the snake-train rushed off in the direction of the distant school, and the army slowly gathering outside its walls.

T he river was a rushing, roaring torrent as it gushed down into the tunnels. Benjamin watched a couple of TVs and a battered photocopier float past, bumping against each other, then dropping over the edge. Miranda pointed.

'There,' she said. 'See that wardrobe? That's our ride.'

'You've got to be kidding me,' Benjamin said. 'This isn't Disneyland.'

'Got a better idea?'

Benjamin shook his head. 'Hold my hand. On the count of three.'

A surge of churning water rushed the old wardrobe toward them—

'Three!'

—and they leapt inside as it dropped over the edge. Benjamin screamed as the ground fell out from under them and they went into freefall through a blurring, scattered darkness. Miranda still clutched his hand, and with the other he found an old tie rack rail on the wardrobe's side. As they tumbled, he couldn't think of what to say or do, other than to wait it out and hope they landed in one piece.

Just when Benjamin thought they were going fast enough to explode on impact, the waterfall flattened out, and they raced through tunnels and caves on a torrent of water, spinning around sharp corners and bumping over rocky protrusions. The wardrobe cracked and splintered, and when they finally came to a rest in a frothing pool, it broke apart, pieces floating away like the tired customers of an over-ambitious fairground ride.

Benjamin kicked to the poolside and pulled Miranda out onto a ledge. Water gushed all around them, bringing with it heaps of junk quickly piling up at the bottom of the pool, pushing deeper the level of the water.

'Where's the light coming from?'

It took Benjamin a moment to understand the absurdity of being able to see clearly so far underground, when he heard engines roaring over the rushing water.

'It's them. They're nearby.'

They followed a section of tunnel that had a glowing light at its far end. When the tunnel opened out onto a ledge overlooking a vast cavern, they stopped and stared.

The tunnel was enormous, big enough for an entire city centre to nestle quietly without even touching the walls, and in the middle of it sat the Bagger, the water level already above its treads, while an army of ghouls and other monstrosities floundered in its depths. There were so many of them, the glow from their eyes turn the cavern an eerie, upside-down orange-grey star field, with the glowing white egg at the Bagger's rear the moon.

'David!' Benjamin hissed. He turned to Miranda. 'He's there. I have to help him.'

Miranda pointed at the rear wall of the cavern. 'It looks unstable. If I knock part of it down, it might create a diversion.'

'No, it's too dangerous. Stay here and keep watch for me. I'll go alone.'

Miranda turned to look at him, and her eyes glazed over as she lifted a hand to touch the side of his face in a tender gesture Benjamin had never seen from her.

'I wish I had a brother like you.'

Before he could reply, Miranda leapt off the ledge, diving like a falling arrow into the churning black water.

'No…!'

She broke the surface, water parting around her as she spread her arms, then the ghouls rushed forward into the gap, stumbling after her as she raced for the darkness at the cavern's rear. In an instant, that side of the Bagger was cleared, then the water gushed back in, catching many of the ghouls in the ensuing maelstrom.

Benjamin caught a brief glimpse of Miranda diving into one of the dark caves leading out of the cavern, and then the roof partially collapsed, crushing the ghouls underneath.

No way could he get to Miranda, but her sacrifice had cleared the way for him to reach the Bagger. Water was already filling the floor, but the nearest ghouls were at the front of the massive machine. He gritted his teeth, holding back tears. He couldn't let her sacrifice be for nothing. He closed his eyes and jumped.

The freezing water was strangely comforting on his burns, and already it was deep enough for his feet to barely caress the cavern floor before he bobbed up to the surface right beside the caterpillar treads of the machine. Gasping, he pulled himself up onto a mudguard the size of a table, then began the climb through the metal struts and components in the direction of the glowing orb overhead.

The climb sapped the last of his strength, but determination and sheer willpower forced him on. The orb was almost within his reach, when a ghoul stepped out from among the girders and swung a metal arm in his direction. Benjamin shrank back, ducking out of its way and slipping past, then kicking it in the back as it tried to turn in the cramped space. With a howl, it tumbled down into the water.

Nearly breathless, he hauled himself up one more girder and stopped.

The orb lay before him, its upper side clear, offering a view of the person lying inside.

'David….'

His brother looked so peaceful, yet so lost. His eyes were closed, hands against his sides, and even his hair looked neat. His body was wrapped in a colourless white swirl that seemed a part of the silver ball.

'You're using him for power, aren't you?' Benjamin muttered, clenching his fists over the metal, wishing he could rip the machine apart with his bare hands. 'When there's nothing left, you'll just throw him away.'

Almost as if reading his thoughts, something dark and heavy seemed to press over Benjamin's eyes. He shook his head to clear his vision, but it was right there, all around him, trying to gain purchase.

He looked at the scratch on his hand glowing a deep, threatening orange.

He feels me. He knows I'm here, and he's coming for me.

The glowing orb fit neatly into a space designed for it like an ornamental plate on a stand, but when Benjamin touched it, its surface felt rubbery and soft.

When he put his right hand on it, nothing happened, but when he touched it with his left, it began to tingle and vibrate. David's eyes popped open with a look of horror.

Bennie?

'David!'

The silver oval exploded in a blast of blinding light, and Benjamin covered his eyes, shrinking back. A deafening cacophony of squeals and shrieks rose up over everything, and he wanted to curl up into nothing and disappear, to leave it all behind.

Then something tugged on his trousers.

'Bennie?'

He opened his eyes. David—or at least something that should have been David—crouched before him, pale and ephemeral, his outline shifting like a cloud moving in and out of shape. He wasn't a human, though neither was he a ghost. He was something in between.

'David? Is that you?'

'Bennie....' It sounded like his brother, right down to that soft, kiddy whine that always made David sound younger than he really was. His eyes pleaded for Benjamin to understand.

'Bennie ... he's coming.'

Looking up wasn't necessary; Benjamin could feel him. Whether the Dark Man had a physical form like his little brother

263

or was something else entirely, it didn't matter. He was coming for the both of them.

'We have to run,' Benjamin said. 'Can you run, David?'

His little brother gave a slow, dopey nod.

'Then run,' he said.

47

SHOWDOWN

E ven though David's hand kept slipping through Benjamin's fingers, David's ephemeral glow lit the way as they raced through the tunnels leading away from the great cavern. As they neared the school, the passages became smoother, with signs of primitive human handiwork, and then bare rock became stonework and bricks, and without warning, Benjamin found himself back in the school's lower tunnels.

'He's getting closer,' David whined, and a flush of heat ran across Benjamin's back.

'Where?'

'Behind us. In front. All over.'

They emerged in a corridor that faced a wide set of steps, and Benjamin dragged David up to a door at the top then pushed through.

He stopped, marveling at a quite different type of cavern.

The Great Hall.

Across the floor from him stood the door he had entered through with Miranda on his first day in Endinfinium. That way led outside, so he half-pulled, half-carried David with him, down through the rows of chairs.

'Come on,' he said. 'We have to hurry—'

Two dozen doors opened and slammed at once. Lights

flickered on in the alcoves, and the Great Hall filled with a silvery moonlight. Beside him, David stopped.

'Child.'

The voice drifted over from the other end of the hall, from a figure in black standing on the stage. Benjamin felt his feet moving against his will, gliding across the smooth floors to come to a stop in front of the stage, David still held tightly to his side.

'Give him. Join me.'

Now, the voice seemed to come from everywhere, a great detached resonance that filled the hall, grating like a speaker system feeding back. The Dark Man's arms rose, spindly white fingers appearing, pointing at Benjamin and David.

'Join. Unite.'

Benjamin pulled David in front of him. 'No! Get away from us!'

His feet began to slide again, and this time he reached out for his power, skin burning as it repelled the Dark Man's magic. The figure on the stage started, appearing surprised.

'We don't belong to you!'

'Is that so?' incanted the booming, omnipresent voice. 'Shall we reveal that truth for you?'

In his arms, David whimpered. Benjamin looked down at the ephemeral, glowing form of his brother, tears springing to his eyes. He felt like he was trying to hold on to something that was rightfully dead, that should rightfully be let go.

'He's not yours,' Benjamin said again through gritted teeth, preparing to reach for his power. He glared at the Dark Man, ready to throw everything at this threat, to repel it from his brother and from the school, even if it meant his own death.

The Dark Man lifted his hands, threw back his hood, and Benjamin staggered. Pearl white hair that fell to shoulders framed an ancient visage. Heartless grey eyes stared out of an eerily familiar face.

'You know me.'

'No!'

Benjamin toppled to the ground, pulling David with him. Clutching the shifting, unstable shape of his brother, he tried to look at the Dark Man's face, but he couldn't.

There's nothing I can do. He will destroy me, and then he will destroy everything. All of Endinfinium will end, and it's my fault for bringing him here.

No.

The second voice was unfamiliar. Benjamin squeezed his eyes shut, holding his brother tight.

David. You can send him back. Destroy him here, and restore him to his own world. He is power. He is strength. Use him. Banish the Dark Man.

Benjamin opened his eyes. Above him, the Dark Man was a blur on the stage, but now he appeared to be growing in size, rising over them like a terrible, demonic cloud. Benjamin felt for his brother, felt his brother's touch, and suddenly understood.

Like Wilhelm, David was a weaver. And without a physical form, he was pure energy, pure power.

Pure strength.

'Leave … here,' Benjamin gasped, drawing on everything he felt inside him and projecting it outward in one immense, unending stream.

The Great Hall filled with light, and the screams of a million souls dying and those yet to die howled at him, while Benjamin's grip on consciousness began to fade. In his arms, he felt his brother shrinking, fading away to nothing.

'I love you, Bennie,' a quiet voice whispered, then everything went black.

'Benjamin. Hear me, and awaken.'

The voice was soft and soothing—the sound of a thousand fathers—and Benjamin opened his eyes. At first, all he saw was blackness, before he realised he was looking at a great circle of blackened wood surrounding him.

He was still in the Great Hall of Endinfinium, but now the stage was empty, the Dark Man gone. His arms were also empty, his brother gone, too.

'Well done, Benjamin Forrest,' came a warm, soothing voice from behind. He sat up, less stiff than what he had become accustomed to, and turned to see a tall, stately man dressed in a long robe. He could have been a storybook wizard, were it not for the translucency of his face, a shimmering that blurred his features and a way of speaking that reminded Benjamin both of a dream world and water bubbling over rocks.

'Grand Lord Bastien,' he said.

'I'm pleased to make your acquaintance at last, Master Forrest. I thank you from the bottom of my soul for what you've done today. For your strength and your resilience, and the sacrifices you've made.'

'Is the battle over?'

Grand Lord Bastien nodded. 'Nearly. The Dark Man's forces are in retreat. When you broke your brother free, you took the Dark Man's focus away from me and allowed the other teachers to break me out. Without their power source, his machines were easy to overrun … thanks, too, to a number of friends you appear to have made.'

'What happened to my brother?'

'He is gone. You used all of him to banish the Dark Man back to the High Mountains. David no longer exists in this place, although you took a little of his soul for yourself.'

Benjamin didn't need to ask what the Grand Lord meant. He lifted up his trouser leg. The burn on his left calf muscle was already beginning to heal. The burns on his face were also healing, the skin prickling as it knitted itself back together.

'Back in England … did I save him?'

'In time, you'll find out, I'm sure.' Grand Lord Bastien smiled. 'Now, I think it's time to reunite you with your friends.'

48

ROUT

With each step he took, Benjamin felt stronger and more agile, as if David's residual power was slowly working its way through him. By the time they had reached the battlements overlooking the field, he had a spring in his step he didn't think he'd ever felt before. Grand Lord Bastien had gone to help the other teachers who stood farther along the battlements—Captain Roche and Professor Loane, beyond them Ms. Ito ... and Professor Eaves. Benjamin lifted a hand to point and call out Dusty as a traitor, when the professor lifted his own hands and brought them down over his head, summoning a swarm of haulocks over the battlements, sweeping up floundering ghouls in their wings and carrying them away toward the distant river. As Benjamin stared in disbelief, Wilhelm came running along the battlements toward him.

'What are you doing here? I thought you were captured.'

Wilhelm shrugged. 'Professor Eaves was asking about you. He thought we were trapped down there, so he got the haulocks to come after us. He's part haulock, apparently. He used them to ferry the rest of the pupils to safety at that study camp.'

Benjamin gave Wilhelm a hug, then, as he pulled away, he narrowed his eyes. 'Do you really believe that?'

Wilhelm grinned. 'Not for a second. I think he got busted

trying to drop us into the sea or something, and changed his plans. Nothing we can do about it right now, but I'll be keeping it on file for future investigation. Where's Miranda?'

'She gave herself up for me. I'm afraid she died.'

Wilhelm shook his head. 'No she didn't.'

'What do you mean? I saw the cavern collapse down on her.'

'Yeah, but she's still alive. I can feel her.'

'What, like Edgar said?'

'Edgar? He's alive?'

Benjamin grinned. 'Seems like it's pretty hard to die here. That must be something the Dark Man was trying to rectify, but I don't think we have to worry about him for a while.'

'Come on, let's go find Miranda. If she's trapped in the caves, we need to get her out quickly before they get flooded any further.'

'How can we get to her?'

'Don't worry, I have an idea. But we need to take a bit of a detour. How tired are you? We might need to run.'

Benjamin shook his head. 'I think I might be able to help there. I have a friend I can ask.'

Half an hour later, they were clutching each other atop Moto's back as the reanimated motorbike sped them quickly toward the ruins of Fallenwood. While Moto still refused to pick sides, Benjamin convinced him that a simple ride out into the countryside could be considered a neutral action, and after some deliberation, the motorbike deemed the conclusion satisfactory.

In the entrance to the old observatory, they were met by Fallenwood himself, and after a few minutes of discussion confirmed he could indeed be of help. Another half an hour later, Moto sped along toward the entrance to the caves, a massive wheel of sticks rolling along behind him. Moto let them off on top of a rise overlooking the river, bade them good luck, then headed back to the school. From where they stood, the cruise-shark was visible lying on its side, half-in and half-out of the water.

'First thing we have to do is restore the river's original course,' Wilhelm said, and the Fallenwoodsmen assembled into a giant wedge, pressed in beneath the toppled cruise-shark, and slowly lifted it up. The monstrous creature snapped and wriggled, but as soon as the water began to flow back underneath it, the ground became slick enough for it to slide back into the river. With a tremendous roar, the diverted river righted itself, and took the cruise-shark away in the sudden torrent. As the current dragged it into deeper waters, it made a lazy arc, then, with a gurgle of displaced water, it dived out of sight.

'The rock under the school is like a giant sponge,' Wilhelm said, 'so the water will run away to the sea eventually. What we have to deal with are the collapsed tunnels.'

The Fallenwoodsmen immediately knitted together into a complex system of scaffolds, rigging, and pulley equipment. Benjamin stared in amazement as they squeezed into the nearest cave entrance to engineer a wooden stairway through the rubbish. Wilhelm led the way as it descended into the depths of the tunnels, knitting in front of them and breaking up behind them piece by piece as the rubbish fell back into place.

They were some way underground when Wilhelm stopped. 'She's near here,' he said and, grabbing Benjamin's arm, screamed, 'Miranda!'

Benjamin joined in, and for a few seconds, they hollered into space. Then, after falling silent, they heard a faint 'Over here!' above the dripping of water and the creaking of thousands of sticks.

She had managed to climb up on to a ledge to avoid the torrent, but the cavern in which the second Bagger was trapped had been packed tight with rubbish from the diverted river, and the tunnels above had become impassible. As the Fallenwoodsmen created a wooden tunnel through the rubbish, Miranda hugged Benjamin and Wilhelm tightly.

None were sure what to say. Benjamin felt ashamed for giving up on her, while Miranda just gave them both a big hug, before patting the nearest latticework of interwoven twigs as if to thank Fallenwood, as well.

Slowly but surely, the Fallenwoodsmen retraced their steps to the ground above, and Miranda looked delighted to see the twin suns again. Even Benjamin felt happy to be outside with both of his shadows for company. After the Fallenwoodsmen had knitted themselves into a rather beautiful wicker carriage, they all headed back to the school.

The battle was as good as over. The remaining ghouls and wraith-hounds had dissolved back into the ground, and the huge Bagger stood silent, its massive chainsaw towering as high as the school walls.

As they bid goodbye to the Fallenwoodsmen, Captain Roche met them out on the field. 'I won't ask what that was about,' he muttered, giving a suspicious glance to the circle of twigs now rolling away toward the forest. 'I'm pleased to see the three of you are okay, and thanks to you the school has been saved. However…'

'However?' Wilhelm echoed.

'You disobeyed a direct order to go with Professor Eaves. You kidnapped another boy, and you entered a restricted area without permission. You stole a boat from the Beach Folk, after, of course, stealing a toboggan from the school garages. On multiple occasions you used … certain skills … without permission—'

Benjamin put up a hand. 'Is there anything we didn't do?'

Captain Roche glared at him. 'You didn't do as you were told.'

'And our punishment?'

'Each rule you broke carries a minimum of one thousand cleans. It has been put to the teachers' union to allow you to take meals in the Locker Room and sleep there in a makeshift dormitory with the sin keeper to keep watch over you.'

Wilhelm shook his head. 'But we saved the school!'

'So?'

'So, doesn't that mean we can get a bit of leniency?'

Captain Roche smiled a grin wider than any of their faces. 'Oh, you have,' he said. 'For each broken rule, you've been allocated a thousand cleans among you. It would usually be a thousand cleans each.'

And with a sigh that suggested he was tired of dealing with them, Captain Roche turned and headed back to the school, leaving them standing alone on the grass with the school's towering walls in front of them, and the beaming face of the yellow sun as it arced its way slowly across the sky.

49

MEETING

L ife in and around the school had settled back to normal. At least, as normal as life could be in a school where everything—right down to the pots and pans, and the sinks in the bathroom, trying to vibrate off the walls—was constantly trying to come alive.

Godfrey's continued absence remained a mystery. After rushing off to join the Dark Man's army with the proclamation that he was a great summoner, he had vanished. The teachers encouraged the rumour that he had been expelled, but no one really believed it; after all, expulsion meant little when no other schools existed. They just weren't ready to believe he had turned to the Dark Man.

In fact, most of the other pupils had no idea about anything. As promised, Professor Eaves had shipped them all off to the study camp, and by the time they had returned, the second huge Bagger had reanimated itself enough to trundle off the edge of the nearest cliff, fall into the sea, and drift toward the edge of the world, no doubt with a cruise-shark in hot pursuit.

Within weeks, the pupils continued the drudgery of classes with expressions no more or less glum than those of a regular, real-world school.

It was after a particularly boring lesson on wildflower

ecosystems that Gubbledon Longface handed Benjamin a message.

Dear Benjamin, it read. *Could you do me the honour of meeting with me in my private apartments in the teachers' tower? Yours with gratitude, Grand Lord Sebastien Aren.*

Since the day of the battle, Benjamin had neither seen nor heard anything of the Grand Lord, and he had begun to wonder if he hadn't disappeared like David had. When he reached the teachers' tower and knocked on the door, however, it swung open to reveal the Grand Lord himself, his pale, ephemeral face wrapped in long ropes and almost hidden by a hood. He leaned on a long, metal pole hooked at the end like a shepherd's crook, and his clothes rippled and shook as if his trapped body were trying to escape.

'Welcome, Benjamin,' the Grand Lord said. 'Come in. Take a seat. We never did have that promised orientation.'

The room was a hive of organised clutter; every wall was covered by shelves loaded with all manner of unusual items—in between rows of books sat the skeleton of a birdlike creature seemingly with four wings, the disembodied head of a stuffed toy bear, a featureless block of something smooth and green, and a dozen other things Benjamin imagined had been picked out of the river or the sea, but why remained a mystery.

'I imagine you have more questions than ever.' The Grand Lord went to the window and pulled back a curtain to reveal a twilight view of the hills, with the river's dark flow beyond. Backing down onto it was the grey expanse of the Haunted Forest.

Benjamin shrugged. 'I guess that, over time, I've answered many of them for myself.'

The Grand Lord nodded. 'That's good.'

'But not all.'

'Of course not. Endinfinium is an unusual place,' the Grand Lord mused. 'A world at the confluence of other worlds; a world that is constantly building itself from what other worlds give away; a world that is timeless yet finite.' He shrugged. 'A world where nothing truly dies.' He turned back suddenly, his face

275

pulsing with a white glow. 'Such a place many might call Heaven, wouldn't they?'

Benjamin shrugged again. 'More like Hell. Full of rubbish and ghouls. It's not really what people want from eternity, is it?'

Again the Grand Lord nodded. 'A good job that it's neither. It is only what it is. Tell me, Benjamin, are you happy here?'

A few weeks ago, Benjamin would have given an automatic, vehement shake of his head. Now he just frowned. 'I guess it is what it is.'

The Grand Lord smiled. 'That's a good answer. But … never stop looking for a way back. One day you might find one. Do you ever wonder what's over the edge of the world, or what's beyond the High Mountains where the Dark Man lives?'

'Every day.'

'That's good. Never stop. Too many have. Acceptance is not a way to survive in this place, but the only way to truly die. There might not be a way back to whatever place you call home, but giving up on the chance that there is … you might as well just get into a boat and sail over the edge of the world.'

'And then I might find out what's there.'

The Grand Lord laughed, a strange sound, like five people laughing all at once, though slightly out of time with each other.

'And now, Benjamin, I wanted to offer you one of the few things I can. A little piece of closure.'

He turned, and hands covered with black gloves took an ancient telephone off of a shelf and placed it onto a table between them. The phone had no wires and half of the numbers in the dial had faded into nothing.

'It's a Western Electric 102 model, popular in the 1920s and '30s,' the Grand Lord said. 'I found it one day, lying in the shallows of the river. In a former life I was an antiques dealer, you know. I do so love old telephones.'

He slipped off a glove, and a pale, translucent hand reached out to touch the telephone. It began to hum as the Grand Lord replaced his hand in the glove.

'Call them,' he said. 'Call your family.'

'I don't—'

'Know the number?' The Grand Lord smiled. 'It is not necessary. The magic of this place is … sometimes … enough.'

The humming phone that had no wire had a dial tone. Benjamin ran his fingers over the grooves in the dial but didn't wind it. After a few seconds, a ringing tone came on the other end.

'Hello?'

At the sound of his mother's voice, Benjamin's heart almost broke. He so wanted to talk to her, to tell her he was all right, but it would only upset her and get the phone hung up on him.

'Is David there?' he asked, slightly altering his voice to sound a little younger.

There was an audible sigh of contentment. 'He came home yesterday. The doctors think everything will be fine.'

Benjamin closed his eyes for a moment, holding the phone against his chest until he was sure he could speak without breaking into tears.

'Can I speak to him?'

'Who's calling?'

'It's … it's Kyle.'

'Oh, from school? Well, I'm not sure he's up to talking to anyone just yet but … hang on a minute.'

There was a slight clunk as his mother put down the phone. Benjamin heard shuffling feet, then a kid's voice said, 'Hello?'

'David?'

The voice became a whisper. 'Who's this? Bennie, is that you?'

'It's me! Are you all right?'

'I woke up again a few days ago. Mummy said I went for a really long sleep and I didn't want to wake up. I told her I met you in my dream and you helped protect me from this really bad man and that you'd be back soon, but she didn't believe me. She told me to stop telling tales. Did that really happen, Bennie?'

Benjamin wiped a tear out of his eye. 'It really happened, but adults won't believe it, so it has to be a secret between just us.'

'Are you coming back soon, Bennie?'

Benjamin swallowed down a lump in his throat. 'No, I don't think so.'

'But why not?'

'Because … that bad man I saved you from, I have to save other people from him, too.' He glanced up at the Grand Lord, who had retreated to the window, and just at that moment, the Grand Lord looked back, his face strangely melancholic, as if in Benjamin's attempt to soothe his brother, he had happened onto an unmistakable truth.

'You're a good brother, Bennie. I miss you.'

'I miss you, too, David. I'll always be thinking of you, wherever I am.'

'Won't I see you again?'

'You'll see me whenever you close your eyes. We'll be having adventures together, only this time, you'll be saving me.'

'Thanks, Bennie. Oh, Mummy's coming back, I'd better go. Do you want to speak to her?'

Benjamin closed his eyes, swallowing down a wave of sadness. 'No … she'll be tired. Take care, David. I love you.'

'I love you, too, Bennie.'

Benjamin put the phone down before he started to choke up, and he stared at it for a long time before he felt able to speak again. The Grand Lord came to stand across from him, arms folded into his robes.

'Did you find it? Your closure?'

Benjamin nodded. 'Some. But I still have questions.'

'Like what?'

'My brother … he sent me here, didn't he?'

Grand Lord Bastien nodded. 'I believe he did. It is my theory that your brother is one of those who has links to both of our worlds. One like … myself.'

'But you can't return?'

The Grand Lord shook his head. 'I don't know how. Maybe it is true that I lie inert somewhere in another life, and that if I die here or there, I will become whole again, but I do not know. And—' he smiled, '—I am reluctant to test my theory.'

'I saw the Dark Man's face. I saw—'

The Grand Lord closed his eyes as he nodded. 'I know.'

'He looked like me. Like an older me. How is that possible?'

The Grand Lord patted him on the shoulder. 'I think for now

that is a secret best kept between us. I, too, saw his face, and the likeness was … uncanny. We know little of the Dark Man, only that your coming stirred him in a way he hasn't been stirred in decades. Perhaps time will tell, but from now on, we will be ready for him.'

Unable to shake the feeling that he was at the centre of a darker plot than he could have imagined, Benjamin just gave a short nod. 'I don't know that I'll ever really understand everything I want to about this place,' he said, 'but in a strange way, I feel safe here in the school, perhaps far safer than I've ever felt.'

The Grand Lord nodded. 'That's good. Now, you had better run along. Your friends will be waiting.' As Benjamin reached the door, he added, 'But remember, I am here to talk to you whenever you need. I might not have the answers, but I can certainly listen to the questions.'

'Thank you,' Benjamin said. He smiled briefly, and went out.

50

FRIENDS

C limbing class had nearly pulled their arms out of their sockets. Captain Roche had taken them to a particularly tough section of cliff known as the Comb-Over because of the way a hooked overhang protruded from an otherwise gentle slope. And while Benjamin, Miranda, and Wilhelm had all passed their climbing test with ease, they spent the whole walk back to the dorms massaging their shoulders.

And worse was to come—in the evening they had a catch-up class with Professor Loane, on the dead-boringly titled subject of Mythology and its Influences on Children's Stories, because all three had flunked the final semester test. Wilhelm and Miranda had fallen asleep at the back of the class, while Benjamin, aware he had failed so spectacularly to study for the test that any attempt to put pen to paper would have been a crime against education, had spent most of the period balancing pencils on their heads.

Now, as Benjamin pulled off his climbing clothes and opened his bottom drawer to get his classroom uniform, he jumped in surprise. An orientation manual sat on top of his shirts, looking pristine and new. He picked it up and turned it over in his hands.

On the front, it said: "To: Sebastien Aren. Welcome to Endinfinium, the School at the End of the World."

He lifted the front cover, and inside was an inscription in ornate script that said:

Benjamin,
  I heard that your copy got a little wet.
  You may borrow mine indefinitely.
  Yours,
  Grand Lord Bastien

'Wilhelm, look,' he said, turning to hold up the book. 'The Grand Lord gave me his handbook.'

Wilhelm poked about in a drawer on the other side of the room. 'That's nice,' he said without looking up.

Benjamin flicked through a few pages that held descriptions of lessons and several pages of truncated school history, none of which came across as remotely true. Then there were menus and school rules. Everything, really, that a regular school handbook ought to have. He smiled and put it back into the drawer to read later.

'Are you guys ready?'

Miranda waited in the doorway. Benjamin stood up, but Wilhelm still poked about in his drawer, right arm almost swallowed up as he felt around for something at the back.

'What are you doing? We're going to be late! Haven't you had enough of the Locker Room for one semester?'

Wilhelm grinned and beckoned them with his free hand. 'Guys … we're friends, aren't we? Friends trust each other, don't they? Friends help each other out, right?'

Miranda and Benjamin shared a glance. 'Yeah,' Miranda said. 'Why?'

Wilhelm pulled a glass jar out of his drawer, where something white and frilly moved about inside, like an overlarge, albino butterfly.

'What have you got in there?'

'It's a scatlock.'

Miranda cuffed him around the ears. 'Where'd you get that from?'

'I caught it outside.'

'Why?'

He grinned again. 'I thought we could prank Professor Loane. I need help, though. You two have to distract him, while I release it in his book bag. I can't do this alone. Who's with me?'

Miranda and Benjamin looked at each other, then both grinned.

'Let's go,' Benjamin said.

'All right!'

Wilhelm stood up. 'I'll brief you on the plan on the way over. And remember, when it comes flapping out in his face, we know nothing. Poker faces. Deal?'

'Deal,' Benjamin and Miranda said at the same time. Then, with Wilhelm taking the lead, the three of them headed off toward their destiny.

END

Printed in Great Britain
by Amazon